D0991977

WITHDRAWN

THE PATCH BOYS

BOOKS BY JAY PARINI

Singing in Time (poetry)
Theodore Roethke: An American Romantic (criticism)
The Love Run (novel)
Anthracite Country (poetry)

THE PATCH BOYS

JAY PARINI

HENRY HOLT AND COMPANY
NEW YORK

Library of Congress Cataloging in Publication Data
Parini, Jay.
The patch boys.
I. Title.
PS3566.A65P3   1986   813'.54   86-4823
ISBN: 0-8050-0047-X

First Edition

Designed by Kate Nichols
Illustrations by Gretchen Bergner
Printed in the United States of America
1 3 5 7 9 10 8 6 4 2

ISBN 0-8050-0047-X

For DEVON, with love.

And for our sweet sons—
OLIVER and WILL.

1

Our teacher Miss Turner was from Hugo, Texas, the home of Rogers "The Rajah" Hornsby. She talked with a Southern twang in her voice and liked to claim that her uncle actually knew Rogers Hornsby and had gone fishing with him before the war. This I doubted, but the class believed her, which kept them in line. Miss Turner put a picture of The Rajah up front on the blackboard between President Coolidge and Gifford Pinchot, the governor of Pennsylvania, so nobody would forget who he was.

"I bet she ain't going to let us go," said Will Denks, my best friend.

"She is," I said.

We always sat next to each other in the back of the class, where you could duck questions. I angled my seat so I could see the blond hair of Ellie Maynard, the principal's daughter, who sat way up front beside Nip Stanton in his last-day-of-school clothes, pressed stiff as cardboard by his family's maid. This really was Nipper's last day, since he was going away to school someplace in New England next September. Good riddance was how I saw it. I decided then and there to refuse the invitation he'd given to the whole class to attend his birthday party in a couple of weeks. To what kind of party would you invite the whole class, even Ethel Bombodino, who weighed two hundred pounds without any makeup on her face?

"Class," said Miss Turner. "Y'all have done good work for me in English this year, and next year I know you'll do just as well for Mr. Romolo in tenth grade. Remember what I said about summer now: Use the library!"

I peeked sideways at the clock. It was two exactly.

"And *because* y'all have been such a good class," Miss Turner went on, "I am going to let you go early."

All of us except the brown-nosers were out of there within the minute. It's amazing how quick you forget things like school and church. I wasn't more than a couple of steps out of the schoolyard when the whole year evaporated from my brain, burned off in the bright sun.

We headed straight to the river, where Will Denks had already been camping for three weeks.

"Why don't you come live with me on the river this summer, Sammy?" he asked.

"Mama would kill me," I said.

"You're almost sixteen years old."

"No matter," I said. "She'd never let Vincenzo live on the river, and he's twenty-six." Mama thought it wasn't right for her children to live in a lean-to on the Susquehanna River when the di Cantini family had a perfectly good house in the patch. In fact, we had one of the best houses up there, a big yellow one with woods and a yard behind it. The house perched on the crest of a hill, overlooking a valley shaded by chestnuts with big fanlike leaves that must have been there when Columbus accidentally discovered America. Those trees covered the lawn with brown nuts every fall, and the patch boys would come in droves to collect them, though nobody ever really knew what to do with a pile of nuts. The house was everything to our family, which was not one of the dirt-poor mining families that made up most of the Exeter patch, one of hundreds of mining neighborhoods in Pennsylvania. We were miners like the rest, but Papa had a rich brother in Jersey who had never married, Uncle Nello. Nello di Cantini died young, without a family of his own, so his money came down to us just after the war, and we bought the yellow house. Papa paid cash for it, and though we didn't have a penny of Nello's money left over, a house was nothing to sneeze at, as Mama said. We all worked hard to keep it up, painting, repairing broken shutters and steps, and making sure nobody threw a ball through the windows, which wasn't easy. Mama would stand on the back porch in a white apron, yelling in broken English, "Don't play no ball here! This ain't no stadium! *Ragazzi,* shoosh!"

We cut through pinewood above the Exeter Coal Company, where Vincenzo and Grandpa Jesse were still at work. Will moved ahead of me, gliding like an Indian, each foot hitting toe first, the weight on the outside and rolling inward; his eyes could pick up animal trails in the soft dirt. To one side of us, the mine shaft threw a long shadow on the gravel and thin grass. A dozen outbuildings crowded around the shaft itself, and the big breaker, with gray siding and many broken windows, stood on its own fifty yards away, hanging like a ghost in air. In the mule barn, they were brushing down the animals, who'd been underground since early morning hauling coal sleds up to a central shaft. A coal train passed, pulling wagon after wagon of anthracite, the hard coal that comes from this part of northeastern Pennsylvania. Will slid down the mossbank toward a bend in the river, and I followed.

"You want to hop a train this summer?" Will asked. Summer freshened him up for adventure.

"Naw." I remembered only too well last summer's trip to Buffalo, back and forth in twenty-four hours, riding in a boxcar

3

full of cowshit. Anyway, I had newspapers to deliver every day, and I had to caddy at the golf course whenever I could. I would also have to wash cars and mow lawns in West Pittston.

"You ain't up for nothing," he said.

As he said that, the river appeared, glistening half a mile wide. It had rained throughout May, and the beach looked washed out, with the pebbles lit like eggs.

"Don't say you ain't going to swim, too?" Will Denks groaned.

I answered by stepping out of my clothes, letting everything—including the pants Mama had pressed especially for the last day of school—fall in a clump on the bank. I took a shallow dive from a ledge. It was freezing! "Get your ass in here!" I yelled back to Will, who stood on the shore with one leg drawn up, staring across the water. He was skinny, taller than me by three inches with blond hair that stuck out in frizzy wild curls.

He shook off the trance and launched himself into the air. "Jesus and Mary!" he screamed when his head exploded through the water. He was an atheist and a Protestant, so he could say those things.

"It's *chally!*" I said, pronouncing the word like Miss Turner.

"You should have tried it three weeks ago."

"Not me."

"You act like a girl," Will Denks said.

"How does a girl act?"

"Negative," he said.

"How do you know how girls act?"

"I know," he said, treading water like a puppy, with hands up front.

Will Denks knew nothing about girls. At least I had a sister, Lucy. She was seventeen and definitely acted like a girl, which accounted for much of her problem.

"So who's the best pitcher this year?" Will asked.

"Vincenzo," I said. My brother's fastball was so fast you never saw it except in your memory.

4

"Hell, I don't mean around here. I'm talking about the majors."

"Walter Johnson, then."

"Nope," said Will. "It's Dazzy Vance. He beats Johnson on all three counts: better won-lost record, more strikeouts, better ERA."

"You put too much on numbers," I said. "Johnson is a classic."

"A *what?*"

"You deaf or something?"

Suddenly a whistle blew. It blew again, an ugly shriek that bounced off the cliffs of Camel's Ledge and carried down the valley. The day, like crystal, shattered.

We waited to see how many times it would sound; as we'd been talking and treading water, the current had carried us south almost to the Coxton Bridge. The whistle blasted seven times in a row—the signal for an emergency at the mines.

We headed back to shore against the current as fast as we could. Will Denks reached there ahead of me, stumbling over the mossy stones and skinning a kneecap. I was close behind him. We dressed on the run.

The most direct route to the main shaft was a thin runnel that led straight up a bank behind the breaker. You could climb it like a rope ladder, stepping in the brown loops of roots, though it was slippery and dangerous. You'd break your neck if you fell backward on the rocks.

We went carefully, with Will climbing first. He did this every day, so he knew just how and where to step. My hands shook and my knees felt weak; I could barely hold on at all. The breaker itself threw a cold shadow down the bank.

When we got to the top, we saw people swarming on the shaft, scared and running, wives and mothers, old men with cloth caps in their hands, children. Someone said, "River broke in but they don't know where." The crowd pressed at the shaft entrance, trucks and cars and the Pittston ambulance moving toward the center of the trouble like hornets coming home to nest. It was all a blur of noise and shouts, the gravel sputtering under tires, the whistle going off like nobody heard it the first time. Only Bing Stanton, who operated the shaft, seemed calm. He stood coolly on the side porch of the office shack, fiddling with his pipe.

"What's going on, Mr. Stanton?" I asked. My own brother and uncle were down there, so I had a right to ask.

He tapped his pipe on his heel. His Panama hat was tipped backward.

"There's water in the bottom line," he said. "It's a new vein."

"Was anybody caught down there?"

"I don't think so. Probably not."

I saw my brother step into the sunlight from the shaft's entrance, just behind his friend Nick Maroni. He wore a side-long mackerel grin and walked with his shoulders swaggering back and forth. People said he walked like an athlete, which meant he walked like his underpants were wet. The mines were no place for Vincenzo.

Grandpa Jesse, who was really my uncle, slumped along beside him. He looked skinny and weird, like always. He wasn't cut out for mining either, but he wasn't good for anything else, so he mined.

Will Denks was talking to him and pointing to me.

As I waved back, a man came up to Bing Stanton to say that nobody was hurt and they shouldn't have blown the whistle. It was foolish to get folks overexcited, and they didn't need bad publicity right now, when the unions were grabbing hold of the men.

"Who blew it?" asked Bing Stanton, obviously mad.

In the distance, Mama and Mrs. Montoro, the widow who lived next door to us, rushed along the road to the Coal Company. The fear on Mama's face showed through even before you could make out her features. She always stooped forward when she ran, her shoulder blades sticking out like wings.

"There's nobody hurt," I told her when she came near

enough. She was out of breath because she had a hole in her heart and was not supposed to run or get excited. Last summer, when Papa was killed, she had passed out cold. When they brought him home in a sack and laid him on our porch, Mama took one look and fell over his body. Her lips and fingers went blue, and it was hard to get her breathing again, even with the smelling salts.

"My Vincenzo. . . ." she said to me.

"He's okay, Mama. He's standing there with Jesse. Nobody's hurt." I realized that I was shouting in her face.

Mrs. Montoro immediately dropped to her knees in the road and began counting rosaries, as I held Mama in my arms, her small bones fragile as a bird's. Her red hair scratched my cheek. Her shoulders smelled of garlic.

All the while, Mrs. Montoro was mumbling, "Hail Mary, full of grace, blessed art thou among women."

2

The miners in our valley came from Wales, Poland, and Italy. Most of the Italians in the patch were from small towns in the south like Campobasso or L'Aquila. The old men at Bo Wilson's store talked about these villages, saying they were no good as places to live because the land was dry and stony. You couldn't get the schooling you needed to lift you out of the poor class. That's why they'd come to America, a country where money and jobs came easier, and where you could get decent schools for your children. I never understood how they could be so happy about working in the mines, but I suppose no work is worse than rotten work if you're proud. Papa said that in Italy life was lazy, and he didn't mind that. In America, laziness is one notch below syphilis on the scale of diseases. So most of the miners went underground without a complaint.

Grandpa Jesse was an exception. He understood that the mines stank and that the miners got a raw deal from the operators. He had been ridiculed as a Bolshevist by the others when he first came over and began to spout his socialism, so now he didn't pipe up much. The mines were tense places with the threat of strikes, the unions, and the way accidents seemed to keep happening. Papa's accident was most on my mind, but there was also that cave-in near Shamokin only a year before, when a dozen miners were trapped and suffocated due to pillar robbing. The law said you were supposed to leave pillars of anthracite every so many yards, to hold up the ceilings. But the owners robbed them. Vincenzo said it was plain greed that had caused the Shamokin accident. Part of the union platform was that miners wouldn't have to rob the pillars anymore, that operators would be shut down for taking that kind of risk.

Another big issue was methane gas, which seeps naturally into mines and explodes on contact with an open flame. Many of the miners still used carbide lamps that worked by squirting water over pellets, which produced gas that was sparked by a flint. Those lamps burned with a bright flame but caused too many explosions. Vincenzo argued for the Elvin Lamp, a version of the old Davey Lamp, once used to detect methane gas. Vincenzo had all the brochures on the Elvin Lamp and preached it up and down the valley. Now we also listened to it every night at dinner. I seemed to know more about mining than sex.

Ventilation was bad in the mines, of course, and Vincenzo had picked up about a dozen different schemes at union meetings for the improvement of air underground, where firedamp, smoke, carbon dioxide, and dust—as well as gas—blend together. Some way had to be found for blowing clean air in and extracting the bad stuff. They used hot-air furnaces with a high stone flue in the past, but these set off more explosions than they prevented and were being phased out. Now giant steam fans called Beadles and Guibals huffed fresh air down the modern shafts. Vincenzo was trying to convince Bing Stanton to buy these machines for the Exeter slopes, which operated along primitive lines and killed or hurt someone every few months. If you didn't get a piece of rock on you, you got knocked over by a coal car or kicked by a mule. Or you simply wheezed to death from lung disease. The worst job in the mines was the doorboys, who held open the big entrance doors for miners or cars to pass. The boys worked such long hours that they'd fall asleep and get run over by cars. Vincenzo argued for rotating shifts to prevent the boys from dozing off. I didn't see how anyone could quarrel with such a simple solution.

Vincenzo was never sociable with me like you'd expect from a brother. His moods were worse than Jesse's, and he could stare into space for two or three hours at a time. Things gnawed at him like they shouldn't gnaw at a man of twenty-six. Mama said to me one night in the kitchen: "The problem your brother has is girls. A boy his age needs a *bella ragazza* or he go silly, *pazzo*." She waved her hands like she did when she talked, especially when Italian words came out.

I often took the opposite point of view with Mama, just to benefit the conversation. "He doesn't need girls. He has his union and baseball. What does he need girls for? They only cause trouble." I didn't bring up Lucy, who was a case in point.

"Sammy, a boy his age needs the girl to be happy. That's why he sits and stares at the wallpaper like it was a burlesque show."

"How about me?" I said. "I don't have any girls."

"Someday you will. You're a young boy now. You got Will Denks."

Mama said that in a way that irritated my nerves, but I let it drop.

"Maybe girls don't think so much of Vincenzo," I said. "You can't tango with yourself."

"That's crazy. He's a nice-looking boy and an athlete. Girls go crazy over a man who can pitch like him. They go to the games to watch him, but he don't even notice them. I know a dozen girls would kill for a date with Vincenzo—like that Rosa Nino. She goes to all his games. She loves him."

I wouldn't have given you a nickel for Rosa Nino, who weighed more on the kneecap than most girls do on the hips, but Mama was correct about girls and Vincenzo. Women had always been drawn to him. I only wished one-tenth of the women who went after him came after me. I'd talk to them about something other than the mines. But I suppose I lacked whatever women went for. Maybe it was the intense look in my brother's eyes that attracted them. The same look scared the bejeezus out of batters. Once or twice I tried walking uptown like Vincenzo, frowning, staring ahead, really fierce. Last spring on a Friday night I paced back and forth, my hands jammed like Vincenzo's into my pockets, swaying as I walked. I screwed up my face, as though my head was bursting with Big Questions. The bigger the better. Then I ran into May Direggio, belle of the eleventh grade. She was loose and hungry, destined for no good. "Hey, Sammy," she said, stopping in front of me. I ignored her, scrunching my forehead to indicate thought. "You got a load of shit in your pants or what?" she said. I went home the back way.

Mama said, "You got something your brother don't got."

"What's that?" I figured she meant my high cheekbones, my best feature.

"A heart."

This embarrassed me. "Vincenzo cares about the miners."

Mama scowled. "He's going to get himself in trouble with the law, I'm telling you the truth. Nobody likes a troublemaker. I'll wind up the mother of two jailbirds one day: Vincenzo and Louis. They're both heading into trouble. You wait and see. If your papa was alive. . . ." Mention of Papa generally brought her voice to a halt.

Vincenzo hadn't gotten over Papa's death, either. It was the beginning of his union work. He said that Bing Stanton was responsible for that death, and I couldn't argue with him on that one. Vincenzo was determined to see that, somehow, Bing Stanton paid for Papa's death and for the other deaths as well. He was building up to a giant strike that would come if

11

change didn't happen quickly, a strike that would shake the whole mining industry in the anthracite country. It would be worse than the strike of '23, which had threatened to ruin everything. Vincenzo said it didn't matter if the mines were ruined, that without proper working conditions, we'd all be better off without mining. Other industries would move in—safer ones. What was mining after all, he said, but a worm's way of life?

"Your brother, he wants control," Mama said. "Since he was a little boy, he wanted to tell people what was what. That's what this union is about."

Mama hated the union, but I took care to say nothing for it or against. I tried to keep quiet about things I didn't understand. Meetings were planned to organize the miners, with Vincenzo behind the planning. The young miners always got together anyway on Saturday nights at Tommy Carlo's Pool Hall in Pittston, but the union meetings would start there in a couple of weeks. "You begin with the young miners," said Vincenzo. "You work up from there. If Bing Stanton loses the young ones, we got him." My brother took a week off without pay to write and print pamphlets that argued for a strike if the Coal Company refused to cooperate with the United Mine Workers, which was already strong in the western part of the state and farther south.

Somehow, Vincenzo roped me into passing out pamphlets through the patch with him. I agreed, against my instinct, to help. Once you got involved in things, you were in danger of getting stuck. It happened when Mike Torrentino asked me to come to a Boy Scout meeting at the Baptist church. I couldn't say no, so I wound up a Life Scout. Papa thought you had to finish what you began. People never expect anything but more and more of you.

We humped two big boxes of pamphlets in a wheelbarrow throughout the afternoon, which brightened Vincenzo. He came home with me happy as a fly in a pig stall.

That night after supper, while Mama and Lucy washed the dishes and Gino, my little brother, ran down to the store for

12

ice cream and Grandpa Jesse went out onto the front porch to read the *Gazette*, Vincenzo and I went out back in the yard. He asked me if I wanted to catch some ball, which he hardly ever did. He couldn't let off full steam without fear of killing me. I knew he was doing this only because I'd helped him with the pamphlets, but I figured he did owe me a favor. Anyway, if I was ever going to get into the major leagues myself I'd have to learn to catch a fastball. I was fifteen years old, almost sixteen. Jimmie Foxx, who was only seventeen, played with the Athletics in Philadelphia. To catch up to him, I'd have to get moving.

"Stand by the tree, Sammy," he said.

I had a big mitt, the one Papa got for me in Scranton. The night before he was killed he was working on his slider with me, a pitch that seemed to stop in midair and sort of hang around before, suddenly, it would come to life again and veer down on the inside. It was weird. Vincenzo said that Papa could have been a big-time pitcher himself if he'd wanted; he never really played the game, but he followed the scores. I kept seeing him before me, not Vincenzo. The leather mitt had a rich smell that reminded me of him, and I wondered where he was now. Was he watching us, cheering away on a cloud somewhere? Some religions think that dead people come back as birds. Maybe Papa was that old crow in the big elm beside us.

"Keep the mitt up, Sammy!" Vincenzo yelled. He knew I was daydreaming. He looked at me with eyes that burned a hole right through you. In dark trousers and a bright yellow shirt, his slow backward windup made you nervous; it took so long to come around, and you couldn't tell when or where the ball would fly. He took it easy with me, but the ball still sizzled and smacked so hard I had to wince. My palm was raw meat after only three pitches.

"How about a curve ball?" I yelled. A curve took longer to get to you, since it had longer to travel, having that little corner to get around.

"Your hand okay?"

13

"Sure is."

"Can I put some pepper on it?"

"Sure can."

Pepper! I thought. Who needs it?

"It'll jump, so watch close," said Vincenzo. "Don't hold the mitt too low."

I was squatting like in a real game, practicing the correct position. It's hard on your knees and ankles, and you feel you could tip forward or back if the wind blew either way. I wanted to keep the mitt up, but the problem was that if you did you had to trust that the ball would rise. It took faith, which meant you were willing to let your balls dangle uncovered. Nothing is worse than a pitch in the balls. It thuds and squishes them, and you feel a large pain widen from your knees to your throat like you just swallowed an ashcan lid. Your eyeballs press out like corks from a couple of frozen wine bottles. Your voice goes up at least half an octave for the rest of your life. So you wanted to keep your mitt over your balls at all cost. Unfortunately, if the ball rose and you didn't get the glove up, you ate it.

"Give it all you got," I said. "I got to practice." That was my head, not my heart, talking.

Vincenzo drooped his glove near the ground, meditating on the spot he wanted to hit. I wondered what the hell he was looking at. My tongue felt like a slice of ham in my mouth, salty and pink. I wiggled my fingers to get as much blood in the hand as I could, hoping that the fluid would act like a cushion. I knew that I'd need to put a hanky in the mitt after one or two more throws. I whispered a Hail Mary under my breath.

The ball started low, about a foot or two off the ground, maybe ten feet in front of me, sailing at a speed where you saw nothing but its streaking tail, before it leaped to waist level. It glanced off the top edge of my mitt, careened sideways, and shot into a deep fern patch at the edge of the woods.

"Hey, kid, you're lucky that didn't bust your jawbone,"

Vincenzo said. He shuffled with me through the ferns, looking for the ball.

"I can't seem to gauge it. The way it jumps. How can you tell where it's going?"

"You can't really know," he said. "A good catcher doesn't really try to gauge. What if it didn't rise? What if it curved, slid, or did something else? How do you think they catch a screwball? Those can go anywhere."

I waited for him to tell me.

"The point is, your hand knows. A good catcher's hand simply knows. It's the last-second reflex. If you just let it happen, you'd have caught it. Your hand *wanted* to go for the ball. It *knew* where it would land, but your head was working too hard; you wouldn't let your hand do the catching."

This struck me as superstitious.

"*My* hand didn't know," I said.

"It did," he said, mad because we'd lost a ball.

We searched hard, but a ball can disappear forever in the ferns. It gets swallowed into the fourth dimension.

We went to the pump and drew icy water from the well that Papa had drilled several years ago. Vincenzo worked the pump slowly, and the water spurted over the flagstones and splashed my ankles. He gave me a tin cup full to the brim, the way Papa would. We both thought of him at once.

"It was only last year about now, you know," Vincenzo said. "It was coming into a real hot spell. This is going to be another hot one."

I hadn't noticed until he said that how hot it was—sweltering. "Don't you believe in God anymore, Vincenzo?"

He said, "No."

"Then you don't think you'll ever see Papa again."

"That's right."

The twilight was coming on now, streaking the sky in the west. Bluebirds shot from branch to branch in the woods. The ground smelled so fresh and strong. I wondered if this was the one, the only world we could ever know.

15

"You still believe in God, don't you?" he said.

"Yes."

"That's okay. You've got to do what seems right to you." My brother's face caught so much late sunlight that his cheeks burned. His eyes, dark as they were, looked bright. He had straight, white teeth and clean skin.

"I got another ball upstairs," said Vincenzo. "You want me to go get it?"

"Naw, it's getting late. I won't be able to see it pretty soon." That wasn't the truest thing I ever said.

"Well, thanks again for helping me with the pamphlets."

"Sure thing, Vince."

Nobody knew Vincenzo very well.

3

Will Denks lived behind the patch with his uncle, Hark Wood, who wasn't really his uncle. Will Denks's father was killed in France in 1918 by a German shell, and Will's mother died two years later, when he was ten. Hark Wood had lived in sin for several years with Mrs. Denks's sister, Eileen Strong, which made Hark something like an uncle to Will Denks. When Eileen herself upped and died of mysterious causes—something like lockjaw—and since there was nobody else in the picture, Hark took over the boy. Some said he did it just for the little pension Will had from being a war orphan, but I never bought that. Hark seemed to like having a son. Several ladies in the town complained that he was incapable of being a father to anybody. The ladies were not, however, upset enough to do anything about it, so Hark and Will lived quite happily together in this loose kind of arrangement.

Hark didn't work. Instead, he got drunk by noon when he

could. People wondered where he got his hands on so much booze, in the year of 1925, but I knew Hark had a still. He made so much hootch there was some left over to sell. I often saw him working the still, tinkering over its mechanism like it was a Pierce-Arrow. His cheeks burned MacIntosh red, and his nose went purple, which Mama said was the sign of a bad heart, something she understood too well. Hark had once been found doubled over a woodpile in agony, and he enjoyed telling us how much it hurt. He hoped it would kill him outright next time; he said: "Ain't no point to living and make yourself a burden."

Their house was a shack among swamp oaks and brush. We called it the Shithouse, which pretty much describes it: weathered boards that stank of creosote, rigged on a square frame without a foundation. Tar paper kept out the rain, more or less, and the beams showed inside like a dinosaur's rib cage. There was no running water, but a well in the yard pumped clear, sweet water. It was lucky the well was fifty yards from the house, since Hark liked to piss out the kitchen window. That made the ground around the Shithouse rancid, though Hark claimed the piss seeped into and improved the flavor of the well-water. Since Will sometimes used a sickle to clear the path, I suggested he get Hark to piss his way home once in a while, just to save a lot of work.

Two small cots lined up on either side of the Shithouse, and a three-legged kitchen table braced itself up against the wall between them, which was near a little window. You could eat and stare out the window or, if you were Hark Wood, you could eat and piss out the window at the same time.

It dropped below zero in the winter, but I never felt too sorry for them. Hark had a big pot-bellied coal stove that threw off good heat and cooked their food. Coal was one thing plentiful in Luzerne County; Hark stole it in bagfuls from the breaker. The anthracite burned clean and long, better than the soft-shit bituminous they sold over in the western parts of the state and down in West Virginia. I came by the Shithouse a lot in winter, and the three of us sat and drank coffee by the fire late into evening. On weekends I sometimes slept on the dilapidated couch, though I hated to wake up cold in the morning with the coffee frozen at the bottom of the pot and my toes blue.

Summer was better, though Will Denks never slept at the Shithouse once the weather turned decent. He camped by the river until October, and Hark Wood hardly saw him except by chance. Mama said it wasn't right that a boy Will's age should be let loose by himself all summer, but there wasn't anybody around who could tell this to Will. He liked his freedom, and he didn't need looking after anyway.

Will had been on the river since he was ten, but this summer he decided to fix things up in his camp. With help from me and Mike Torrentino, he constructed a floating dock out of rusty oil barrels and scrapwood, strapping it with waterproof gut wire. The wood needed to be soaked and straightened, but Will had a knowledge of such things. He worked slowly with a book propped up for directions: *The Construction of Docks* by Harold T. March. It took us a whole week to get it right, but she floated, anchored down with a heap of rocks and old tire irons. The camp was cut out of the woods at a bend in the river just north of the Coxton Bridge, and Will slept in a lean-to thatched with hemlock branches, tar paper, and mud.

I usually went down to the river by day, getting up early and slipping out before breakfast. We ate well—squirrel, rabbit, and fresh fish grilled over a fire. We ate lots of beans and corn, stuff that you wouldn't normally think of as breakfast food, and drank coffee after breakfast, sitting like lizards on the flat rocks by the river. From there you looked up to Camel's Ledge, a chalky bluff named after the famous American pioneer, Camel, who got himself chased by Indians right to the edge and had to leap, horse and all, into the river. That was the story as Hark Wood spun it, though I never imagined a horse could jump so far and not kill itself and the rider, too. It would take a Sopwith Camel to make that leap.

Swimming was the main point of most days, and Will and I never had suits on, of course. Bare-ass was the only way to swim. You felt fishy and free. There is a particular feeling around the balls that needs no explanation for those who've known it. We made some lovely, long mornings out of that river, floating south toward Wilkes-Barre under a dozen iron bridges. The real work was swimming back, upstream, especially when you couldn't stop on the shore for a rest because of your bare-ass figure.

I wasn't a natural swimmer like Will, who was born for the water. He was skinny as a twelve-year-old at fifteen and a half, and beautiful. I tried not to look at him too close when he laid down on the rocks. He had those blond—almost white—curls, and from a distance you could take him for a girl. There was no hair on his body, hardly any between the legs, though he was past puberty. His voice hadn't so much changed as mellowed. When he spoke, it was soft and reedy.

I looked old beside him, since I'd needed to shave from the age of twelve. My voice was deep, my hair black and thickening on my arms, legs, and chest. My short, broad body seemed less graceful than Will's. But I was strong, which is something. "You're built for the mines," said Will, once, to tease me. "A real mule."

Will knew nothing would drag me down the mines. I used to walk my father to work in the summer, at six in the morning, and hold his lunch pail and sometimes wear his hat. With the sun up and dew in cobwebs on the grass and corn, the miners would leave their small houses in the patch, saying nothing to one another as they trudged, as if already exhausted, to shaft #8. They stared down at their feet or straight ahead, afraid to notice how lovely the day was, since much of the loveliness would be drained out by four, when the whistle blew. They had spent ten hours in darkness, eight of them in sleep; now they would spend more hours under the ground in seeming night, lying on their bellies, picking away at the coal face, loading hunks into railcars, watching for the rats to run.

If the rats ran, they ran. There were so many cave-ins now. I guess one reason why nobody talked much on the way to work was the thought of dying. It would hurt too much to notice the world and think how beautiful it was, knowing that this might be your last sight of it. I had walked Papa to work the day last summer that was *his* last time alive on the world. He never talked to other miners, even if they went beside us, but he always talked to me. He said he would take me to see Connie Mack's Athletics in Philadelphia some day. I was going to be a good catcher, he said, maybe better than Vincenzo was a pitcher. He knew I didn't like to box, so that was out. But baseball was my love. I said I would be a catcher in the majors one day—or a lawyer. Papa said either career was a good one, and that maybe I could be both. You have to retire from baseball by thirty or thirty-five, but since men live until sixty or seventy, you've got to do something. Maybe I could be a baseball lawyer, he said. I loved Papa, but some thought it was weird that a fourteen-year-old boy wanted to walk his father to work. I didn't care. We both knew I would never go into the mines. I would leave the patch as soon as school got finished and go to college or to New York City like my brother Louis had done.

It took three days for them to dig Papa out. They said he was killed instantly when the roof caved in on him.

Papa liked Will Denks because he was so smart, which didn't mean "booky" to Papa. He thought Will had common sense and admired his independence. Will came to the house a lot when Papa was alive, but now that Grandpa Jesse and Vincenzo were in charge, he usually stayed away. Vincenzo knew Will Denks didn't have much interest in miners, and he felt nervous around people who didn't. Jesse said Will was a wild animal to live in the woods like he did, but he smiled at him when he came to the house as if to say it was all right to be a wild animal when you are young. He had been one himself, back in Italy, getting himself into trouble with the Italian police because of his socialism; he escaped into Switzerland to avoid being jailed, and somehow got himself to America ten years ago. Because he was an outlaw, and his real name was Giuseppe, we called him Jesse after Jesse James. Now everybody called him Jesse, and he loved it.

Will Denks still occasionally had dinner with us at home, but he couldn't digest Vincenzo's speeches. Opinions didn't interest him, so he told me in private, but facts did. Whether you wanted to know Dutch Leonard's earned-run average or the exact number of pounds in a ton, Will Denks was your man. He wanted details, facts. Opinions he could form himself. As a result, he never said much of anything at our house, so nobody realized how smart he could be.

I preferred being with Will Denks down by the river, where politics had no place and you could just eat, swim, joke, and smoke Fatima Turkish cigarettes, as many as you pleased. I was helping Will construct a proper latrine according to a special army manual, making sure that the hole was a decent number of yards from the river, so you didn't stink up the water.

"Why does everything have to be done like it says in your book?" I asked, digging away one afternoon.

"The experts have worked out what makes a sanitary latrine and what doesn't."

"The animals piss where they like, don't they?"

"We're not animals."

"What are we, then?" I didn't mind being an animal, at least not for the summer.

"We're intelligent creatures. The size of our brain separates us from the rest. We're the only conscious and reasoning creatures in the whole galaxy." Will looked very satisfied by this comment.

He admired intelligence more than anything, not book learning, but practical know-how. Whatever had to be known—how to make a lean-to, cook catfish, build a bridge across a stream—Will Denks knew.

"You got to pay more attention to details, Sammy," he said.

"Bull. There are plenty of people who know details. Why should I?"

"You won't know *anything* until you do."

"Bull." I kept shoveling the latrine. But I felt weak inside, a little scared of Will Denks, who stood straight-backed beside me, his blue-green eyes cold to look at. He didn't take it lightly when I disagreed with him.

"You say that, Sam, but you know it ain't so. Details make up the game. Life is details."

"For Crissake, okay. Lay off."

"What kind of lawyer do you think you could be, huh? I wouldn't bring no case your way."

Will Denks liked to dig the knife in as deep as he could, then twist it, so long as he stayed on top. I almost wanted to lay into him. "So what are you going to be?"

"When?"

"When you're an adult."

He smirked at me. "Nothing more than I am now, probably." He picked up a shovel. "Why does anyone have to *be* something? You're so goddamn big on what somebody is or ain't. Maybe not everybody gives a shit. You ever consider that?"

He got me so upset I couldn't speak to him. We didn't used to fight so much, not so cutting. Will always kept the upper hand, and I let him, but he wouldn't give me an inch today. Not a goddamn inch.

When we'd dug for several hours, Will brought out the lemonade, which had been cooling in the river. We sat on a big rock, dangling our feet in the water.

"So who's going to Nip Stanton's party?" I asked Will, knowing he'd never go. The social life didn't interest him.

"Nobody ain't," he said.

"I sure won't go. Do you think Ellie Maynard will go?"

"She's his girl, ain't she?"

"You got to be nuts," I said. What a notion!

"I seen them together up Pittston, drinking soda."

This news sickened me. I felt weak and thought I might

topple forward into the river. The fish scum that gathered in the reeds at the water's edge filled my head with its rank smell.

"The Nipper has quite a house, they say," Will Denks added. "I walked by there a few times. Nice brickwork."

It struck me that Will Denks was capable of attending the Nipper's party just to look at the brickwork on the building where it was held.

"Who would you say's the best pitcher in the American League?" I asked.

"Now?"

"Yeah, right now—1925."

Will spat lemonade on the rock to watch it dribble into the water. "Ain't nobody like Joe Wood. He was 34 and 5 in 1912," he said. "Walter Johnson's a flash in the pan."

I said, "What gets me is how everybody knows everything about pitchers. What about catchers?"

"Catchers don't count."

"Why the hell don't they? The catcher's the one who calls the pitch. It's their brains that win. If it wasn't for catchers, a pitch might just keep going. Who knows if it'd ever stop?" I sipped the lemonade. Will Denks never liked my crazy notions and ignored me. "They call the shots. They control the pace, don't they?"

"The pace ain't what matters. Runs matter. You don't win a game on pace. That's why the Babe is Baseball Himself."

Sometimes Will Denks was downright obstinate. I decided to drop the subject altogether.

"Ain't your brother pitching this Saturday against the Wings?" he asked.

"Yep. He's ready for them." I had seen Vincenzo practice a lot lately, pitching in the backyard until the sun went down. The patch boys would gather after supper to watch him. Vincenzo's fastball took their speech away. The last few nights I sat there on the grass with Mike Torrentino and Billy Shawgo, waiting for the lightning bugs to come out. That was Vincenzo's signal to knock off for the night, since it was hard enough to see his fastball in broad daylight.

"He'll get a bid from the majors this year," said Will. "You wait and see. There were scouts at his game last year. I saw them."

"He knows."

I loved having a brother who was almost famous. Louis, who hardly ever came home now, was almost famous, too. He made big money in business in New York City, and he sent a check home every month. Mama didn't trust this money, though, and put it in the bank, where she had a special account with his name on it. "Business," she often muttered to herself. "Nobody believes me when I tell them he's in business. *'Non è vero,'* they say. *'Non è vero.'* "

"I bet the Yanks grab Vincenzo," Will Denks said.

"He'd like to go to St. Louis."

"Naw, the Yanks could use some good pitching," Will said. "Hey, is Vincenzo religious?"

"Nope," I said. "He gave up church a long time ago."

"I know that, but I seen him crossing himself on the mound. What's that about?"

"Just superstition . . . habit."

"Vince ought to turn pro this summer, Sammy. He could do it," Will said.

"Probably."

"But he'd have to change his name. How many wops get into the majors?"

It was true. There weren't a lot.

"*Vincenzo* is a weird name," he went on. "It sounds foreign."

"Hell, what about Bill Wambsganss?"

"He made an unassisted triple play in the Series. Nineteen twenty. Dodgers against the Indians."

"What about his *name?*"

"He must be Jewish."

"I don't know. He's something funny."

I'd never thought too much about being Italian and how it might hold me back. I liked plain names better—Ed Sutton, Ben Worth, Mick Johnson—three guys in our class. But most

25

of the patch boys had Italian or Polish names, so I never worried about it. But now I wondered about Ellie. Did she think of me as Italian? Did she prefer the Nipper because he had a clean, swift name?

"The Wings are the best team in the valley," said Will Denks. "Ain't Vincenzo worried about them?" The Wyoming Wings had come in second to the Eagles for three years running. This year they had Lester Manubo, a big hitter who had moved in from New York. He had played briefly for the Dodgers, but he was working in the mines now.

"Vince will kill them," I said.

"Want to bet on it?"

"Two bits."

"You're on," I said, but my heart was not on baseball.

The Saturday of the game between the Eagles and the Wings—the first big game of summer—started off poorly. It was blazing hot when I woke up, the air crackly like before a storm. The previous night, heat lightning flickered from ledge to ledge in the hills as I stood at the window, sleepless and thinking about the game. A big game was like a block party, where you met everybody from school and went downtown afterward. Mama would be making a mint in the cellar; she ran a speakeasy on Friday and Saturday nights, and you could never get to sleep before two or three in the morning because of the noise.

"It's going to storm," said Grandpa Jesse at breakfast. "Ain't going to be no game." He had an ugly way of curling his top lip backward when he said things like that. I looked away.

"So long as it don't lightning," said Mama. She hated lightning. When she was a girl in Savona, a man had been struck dead right on the street in front of her house. She never lost the chance to tell you about it. "He was a young man, maybe twenty-five," she would say. "His Aunt Valeria lives in Kingston now. His eyeballs were burned out of his head—they were charcoal pits. I saw smoke blow from his ears!" Before we

26

were six or seven, she made us hide in closets when it light-ninged, but later we wouldn't do it.

"Anybody's got as much chance of getting killed by light-ning as they do dying of piles," said Gino, who liked to make fun of Jesse's ailment. My little brother was so fat he had to head off insults with some of his own.

As long as there was food on his plate, Jesse never took offense. He snuffed down scrambled eggs and crisp bacon slices.

"I hope it don't rain," said Vincenzo, "since this is my last game."

At first, it didn't register what he said. Then I noticed nobody was moving. Jesse even stopped chewing.

"What are you talking about?" said Gino. "It ain't only the start of the season."

"That ain't fair," said Lucy. "It ruins everything." She had on a sexy dress and red lipstick. "I got all these dates lined up to go see you play, and if you ain't pitching, who's going to go with me?"

"I'm sorry, Lucy, but I had to make a decision," Vincenzo said, his voice deep. You could see he'd thought up sentences in advance. "We're getting close to a strike, and Bing Stanton ain't going to give in. We're going to have meetings to organize the miners on Saturday nights from now on, and the games don't end till after eight most nights. It just don't leave me enough time."

I didn't see how all that talent of his—and the practice every night with the cans and bottles—could be wasted on a union. Vincenzo was throwing his life away.

"Give up the union," said Mama. "You going to lose that job, it's for sure." Her cheeks became roses, blushing.

Vincenzo was used to Mama's outbursts and paid her no mind. "I'm going to tell the team tonight," he said. "After the game."

"They ain't got another good pitcher," said Gino. "Who they got?"

"Al Medino can pitch," said Vincenzo. "He's really coming along. Anyway, I'm getting too old."

"Twenty-six ain't old," said Lucy. "Sally Fero's brother is thirty-four, and he plays ball."

"He plays like a corpse," said Gino.

"What about me?" said Jesse. "Think how old I am."

"You're lucky you ain't dead," said Gino.

When I told all this to Will Denks, he wouldn't believe me.

"He's kidding," said Will.

"No, he ain't."

"He is."

"How can you say he is, when I heard with my own ears he was quitting tonight?"

"Because nobody puts in that kind of practice and quits. It don't make sense."

I was nearly convinced by Will Denks, who talked with that teachery tone of his. We were on our way to the game, to be played at Exeter Field behind the school. The field had been strip-mined awhile back, then made into an athletic field by some local clubs. It had a tall backstop, made of wire mesh, and a few bleachers running down the first and third base lines. There were no fences, so a home run wasn't dramatic like in the big leagues. All you had to do was put the ball between two outfielders, scoot like hell, and the run was yours. The outfield quickly turned into a swamp, and if the ball made it to soggy ground, that was that. Beyond the swamp was a ridge of culm, large flakes of slaggy stuff that smelled bad, especially when the wind came from behind. On nights when a game would go into extra innings, the twilight would deepen over the culm dumps and they would take on a brighter glow; Exeter Field seemed like Mars then, red and burning. The sulfurous smell rolled in layers over the dry dirt, slowing the players and the game down so that each inning took longer. The players' faces would get red and shiny, and I used to think that if they played right through the night, nobody would recognize them at dawn. Their faces would have grown decades older, from breathing in that culmy breeze.

Sure enough, the game was delayed that night as rain poured

in from the west, a hot rain that drilled the ground and ran muddy water into the mines. You always worried about flooding in the mines. Not five years back a wall broke in, letting the river run through; eighteen men drowned in a flash. But this was a short storm tonight, the kind that soaks everything for an hour, then leaves the sky blue and bare, the grass like raw wet hair.

The Wings had a big lineup—with Lester Manubo batting fourth. He came up against Vincenzo for the first time at the start of the second inning, and he caught the second pitch inside, nearly on the fists, and sent a line drive right over the first baseman's head and down the line. He made a double out of it, but that didn't help the Wings, who didn't even get a piece of my brother's fastball for the next five innings. It was in the eighth that Manubo showed what he was: a boomer. It was getting darker, which usually worked in Vincenzo's favor. When the dump started to burn, you could forget it; nobody was going to get wood on anything. But Lester Manubo found a sweet spot on the outside corner, and the ball sounded like a head-on collision between a truck and a bandwagon. It cleared the swamp and landed, way off, in the dumps. The fielder never even chased it.

The problem was that the Eagles couldn't get a piece of anything thrown at them by Bob Sevensky, a little Polish guy with a large nose and a smart head. His slider slid under everybody's swing. His change-up nearly broke several backs, they swung so hard. His knuckleball made half the team feel like giggling: a ball that took that many dipsy doodles was more fun to watch than swing at. Sevensky was new in the area, like Manubo; he had moved in from Chicago. I knew in the eighth inning that the team of Manubo and Sevensky would cream everybody up and down the valley that summer, even if Vincenzo changed his mind to stay with the Eagles. The Eagles didn't have any big boomers.

Lucy sat near me. She had come to the game with a creep called Bonino, who was courting her like crazy. He had a big

Buick, which she loved, even though it wasn't the fanciest model and was old. She always fell for a Buick. In Lucy's mind, tonight, a lot rode on Vincenzo's right arm. Gino and Jesse stood with their noses pressed to the mesh behind home plate.

It came right down to the bottom of the ninth and the last batter. George Cizzo, called "The Sisler" because his name sounded something like George Sisler's of the Browns, got lucky and caught a slider at the knees. George was a little nearsighted and often swung low, which paid off here. He put a hard grounder between the right and center fielders. The ball rolled into a thick wad of vetch, where nobody could retrieve it. The score was 1–1, and the game went into extra innings.

I knew my brother too well to think he'd let them down now. This was his last game, and he wasn't going to lose it. He bore down, firing faster as the sun fell. It was nine and nearly dark in the fifteenth inning when he came up to bat. Sevensky knew that Vincenzo wasn't a great hitter: he wasn't *bad,* but he wasn't great. Why, I don't know, but Sevensky let one float up near the chest, a soft, bosomy one, which Vince cannonballed over the left fielder's head. It didn't go way out, so the guy caught up with it—but too late. The throw missed Vincenzo at home by a split second. The game was over, the sky blazed deep purply red, and washed by the rain, the air seemed sweet as apples.

"So you ain't telling me he's quitting baseball," said Will Denks.

But Vincenzo soon had them all in the dugout. You could tell he was saying something unpleasant by the look on their faces. They did not seem like a team that had just won a game in fifteen innings.

"Shit," said Will Denks. "He's got to be crazy."

4

On Sundays we went to mass and, in the summer, had a big family picnic by the river. Papa had a special private place where he always took us, and we still went there. It offered us another way to remember him. The day after the ball game, everybody went to mass as usual, everybody except Vincenzo and Jesse, who were atheists, though they never said so. They hadn't been to mass since Papa died. I prayed that God would show them that being an atheist got you nowhere, though I never imagined they would go to hell, of course. Heaven and hell were impossible to think of, sort of like New Jersey. Papa once promised to take us all to New Jersey to visit the grave of Uncle Nello, near Hoboken. I spent months thinking what New Jersey looked like, what its smells were, how it would *feel* to be in New Jersey; I woke up early on the morning before we left and thought New Jersey was as real to me as the patch, that when I got there and finally saw it, it would seem old hat.

As it turned out, New Jersey was nothing like what I had imagined, which suggests that the mind has no power to reach ahead in time. It's lucky enough to go backward with any accuracy.

Father Francis, our priest, spoke about Doubting Thomas on the Sunday morning after the Eagles beat the Wings. Thomas could not believe Jesus had come back from the dead till he actually laid his hand where the soldier's lance had cut through the skin. You wouldn't have got me to stick my hand there for any money. But the point was that some people need visible evidence, while others rely on faith. Mama, for instance, was faithful. She never doubted God for a minute and accepted things with arms wide open. She would kiss Louis when he came home no matter what he did in the outside world. He could have murdered a helpless old lady or robbed a convent, but she'd still hug him. Lucy could come home pregnant with quintuplets and Mama wouldn't turn her away. She had faith in her own. To her, Jesus was like a second-cousin in Italy, one who might turn up one day with a bagful of groceries. Mama was the angel of our household, and God hung over her like a strong perfume. He was there in her bright red hair, which she wore piled up high in back—"the burning bush," as Gino called it ever since Father Francis told us about Moses in the wilderness. Mama refused to have her hair bobbed like Lucy.

Lucy had faith, I ought to say. She was too lazy to doubt. Doubt requires a certain effort, and Lucy's efforts were concentrated on boys. She had a beautiful high forehead and sharp features. When Papa was alive, boys came softly to the back door, polite and courteous. Now they jammed the front porch, night and day, and nothing frightened them away—not even Jesse running through the house in Mama's yellow scarf. The patch boys understood that, for a seventeen-year-old girl, Lucy was tops. Her breasts stood up, large and tight, though she tried to suppress them to look like the girls in the magazines. Her waist was as narrow as Will Denks's, but her hips widened out nicely. Her legs dropped lovely to the calves; her black hair cut across her forehead like a crow's black wing and fell straight at the sides.

Some nights I dreamed about Lucy, and I told this to Father Francis several times in confessions. I knew how bad it was by the time it took Father to respond. When he did speak, it was in a strained voice, higher; he gave me more Hail Marys for those dreams than for abusing myself six times in only two days during Lent! "Ask the Lord to cleanse your mind," he said. "The Devil has entered your mind, and he must be cast out. Pray to the Lord."

The Lord was a man, too. He would have understood about girls, how their legs move like scissors sometimes, drawing you toward them. He'd have understood about the way their hair smells after rain. About the way a belly ripples. About how they look from behind, especially when lying on the floor. Lucy occasionally had her friends over to sleep the night, and they would lie on their stomachs on the living-room rug in snug flannel nightgowns. I would sneak my looks, secretly wishing I could spray a gas that would stun them all, blank out their brains, so that I could enter the room and lift their nightgowns, one by one.

I should never have added this last detail in my confession to Father Francis. He probably thought I was some kind of pervert. But my head was swirling with evil thoughts.

"Do you ever think about girls, Sammy?" Lucy said to me, helping to get ready for the picnic by packing the basket in the kitchen.

"Me?"

"Yeah."

"Not except once in a while."

"You're about that age, so I just wondered."

I suppose she hoped I was as snarled in sexy thoughts about girls as she was in sexy thoughts about boys. Now that Vincenzo wasn't pitching, she figured her sex life was over.

"Sammy don't need no girls," said Mama, who had been

on the back porch; she heard us through the screen door and butted in. No conversation was not *her* conversation, too.

"It ain't nobody's business what I need," I said.

"It's my business," said Mama. "Anything my kids do is my business."

"Sammy never gives you any trouble, Mama," said Lucy. I couldn't believe she said a word in my favor. Her method was usually to draw attention only to the rotten things done by other members of the family, hoping this would divert attention from herself.

"Lucy's right," I said. "What do I ever do wrong? Maybe I don't do enough."

"You'll do plenty when the time comes," Mama said. *"E altro."*

I let this pass. Mama said a lot of things that made no sense.

We were all in a good mood because Vincenzo and Jesse said they would come to the picnic. This summer, they had been making up excuses, like they didn't want to hang around with us and waste their time on something stupid. But Papa always believed in the family as a group who did things together.

As we set off for the river like a camel train, Lucy took me aside. She and I were behind Mama, Gino, and Father Francis. Vincenzo and Jesse came behind us.

"I need this dress I saw in Pittston," she said. "It's in the window of Stauffer's."

Stauffer's was *not* the sort of store Lucy should have been shopping in. It was strictly for the people from West Pittston— the lawyers and bankers, the mine operators and doctors.

"You *need* it?" I said.

"That's right."

"I saw plenty of dresses in your closet last time I looked."

"What were you doing in my closet?"

"I helped Mama put up the laundry last week."

"You stay out of there." She explained how she had a date to go to a fancy restaurant in Wilkes-Barre with Bonino, this

34

new boyfriend. Nobody ever called him anything but Bonino, not even his mother. He was tall, thin, and slimy—a real Sicilian. His chocolate brown suits were the joke of Luzerne County.

"He ain't worth a new dress," I said.

"So how is it you know everything about Bonino?"

I didn't want to tell her everything, but the patch boys knew he was an ass. He came from down the line, below Wilkes-Barre, though he hung out in Pittston. Nobody knew where his money came from, but he was known to have a brother in Trenton who had made a ton in bootleg and gambling. Bonino sometimes turned up on Saturday nights at our speakeasy, but Mama never let him in. She figured that her cellar was a private club; whoever came for a drink was her guest, and she never let just anybody through the door. The cops knew about Mama's operation, but nobody bothered about booze. They figured the miners earned a good time once in a while, and Mama's gin wouldn't make you go blind like Grandpa Jesse's wine.

"Mama doesn't like Bonino," I said.

"She told me that, but it ain't her that's been invited out."

"He's too old," I said.

"He's twenty-seven. That ain't old."

"You're only seventeen."

"I'll be eighteen in December. And I'm quitting school this fall, but don't tell nobody yet. I want to get a job before I tell."

She only had a year to go and she would graduate, so the idea of her quitting made me mad. Papa would not have allowed it.

"So can I borrow ten dollars?" she said.

"Ten dollars!"

"For the dress."

The family knew I'd saved up nearly twenty dollars, which meant they could tap me for a loan when it pleased them.

"I don't think that's fair, Lucy. Ten dollars is too much for a dress."

"It ain't nothing for a dress these days. You should see the prices." Lucy read all the magazines, so she knew.

I should have explained to her how many hours Vincenzo and Jesse would have to work in the mines to make ten dollars, or how many customers Mama would have to serve in the cellar, but I held my tongue. Girls don't think logically.

"Okay," I said. "But you have to pay me back."

"I'll pay you back in two weeks. Ethel Gryzbo owes me money. I'll get her to pay me back, then I can pay you."

The Gryzbo family were so poor they ate nothing but coffee-soaked bread for supper. Lester Gryzbo, the father, had a wooden leg and was near blind, so he couldn't work. I didn't doubt that Lucy had loaned money to Ethel, but I did doubt Ethel could ever pay her back.

It was a swell day by the river, with the sky clear enough to squeak if you ran your finger from one end to the other and a few clouds, like puff pastry, floating in the blue. Father Francis, standing with his paunch up front like a pregnant woman, smiled like he'd just met Jesus on the path. He talked away about nothing, like ladies do in the church kitchen, sometimes saying things that a priest oughtn't to. Gossip was his downfall. I listened and began to regret some things I'd said in the confessional.

Mama fussed over the basket, unwrapping the sandwiches and cookies. The tablecloth with "Home Sweet Home" across it in cutout letters she spread neatly over a flat rock, and her yellow-and-white flowered dress puffed out, like a tent, around her as she sat at the center of us, the ringmaster.

The breeze carried the familiar smells: the foamy odor of mud, the leathery moss. The river itself was high now, brimming its banks, and it moved slowly through this bend in the river. The path here was the kind only Papa could have found, since it didn't look like a path from the road. You had to push between two bushes to see it, and then it looked like a faint trace, more the recollection of a path than a path. Papa had a sense for hidden things. He could ferret out rabbits where nobody guessed they would hole. He saw a bird's nest long before anyone else did, just like he understood what was bothering you before you did yourself.

One by one, Mama unwrapped the bologna sandwiches and passed out plums, which produced a lull in the day's chatter.

Father Francis was the first to finish his food, and he decided to stir things up a little: "So how's that young man of yours from down the line, Lucy? I refer, of course, to Mr. Bonano."

"Bonino," she said.

Mama could not help scowling. This topic did not suit a beautiful day for a picnic.

"So how is he?" Father Francis pressed.

"Good."

"He don't eat enough," Gino cut in. "That's why he's so damn skinny. They should call him *Banana*." Only he found this a rib-tickler.

"Shut up, Gino," said Lucy. "You're too damn fat. It disgusts me."

"Fat is better than ugly," he said. "At least I can go on a diet."

Mama was not going to allow this. "*Basta!* I don't want no fights." Her high cheekbones flushed.

Father Francis seemed to have heard none of this. He said, "I hear Bonino is polite."

"He's a nice guy," I said, feeling warm toward Lucy and wanting to take her side this afternoon.

"He ought to get a job," said Jesse.

Lucy looked upset, so I tried again to help her.

"He knows a lot about cars," I said.

Lucy smiled at me. "Sammy has good taste in people."

"She's just softening you up," Gino said. "She wants a loan."

This did not pass by Father Francis. "I understand you're quite the wizard with your money, Sam," he said.

Just because I worked hard at selling newspapers and made some cash that I didn't squander, they all figured I was a millionaire.

"He's going to be a rich man," said Mama.

"A lawyer," I said. It suddenly seemed plain to me that I'd never get a spot in the majors, since I didn't even play in a league. No scouts would ever see me perform. I might have tried to get on a sandlot team, but Will Denks persuaded me not to bother. He wanted me to swim with him this summer.

"I see," said Father Francis. "Law is a distinguished profession."

You had to hand it to Father Francis, he had a beautiful way with the language. Nobody talked quite like him. I admired that, as Papa had. He told me to listen and try to talk like that. I once asked Father Francis where he learned his fine speech, and he gave me a little book called *The Elements of Eloquence* by a professor from Princeton. I read it twice, and it helped. People commented on my educated talk, and Vincenzo said I would make a great orator one day. I loaned him *The Elements of Eloquence,* although he never had time to read it.

"I'm going to be a fighter," said Gino. "Like Dempsey." His cloth cap was cocked sideways, mean.

"You could be the fat man in a circus,"said Lucy.

Gino nearly popped a vein in his neck. Looking at him, I was glad not to be fat. You have to be generous with people, since most of them don't have any luck. Gino couldn't help that he was hungry day and night.

"He must have a tapeworm," said Mama, "the way he eats."

"I ain't got no goddamn worm," said Gino. "If anybody's got a worm, it's her. Bonino's a worm."

"I'm getting too old for a son like this one," said Mama. "The way he talks."

Father Francis suffered a milder case of constant hunger. He ate everything he could lay his hands on, so his fingers got that pudgy look. Skin rippled around his holy ring. If you touched him, he dented like bread dough.

"Choose your young men carefully, Lucy," said Father Francis. "The choice of one's lifemate is the most important choice one ever makes." This remark pitched Gino into giggles.

"Have a cheese sandwich," Mama said to Gino.

Lucy once told me she didn't think that priests had any right to talk about sex and marriage, since they didn't know a damn thing about either.

"I'm going for a swim before I eat my sandwich," she said. "I don't want no cramp."

"I won't save you if you drown," said Gino. "I don't think nobody would."

We sat and watched her, all except Father Francis, who stood. She wore a bathing suit under her dress, a silly one that ruffled around her knees and came down to her elbows. Hanging her dress in a branch, she waded slowly in, then dove when the water reached her navel. There was silence while she swam, as though she might really drown or something. Everybody— even Vincenzo—was waiting for her to step, wet and glistening, from the river. A wet girl is a beautiful sight, even if it is your own relative.

"Sexy, sexy," said Gino in my ear as Lucy came on shore.

"Shut up for once, will you," I said.

"Want to fight?" he said.

"Sure."

The eel grass opened into a small clearing like a boxing ring.

"Come on. Jab!" I said, boxing the air. I darted around Gino like a pro. He took off his cap.

But Gino was too fat to be a fighter. If he ever connected, it would sting. It might even knock out a tooth or crack a jaw. But his swing came too slow and his arms could barely reach me. I held him off like a puppy, though he threw everything at me but the kitchen sink. He finally gave up and sat down to his sandwich.

Father Francis said, "You've got to vary the pace, Gino. Hit him low first, real low. When his guard is down, come across with a right, a high right cross."

Gino's jaw stopped munching.

39

"And don't circle the same way over and over. Go one way, then the other. Keep him off guard."

"How'd you learn that?" he asked.

"I used to box."

"Really?"

"Yes. At the Carbondale Y." Carbondale was a dozen or so miles north of Scranton, a mining town famous for its fighters. Len Lapuzzi came from Carbondale, and Father Francis had grown up there, the son of a mining engineer. "I wish I kept in better shape," he said. "I'm a wreck."

"You're a nice-looking man," said Mama. "You got nice teeth."

Nice teeth is to a man what nice personality is to a woman: an excuse for a compliment.

"Thanks to Ipana," he said, stupidly.

"How was the water, Lucy?" asked Vincenzo, undressing, looking more relaxed than I'd seen him in months. He wore a long-sleeved striped bathing costume that he bought mail-order from Sears, Roebuck.

"Cold," she said.

"Good," he said. "I like cold water."

We all watched, dazzled, as Vincenzo dove shallow and glided, turned, and swam backstroke far out. He grinned and waved, and we waved back.

The sun poured down, flooding the grass and river. Jackdaws and bluebirds flapped overhead. You could feel the whole world turning like it does, slowly, with terrific sureness.

When Vincenzo came in, Mama started talking about Italy, and we all leaned back to listen. She had wonderful stories about growing up near Savona, which I planned to visit one day when I was rich and famous. My relatives—dozens of them there—would roll out the red carpet for me. I lay back in the dry grass with my feet up and munched chocolate cookies, letting the sun warm both cheeks. For a moment, it seemed like summer would go on forever.

5

The Saturday of the first big union meeting, early in July, was a scorcher. After a busy morning on the golf course at Fox Hill, where we both caddied sometimes, Will Denks and I spent a lazy afternoon in the sun. We fished a little, pulling out six perch and three bullheads, which stank in the pail. They'd be our supper. We also did some reading—Will Denks on hydroelectric power and the use of dams, me on *Ivanhoe,* a long book about knights. Will Denks had a pack of Fatimas, so we smoked them one by one as we sat under a tree, banked against it from opposite sides. The tobacco made us dizzy, but we made ourselves extra dizzy by guzzling half a bottle of Hark Wood's piss-oil bootleg, confiscated by Will from the Shithouse.

I loved it when Will Denks got a little drunk. He was normally so cool and reserved, which I admired. But alcohol loosened him up, as long as he didn't get testy.

"Don't you wish it was always summer?" he said.

"Yeah."

"And there wasn't no school or mines or unions. Just people doing what they like best."

"Maybe in heaven," I said.

Will Denks was about to scoff, like he did whenever I brought up religion, but the alcohol made him mellow. "You really think there's a heaven, don't you?" He was pointing at the sky. "Right aways up there."

I said I didn't know where it was, up or down.

"Maybe you're what's called an optimist," he said, getting downright philosophical. "I'm a pessimist. I don't think anything ever works out for people. That's why you got to be selfish."

"If nothing ever works out, you got to feel sorry for all the people in the world."

"I don't feel sorry. Just pessimistic." He blew a smoke ring into the air, a perfect circle that lost its tightness and perfection as it rose. I studied his hard features, the crazy curly hair, the tallness and slimness that had always set Will Denks apart. Even Nip Stanton was a little afraid of him, maybe because Will had nothing to base anything on but his own hardness. He had nothing to lose. And he took no shit from nobody.

About five we fried the fish. The excitement about going to the pool hall for Vincenzo's speechmaking had us percolating.

"What do you think about this union stuff?" I asked him. It struck me that Will Denks hadn't said much on the subject, and I was curious. You never could figure his mind unless you asked.

"I don't think about it."

"But what about the conditions?"

"Which ones?"

"In the mines. The ventilation, the gas, all that."

Will Denks looked cross at me. "You got to take a long view on the mines. They're a business, and they run for profit.

42

If you go fixing up ventilation and buying new lamps and upping wages, you know what you get? You get out of business. And when you get out of business, people who once had jobs get out of work and starve."

"Vincenzo says it's better to starve than be a slave."

"If that was the case, do you think people would've come across from the old country?"

He had me stumped.

"If there's another strike, there will be no work, and the mines will close. When that happens, the county will go downhill. You'll get riots in the streets." Will's blue-green eyes popped: "And then—*war!*"

The prospect of war excited me. I wanted one. It frustrated me that the Great War had come when I was just a kid. I never forgot the fancy parade in Pittston when the doughboys came back, the crowd thick on both sides of the street. I sat up on Papa's shoulders and threw rice. They looked fresh and proud in their helmets and uniforms, carrying rifles, marching to a bugle and drumbeat. It was better than football.

The speech wasn't scheduled until eight, but we cleaned up the camp by six and took a late swim. We laid our clothes under a tree. Will, as ever, piled his neatly. He was like an old lady when it came to neatness. I dumped mine in a heap and waded, beside Will, into the lukewarm water, which slid like glass sheets over the pebbly bottom. The light lay on the surface of the river, having a velvety sheen by this time of day. The hills on the other side got deeper, grape-deep, and cool. The smell of pine got richer as you breathed it. I stood knee-deep in the current, letting the minnows nibble my toes. The sun bobbed between two hills on the west bank, flashing on the girders of Coxton Bridge.

Will went ahead, taking a shallow dive, and swam briskly to the middle, where he turned and waved. He wanted me to join him, but I was caught up in the notion of rivers. A river has its own story, moving in one direction, powerful but without show. I imagined that each man was himself a river, flowing in the banks of his life, running out to sea. The sea is like death, and nothing stops our flow in that direction. Papa had made that journey, and I could imagine him floating in space, happy forever in his last real home. I'd thought about people as rivers and the sea as death before this, and once almost brought it up to Father Francis after catechism but changed my mind. Father Francis might think my idea was atheistical, which would set him off. He hated atheists worse than Protestants. But I was not an atheist. I just had a different way of looking at what they taught you in church. My feeling was that religion ought to make sense, which it never did unless you said it in your own words.

I didn't swim that night but was satisfied to sit watching as Will Denks paddled in closer and stood up with his hair wet and his face sharp as a blade. His long arms dangled from his shoulders. His knees knocked together.

"What are you staring at?" he said.

"You."

"What for?"

"You're funny-looking."

At this, Will dove for my ankles. He knocked me hard back against the pebbles: We rolled over each other, painful, into the water. Catching quick breaths, gulping, we wrestled each other to the bottom. We might have been under for days, so it seemed, floating in a dream. I held Will hard around the stomach, floating behind him, trailing like seaweed.

"Let me go, you bastard," said Will, when we came up for air.

It felt good that I was so much stronger than Will, and that he knew this and would let me wrestle and beat him in the water.

Light spread across the river like an oil spill, and the world was on fire everywhere, even in the woods, backlit through the trees. The waxiness of the poplar leaves caused them to shine, as their loose wrists dangled. The white pines brushed the sky with their long, hairy needles, which Will Denks sometimes chopped up and boiled to make tea.

"We can shoot some eight ball tonight, from what I hear."

"What'd you hear, then?"

"Bo Wilson says there'll be trouble."

Bo Wilson made like he knew everything. Because he owned the general store in the patch, he sat there telling people what they needed and what they didn't.

"You're coming with me?" I said, making it half a question and half a statement.

"Sure am," he said, like who was I to doubt Will Denks?

As he dressed in silence, I began to worry about the way we had wrestled in the water. Had I made him mad or something? He could be touchy.

"You're kind of quiet tonight," I said.

Will shrugged his shoulders. It was clear he had a mood on him, but you could never fathom his moods. You had to let them gloom over him, knowing they'd clear when the time came.

We walked glumly along the road into Pittston. The Coal Company sheds lined the road, and boxcars huddled in the rail yard like old horses, asleep on their feet. One train, its twenty cars heaped with coal, bullhorned across Exeter Avenue by the biscuit company. I broke off a chestnut walking stick and dug it in the road as we marched, a tiny army, with a dozen others, all miners. It reminded me of heading across the bridge for a big football game in the fall, except that a strange weather hung over everybody, not only Will.

We crossed the Fort Williams Bridge, making our way down Main Street to Tommy Carlo's. It was seven-thirty, but already people hung out in the doorways: the crowd of young miners was scattered through with a few salt-and-pepper heads. I smelled booze on a lot of breaths and felt the tension in the room, already too thick with smoke to see through without a squint.

Will and I squeezed past a barrel-chested union man who glared at us like we weren't supposed to to be there. Only miners were allowed in tonight, he seemed to be saying. No kids. But we pretended we didn't notice and went to the farthest corner of the room, where one table was racked for eight ball. The velvety green table glowed, and Will took a long, straight cue from the wall and chalked it, slowly, as if life or death depended on a clean break. He arched against the cushion with his butt angling upward, then fired. The crack came clean, scattering the balls so a dozen good shots appeared if you had an eye for them. Will did: he found stripes like sitting ducks in each corner and on the lips of the opposite side pockets. Choosing solids, which clustered like grapes in the center of the table, he picked off my jailbirds one by one, working slow as a dentist, drilling the holes with short, neat jabs. A few of the youngest miners drifted our way to watch the spectacle of my defeat (I never got in one goddamn shot) as we waited for the chimes of eight.

I'd been so lost in the eight ball, in my own helplessness in the face of Will's methodical victory, that I didn't notice how the crowd had become a mob. The noise level had risen with the smoke. My eyes stung as I scanned the room for my brother.

The cops, who'd planted themselves in different places, watched everybody close. Some of them weren't real cops but the Coal and Iron Police, the C&I, a private army hired by the mining companies to protect their property. Their faces were unfamiliar, which made them more frightening than they should have been. They were, after all, just human beings.

Nick Maroni dragged a crate onto the floor center near a wall as a platform for Vincenzo, who hadn't yet shown his face. He knew you should let the excitement build, then come on gangbusters. You could always trust Nick Maroni, who was a good friend of ours, to do things the smartest way.

It was ten past eight before they cleared a path from the cardroom, where Vincenzo waited. It surprised me how his simple entrance hushed the mob to a matter of coughs and spits.

"Vincenzo di Cantini will talk on behalf of the United Mine Workers," said Nick Maroni. Maroni wasn't a good talker or he'd have given the speech himself. He was a kind of godfather to Vincenzo—a man of forty with a wife and three boys who

46

had devoted himself to the union. Almost everybody except the operators liked him, including me. Maroni used to play catch with me when I was small, even though he had all those sons to play catch with.

My brother looked darker now than ever, his eyes sunk in their caves, his cheekbones prominent, the chin and lower jaw unshaven. His hair was slicked back as usual, but a loop of it came unstuck when he jerked his head to speak, and it dangled across his forehead, the kind of thing that drives girls berserk. He held his cloth cap to his chest.

"My friends," Vincenzo began. "You know why we are here tonight. We are here because Mr. Bing Stanton is trying to squeeze out the union—our union. I say *our* union not because you all belong to it. You don't." The crowd grunted in response. "I figure we got less than ten percent of you in this room. You are here, I assume, because you know your rights are being denied. Your rights as men and workers. Your American rights."

"Bullshit," somebody yelled from the back. I couldn't see who it was, but the atmosphere tightened and brought steel into Vincenzo's voice.

"It's *bullshit* what we got to tolerate for conditions in the mines, for wages and safety and benefits. *That*," he said, "is what I call bullshit!"

A small cheer went up from the section of the miners who belonged to the ten percent, but you could feel approval crackle across the room.

"I'm here to lay down some plain facts. You tell me if they are true or false. I'm talking about robbing the pillars, first of all. Is it true that thirty-seven men died last year in cave-ins in Luzerne County alone—miners crushed because of cave-ins that would not have happened without robbers? Thirty-seven dead, and thirty-seven families without a source of income." He paused. "My own father, as you know, was one of those killed last summer."

The crowd responded, muttering their yeses. Most of them knew Papa. He got along with everybody.

47

"What about ventilation, about open flame lamps, about gas? We've had I don't know how many killed and injured in explosions. Is that true or false?"

Everybody knew it was true. They didn't need the exact numbers. But the man who had yelled "bullshit" before said, "That's a goddamn lie, di Cantini!" He had support this time. A man next to him yelled "Liar!" Somebody yelled "Bolshevik!" I don't know what else they yelled, but my brother had run into trouble, though he showed no sign of backing down. He stood up straighter and clenched a fist, which he raised, not as a threat, but more like a magic wand. The fist flared in the dim, smoky room and quieted the men. Vincenzo just stood still, glaring them down to a soft rumble, then into silence. You could hardly believe he was just twenty-six.

"Nobody in this room has ever had a decent day's wage for the work he's done," he began. "And nobody here goes down into the ground without thinking that maybe he won't come up at the end of the day." He paused to let the truth of what he said sink in. It was like watering the grass. His talk fell cool as rain on them and washed to the roots; they came up green on him, one by one, murmuring yeses in the front few rows before the assent spread backward.

"All we want is proper wages, proper conditions of safety, and some guarantees," Vincenzo said, a calm, reasonable tone flowing through his words. "And if we don't get these . . . If we don't *get* them, then we're going to have to *take* them!"

At this the bastards in the contrary corner started up again. I couldn't make out what they yelled, but the sense of it was that Vincenzo spoke horseshit. Pure unadulterated manure.

"What are you going to do if Stanton don't agree with you?" a man in the middle of the crowd hollered.

Vincenzo screwed up his brow and said, "If Bing Stanton won't listen, we won't work. We'll *strike,* that's what we'll do. On September first, we will strike."

The word *strike* always fell like a stone into the well of any crowd. The memory of '23, with its terrible eighteen-day strike, settled personally by the governor, Gifford Pinchot, still felt like a gash that wasn't healed. Most of these men remembered the last four or five strikes, in fact: '22 had been the worst, with the miners out for 163 days until forced back by President Harding, who said the army would work the mines if the miners didn't. They remembered how Woodrow Wilson had tricked them back to work in '20, making concessions that he then went back on without even an apology. Wilson had been a damned liar, as Jesse said. A few of the older men in this room could recollect '02, when they sent in the National Guard to Shamokin, outside the Royal Oak Colliery, forcing the miners to work at gunpoint. Jesse would tell me this stuff like it was fresh news.

"I said we'll *strike* if Bing Stanton won't listen to what we got to say!" Vincenzo repeated.

This set off a small brushfire, and the hostile camp screamed "Bolshevik!" at my brother, provoking some of the youngest miners near the front to turn on them. I don't really know how it started—you can't ever tell in a mob—but in seconds the brawl spread, a jumble of fists, screeches, yells, thumps. I got pushed from behind and thrown into the bunch ahead of me, who thought I'd jumped them and turned on me, swinging. I caught a round one on the jaw; it came into my neck first and slid upward, cracking my teeth together so hard it didn't feel but numb at first, though it knocked me dizzy. I fell to the floor and looked up for help from Will Denks, who was tough as anybody when the situation called for it. He caught my eye for maybe half a second before plunging backward into the dark. I don't know how he got out of there or why he didn't drag me with him.

The C&I came crashing forward, knocking the crowd around with their rifle butts; the cops didn't hold back either. The place became a henhouse, fluttering, as if besieged by a pack of wolves they hadn't really known were there. Sick and bloody, I crawled through a tangle of legs and escaped by a side door into the back alley.

6

It puzzled me why Will Denks had cut out when I was in such trouble. It hurt me, but every time my mind slipped too close to the cliff edge, it pulled back toward the safer woods of confusion. I might have been crippled in that mess, but I figured I should just forget it; Will Denks had no family connections to keep him there, as I did. Nor did he have any interest in the miners or what they got paid or whether someone robbed pillars or made the miners go underground with an open flame on their hats. When I could stand, I took the shortcut to Will's camp, crossing through some of the fanciest gardens in West Pittston. They poured the smell of flowers into the air, none of which I could name. The big old houses were lit up like jack-o'-lanterns, and you could see through their windows to the rosy wallpapers, the dark woodwork, the china vases filled with flowers.

Near the river path, I caught sight of the breaker in the

distance, the air heavy with dust. Empty cars waited to be filled beneath coal chutes that rattled and rolled, big slippery tongues. Culm was piled up, heaped, beside the pits and burned slowly; the fumes would sting your eyes if you got too close.

Will sat on his haunches, squat by the fire, in deep thought. Leftover coffee was heating on the grill. He looked at me slantwise: "You get hurt?"

"Naw, just banged my ear on somebody's goddamn boot."

He stood up to inspect the damage, fingering the lobe. "Sliced you pretty good. You better wash it off."

"Yeah, guess so. It doesn't hurt."

"You don't want to get an infection. I got a thing of methiolade in the lean-to. You go wash it out first. I'll fix you up."

Only Will Denks would have had methiolade right there.

I went to the river and lay on a flat rock. The stream swirled twigs under my nose, and the water smelled fish-oily, but I dipped my whole head under and let the current luff out my hair and cool the skin under my collar and sting the cut on my ear. I stayed under as long as my breath held out, flushing the germs.

Will came down to the river with a towel and wrapped my head; when my face and hair were more or less dry, he daubed my ear with the red juice. It sent shivers down my neck. "Thanks," I said. It wasn't his job to look after me. I was stronger than him anyway, so why should he have hung around to get beat up like me? So I told myself.

We went back to the fire and drank coffee without talking. Will stared ahead, looking guilty and upset. I hated to see him like that, but what could I do? I felt terrible inside too, afraid that Vincenzo had been hurt. With Papa dead, we needed Vincenzo. His help wasn't anything obvious; in fact, people like Louis said that he didn't do a thing to help the family except give us a little money every week for food. But Mama, Lucy, Gino, and I felt his support. It was like the invisible beams behind the walls: you can't see them, but if you took them away, the house would crumble. Papa had been like that—

never obvious, never forcing. Vincenzo wasn't much like Papa, but he was there at the right time, like when he heard me crying in my room one night after Papa died and came in. He didn't say a word but sat on the bed and held me; when I stopped crying, he just left.

"You ever been into a mine yourself?" I asked Will.

"Nope."

"I was, once. I never told anybody before. It was down near the ball field. I sprang open the door of a worked-out shaft and went in as far as I could. The light pretty much trailed off, but my eyes adjusted after a bit. I kept following the mule tracks, keeping one ankle close to the rail."

Will appreciated adventures. "What's it like, then?"

"Scary," I said. "The walls kind of . . . seep. The air gets you in the nostrils, and you hear the bats and spiders, rats and other things. They all squeak together. I saw eyes in the walls, lots of them, peeping and wondering who I was to think you could just come down there for no good reason." Will's eyes widened. What I didn't say was I'd gone down there just after Papa had been killed. One day I walked out beyond the patch, into the woods. When you get upset, the woods can settle you. I was the worst I'd ever been that morning—wild—when I came on a shaft and the sign on the door that said, DANGER, KEEP OUT. I knew I had to go down there. I half thought I'd find Papa there if I could only go deep enough. Maybe it was batwings, but the dead seemed to whisper at me from the walls. I pushed as far as I could, coming to a place where the ceiling dropped and the walls narrowed and you had to get on hands and knees to go on. I'd have gone further if slush hadn't risen, a scum like the Devil would puke up. It stopped me, but not so I couldn't yell to Papa across the water. He was there. I knew he was there behind the wall and screamed "Papa! Papa!" and listened by the wall.

He really heard me. The silence that morning, so strange, was like a barely held tongue. Papa was across the water, locked in the black seam. If he had said anything, one word, I'd have gone for him through the slush. But it would have drowned me. Papa knew my duty was aboveground, where Mama and Jesse, Lucy and Gino needed me. So he held his tongue to let me live.

"You wouldn't get me down no mine," said Will Denks.

I studied the outline of Will's jaw against the trees: the sharp, delicate line as he sat forward, resting his chin in his hands, his elbows balanced on his knees. His bare legs caught the light queerly.

"I'm glad you're my best friend," I said. The words came from nowhere, but they seemed urgent.

Will looked at me hard but said nothing.

"I wanted to tell you that," I said. My hands trembled a little.

"Why?" He said that coolly, almost as though he were asking why the sun shines or the river flows.

"Because I'd be alone without you. You got to have a person you can trust. You trust me, don't you?"

"Sure."

"I used to have Papa. But since he was killed, it's been different."

"You'll get a girl to talk to soon," he said.

"You're the only one who—"

"Naw, it's okay. You don't need to explain it."

I walked over and stood behind him as he sat there, and hugged him. His skin was clean and warm. I hugged him tight, and he bent forward and let me do it.

"I better get home," I said.

The sun was gone now, the air around us hot and gray. Crickets drilled the woods deep like they sometimes do in summer, too loud to hear yourself think. Mama would be in a state by now, and she'd want me there. She didn't know where I was, anyway—in jail, dead, in the hospital. She might not know where Vincenzo was.

"You coming back later?" Will asked.

"Maybe."

"You ought to. It'll be crazy over your place."

"I bet."

"I'll wait up for you," he said. "You'll see the lantern."

I dodged Slocum Street, going home through the patch so as not to pass Bo Wilson's store. Sometimes you want to avoid all looks, questions, comments. I went behind the Slocum estate, a mansion on the corner where the Widow Slocum still lived—or half lived. Death would bring about no change in her outward appearance. Ducking beneath her hedgerow, I climbed the hill and came around back into our yard, where I stepped carefully through Mama's cabbages and kale, at one point shooing off a rabbit.

The house was lit up in every window like the night Papa was killed, a pale skull with its porch-mouth frozen in a frown. My belly knotted as I climbed the steps.

"Hello, Sammy," came a voice from a dark spot. A large shadow stepped forward and the floorboards croaked. It was Father Francis, sweaty-faced and fat. I smelled the booze on him.

"Father!" I said. "You scared me."

"We've been worried to death on your behalf," he said.

I said, "Is Vince here?"

"No, he isn't here."

The air cooled around us. "Where is he, then?"

"In the hospital. They're keeping him there overnight. He's pretty well bruised, I'm afraid . . . but nothing serious. We may all thank our Lord for that."

"The bastards!" I said.

"Your brother is quite a lad," Father said.

"You don't see many like him."

"True enough." He squinted at me. "You'd better go in and talk to your mother. The police were just here." He swayed from side to side, as if testing one leg and then the other to see which would hold him best.

"Okay," I said, glad for a chance to slip away.

"Sammy?" he said.

54

I halted with the screen door half open.

"Could I have a brief word with you?"

I paused.

"Come here." He motioned to a couple of rockers.

I let the door slam and we sat down.

"Sam," he said, "I suppose in your own heart you know that you haven't been to confession in several weeks." He looked at me priestly, his cheeks crinkling at the corners, his hair glowing in the dark like an angel's. The fat overlapped his white collar. My guess was that he had proven too ugly for sex with girls and had ducked into the Church as an escape from rejection. He lived well, too. Better than anybody in the patch, except for Widow Slocum. If he turned up at your door, which he often did around suppertime, you *had* to feed him— or risk what God might do if you didn't.

"I haven't?" I said, pretending like the information took me by surprise.

"Not in three or four weeks."

I fumbled for an excuse but failed. "I'm sorry, Father." The summer always messed up my routine. I tended to skip confessions when possible; it was too much like going to school.

"Don't apologize to me, Sam," he said. "Apologize to God."

That made my flesh creep. "I pray every night before bed, Father."

"Good, Sam. That is very good to know. I've thought for some time about you and God. You know, you did very well in catechism this past year. Very well."

"I know," I said.

"In fact, you're intelligent, Sam. Not so many boys have your gifts, which are the gifts of God."

This struck me as true, and I warmed up to him. "Thank you, Father," I said, my eyes drawn downward in a humble gaze.

"Sam, you must come talk to me soon. I have something very important to discuss." The wicker rocker squeaked.

Blood shot through my earlobes. What did he have on me now? Did he know I planned to ask Ellie Maynard, the principal's daughter, up to Hatchet Pond for a swim? How could he know that? Had Mike Torrentino, that snake in the grass, said something in confessions about my plan? I should never have mentioned that plan to anybody. My first real move with a girl, and everybody knew!

"It's nothing bad, Sam," Father added. "In fact, it may be something very good."

That didn't explain what he wanted, but it eased my mind. I tried to think. What good works had I done? I didn't help any old ladies aross the street, not since I quit the Boy Scouts—though I had fetched groceries for Widow Slocum. But that was for money. I'd said plenty of lousy things about people behind their backs, stolen corn with Will Denks, and once, on kitchen duty with Mike Torrentino at a holy-day breakfast at the church, I blew my snots into the scrambled eggs. My brain sizzled with sexy notions, too, a couple of which I hoped to carry out. But what *good?*

"Why don't you come and see me next Saturday. At four?"

"Okay, Father."

"Good boy," he said. "I'll look forward to our little conversation."

Inside the house, Gino perched in front of a gigantic slice of rhubarb-and-apple pie with dollops of fresh cream piled on for good measure. The kitchen smelled like cinnamon.

"Want some pie?" he asked.

"Nope."

Gino had a round face, short licorice hair, and red lips. His oval eyes were black as Vincenzo's. At ten, he weighed one hundred twenty-three, too fat for a boy of his height. But Mama just let him eat and eat. Boys, she said, fall into two categories: those who eat and those who don't. This one ate.

"Where's Mama?" I asked, sitting opposite him. I never spent much time talking to Gino. He didn't like to discuss serious things.

"She's upstairs, crying. There's not nothing to cry over. At least he ain't in jail." With a fresh mouthful of pie, he added, "Somebody told her they seen you on the floor at Tommy Carlo's, all mangled." He stared at me. "Are you mangled?"

"I only scraped my ear." I pointed to the methiolade splotch. "That's not mangled."

"Why were you down there, anyways? You ain't a miner, not yet."

"I come and go as I please, don't I? What's it to you?"

He chewed for a moment before answering. "Nope," he said. "You don't have no right if you ain't a miner."

Kids repeat what their elders say, so I figured he had been within earshot of Mama and Grandpa Jesse on this topic. This, plus his awful grammar, grated on me.

"Listen," I said. "Nobody tells *you* where to go, do they? You disappear in the morning and don't come back except for meals, and nobody asks any questions."

Gino kept chewing, ignoring me altogether.

"Well, I'm almost sixteen now. I got a right to go as I please," I said. My voice was high now, and loud. Gino was not worth trying to convince.

"Sammy," he said. "You think Vincenzo's got any sense about this thing?" His lilting boy-voice didn't match the adultness of his topic.

"I think Vincenzo is *very* right. Your brother is a leader of men, and you should respect him."

He seemed to appreciate this and smiled. "I always did like him. But he don't like me much."

"That's crazy," I said. "He likes you fine."

"He never says nothing to me."

"That's just his way," I said. "Vincenzo's got too much to think about these days."

He shrugged, then dug into a second slice of pie, cutting it so that the inside goo from the next slice fell onto his own plate.

I walked upstairs, tired, to Mama's room.

"So you joining him, then?" Mama asked. She hardly seemed to be alive.

I didn't look directly into her rosebud eyes, now swollen up from bawling. Her hair fell over her forehead as she propped herself up against the lacy pillow.

"Huh?" she said. "You joining them against me?"

"I haven't joined anybody."

"They say you went to the meeting, and that you got knocked on the floor." She looked hard and cold. *"È vero?"*

"I went there with Will Denks to shoot some pool and hear the speech, that's all."

"That's all! That's all!" She threw a book that lay on her bed table right at me, flinging it hard. I noticed it was her Italian missal, which in normal circumstances she would never have flung. She was hysterical because the cops had come to talk to her, and cops always sent her off her head.

"I didn't mean anything," I said. "I got some rights, don't I?"

"Rights!" she screamed. "Go away!" She turned and sobbed into her pillow. *"Da quanto tempo?"* she asked herself. How long would she be forced to put up with this miserable life? I would have sat down beside her to talk—that usually calmed her in the past—but this fit seemed too hysterical for conversation, so I left the room.

I went outside through the front door to avoid Father Francis, skipping past the living room, where Jesse and my sister argued loudly about Vincenzo. I ducked into the woods, where I could look back from the hill behind our yellow house. The dark suit of Father Francis made him invisible on the back porch, though I could faintly make out his white collar and white socks. Overhead, the constellations that Papa taught me to recognize were perfectly in place: Orion, the Great Bear, the Little and Big Dippers. They crackled in faraway space, studding the sky with diamonds that could not be bought or sold. Unlike people, they were beyond negotiation, permanent and perfect. My papa loved these stars, and I went out to watch them on the day he died. The house was jammed with neighbors, who brought cakes and meat pies and fruit baskets. They all said how sorry they were for us, of course. Father Francis was there, too, with his talk of heaven. But *there* was heaven, overhead: twinkling and brilliant, full of stories, legends, the faces of the dead.

7

Ellie Maynard was the girl I loved. This was not only because her father was the high-school principal and a man I admired. I had loved Ellie since the seventh grade, especially her blond hair and green eyes, green like a pond in late autumn when the weeds grow thick at the bottom and the sun mellows through the water. I loved her outline in the distance when she crossed the schoolyard or walked home, usually by herself. She walked as if a puppet master dangled her from a set of strings.

Nobody knew how I loved her, which suited me fine. I never took her out or ever talked to her about anything more serious than baseball scores. She was the only girl in Luzerne County who cared about baseball. Her favorite player was Sam Rice, who had had a thirty-one-game hitting streak for Washington last summer. Ellie wore a big 31 on her sweater all year to honor Sam Rice, though the other girls thought this wasn't ladylike and made fun of her behind her back. I made a point of praising Sam Rice to her face.

I also loved how she stood alone by herself in the schoolyard at lunch, outside the gossipy circles and kiddy games. She lived on Exeter Avenue—a pretty fancy street. But it wasn't that she was stuck-up about her money. The other girls just seemed to despise her for her bright curls, her green eyes and pink lips, her slight, girlish body. How many nights I pictured her body naked in my bed, hard against me, hot and needing my sex in the worst way. I tried to imagine exactly what it would be like to do it with her, focusing on small details to bring the picture to mind—the way her hair would smell, the feel of her hands on my back, her teeth ticking against my own as we kissed. We met frequently in my dreams, and I learned how to recall them quickly upon waking. If I didn't catch them right away, they slipped back on me, into the lost night's sleep. But I really did meet her: it wasn't my fantasy. She would have the same dream at the same time, and in school I would watch for some slight nod or wink to say, *I know, I know.* Once in a while it came, followed by a brief embarrassed smile, so I had no doubts about these dream meetings.

Ellie lived alone with her father in a tall, thin house just where Exeter Avenue crossed into West Pittston, three blocks from the biscuit company and the railroad tracks. Her mother had died of influenza seven years ago, when Ellie was a small girl, leaving her father to raise her. Mr. Maynard was tall and thin like his house, with a blond moustache that would get gooey fom pipe smoking. He had been a flyer in the war, which attracted me to him. Each year on Armistice Day I would see him march through Pittston in his jacket and leather helmet.

I made a point of talking to Mr. Maynard, who seemed to like me. Whenever I could, without seeming a brown-noser, I stopped by his office at school. Most kids hated the principal, just because of who he was. But he never paddled anybody without good reason. His office was always dusty, with a big oak desk pushed into the center of the room. A high bookshelf sat against the wall, and when I talked to Mr. Maynard I would try to read the titles wihout seeming rude, like I wasn't listening to what he said. He liked Charles Dickens a lot, and there was a whole set in green cloth binding. I asked about it, and Mr. Maynard gave me one book called *Great Expectations,* which I read every day for three weeks, even during classes. I guess the teachers figured if I was reading I was quiet, and they didn't say anything. I had in reserve that Mr. Maynard, their boss, had asked me to read the book. The girl in that story reminded me of Mr. Maynard's daughter; her name was Stella, but she was mean to Pip, and I knew that Ellie would never be mean to me. Mr. Maynard also had a book called *Stover at Yale,* which I planned to borrow from him someday. Yale was my favorite football team, and I would maybe apply there to college if my brother Louis came up with the money. I wanted to be the first boy from the patch to go to college, and I told this to Mr. Maynard, who liked to hear a thing like that. I hoped he would tell Ellie about my ambition. Girls liked ambitious boys, usually.

I sometimes walked partway home with Mr. Maynard, and we would talk about the war. He once told me that when he heard the war was over he took his plane up to fly over the trenches, hoping to get a good look at the Huns, but it had been cloudy that day and he saw nothing. After that, he never wanted to fly again. Sometimes we would talk about *Great Expectations,* too. He liked the part about the lawyer in London, who washed his hands a lot and fingered his nose. I said maybe I would be a lawyer, and Mr. Maynard said I'd make a good one but it wasn't the best thing to wash your hands every hour and put your finger in your nose. Clients might discover these habits, he said, and take their business elsewhere. Mr. Maynard said I should visit him in the summer, and I said I would. It couldn't hurt my chances with Ellie.

Ellie also let me catch up to her on the way home from school sometimes, which is how we struck up our friendship.

I kept this friendship pretty quiet, though Mike Torrentino tried to drag it out of me. He loved details of this kind.

"You get laid yet?" he asked me in the schoolyard one day.

"Shut up, Torrentino."

"Come on, Sammy. Tell your Uncle Mike."

"It isn't your business."

"Ha! You admit it!"

"I don't admit nothing."

"You banged Ellie Maynard, I know it. I seen you to-gether."

"I didn't bang nobody."

"That the truth?"

"Cross my heart."

"I don't believe it."

"Don't care if you do or don't. It's the truth."

Mike seemed satisfied with that. But then, even if I had banged her I wouldn't tell him. Might as well take out an ad in the *Wilkes-Barre Record*.

I did bang her plenty in my dreams; it was a wonder she could tolerate so much activity. When she looked drawn at school, I understood why and felt sorry that I had been so thorough with her the night before. I knew every inch of her body, its hills and crevices, the crotch hair soft as cornsilk, the little belly.

She seemed to like my jokes and stunts in class, like the time I got everybody to stare at the ceiling when the clock struck a certain hour. It drove Miss Beattie, our history teacher, nuts. Whenever I saw Ellie in the schoolyard, she giggled or smiled. Her laughter hung in the air like sleigh bells on a winter night, ringing in my heart for days. I took to calculating every remark way before class, hoping to impress her with my lively talk. I did a very funny presentation one day on President Grover Cleveland's mouth cancer. Miss Beattie was not amused, and she said so point-blank. Ellie Maynard, however, seemed to like it. She sometimes blew out her left cheek when she saw me in the halls—just like I had done in front of the whole class while explaining the difficulties of giving a State of the Union address with your mouth full of tumors.

Now that school was out, I had to plot hard to see her. She spent the afternoons as assistant at the West Pittston Public Library, a chalk-white little brick building with green shutters and a small stone porch. Her father must have got her the job. There she sorted and stacked books, sometimes getting to stamp them at the check-out desk when Mrs. Dietrich, the head librarian, took breaks. This all impressed me. I hadn't realized how intellectual Ellie was, although Will Denks long ago said he considered her smart for a girl.

I acquired a library card fast, pretending to need some reading on airplanes, which was not completely untrue. A barnstormer had dropped out of the sky near Harding last April, when I was there. He shook my hand and showed me the inside of his two-seater, then let me try on his leather flying cap. It had a sweet, gamy smell. I decided to follow up on this interest because women appreciate men with interests, and airplanes are better in this line than stamp collecting or dinosaurs. Baseball did not count as an interest, since every boy in America had it. A girl ought to be selective.

Ellie was bent over a stack of books when I came in, stooped but well balanced, wearing a gray-flecked cotton skirt and a white shirt. The shirt was her father's, with the sleeves rolled up. I noticed the straight line of her backbone and the blond hair coiled behind her, short but full. Two neat patches of skin showed above her socks and saddle shoes.

"Ellie!" I said.

My voice hollowed the room, causing Mrs. Dietrich to glare at me. Her pince-nez, which in French means "pinched nose," slipped down the bridge; she peered over them.

Ellie motioned me into the adjacent room, which had more magazines than a barbershop. Mrs. Dietrich couldn't see us here.

"What brings you here?"

"Airplanes."

"What about them?"

"I've got to learn more . . . you know?"

"Why?"

"The Pacific," I said.

"The Pacific *Ocean?*"

"Yeah, that's it." She looked skeptical. "I might try to fly across it someday. Single-handed."

"What for?"

"China. It's the fastest route. You can get to the East by flying west. Remember Columbus?"

She knew I was just talking, but she said, "Well, we can ask Mrs. Dietrich about our selection. I don't think we're very good on airplanes here."

She started for the desk to consult Mrs. Dietrich, but I put my hand on her shoulder.

"Ellie?"

"Yes?"

"Would you want to go for a soda later on, after work?"

"I don't drink soda." She grinned like in the toothpaste commercials in the *Post.* "My teeth."

"Teeth?"

"It rots them."

"How about milk?"

She nodded, and I arranged to pick her up at five, though I didn't see much in the way of enthusiasm for my proposal.

After work, when light hung in the trees like cobwebs, we crossed the bridge into Pittston, stopping for a moment to look into the river. It had a gold tint, though near either shore the hemlocks darkened the shallows. Camel's Ledge was visible from the bridge, its toothy smile above the trees. You could make out the distant coupling of boxcars in Coston Yard and smell fumes as the dumps burned, invisibly in daylight, along the river. Because I was nervous, I said the first things that flew into my head. I told her about Vincenzo, how he quit the team when he could have been a big-league pitcher, and I talked about the mines. Ellie asked me if I didn't want to work there,

65

since my whole family was miners, but I tried to explain that we *weren't* really miners. Not at heart. Vincenzo should have been a ballplayer. Louis was in business. Jesse was a miner almost by accident, since there was nothing else for him, and Papa should have been a schoolteacher. He had been the smartest man in the patch.

Ellie talked, too. She talked a lot about her father, and I encouraged this. I wanted to find out everything about him—how he got to fly in the war, what college was like. Mr. Maynard came from Massachusetts, and I wondered what brought him to Exeter. It didn't seem likely that a college man from Massachusetts would come to this part of the country for work. I wondered, too, if Mr. Maynard read all those books on his shelf when he got home from school. If you didn't work in the mines all day, you wouldn't be so tired when you got home. You could read. I even wondered where Mr. Maynard bought the green suit he wore at school, with the vest and pocket watch. One day I would have a green suit with a vest, too. And maybe I would smoke a pipe, too. Only real gentlemen smoked pipes. As for the watch, I already had the gold chain to hang from it—my father's gold chain. The watch that hung from *that* chain went to Vincenzo, who had asked for it especially. I asked questions and listened to Ellie talk, aware that a lot of people at the soda fountain knew us and were curious, sneaking looks while they ate ice-cream sundaes.

I knew a waitress there, Maud Muncy, who gave me extra helpings of anything I ordered. She was a Catholic girl, and her family belonged to our parish in Exeter. We sat at a marble table on cane chairs, a full-length mirror on one side. I didn't like seeing myself that close, with a pimple on my nose, so I kept turning toward the counter, away from the mirror. When Ellie was done talking, I put it to her.

"So, do you like to swim?"

"Sometimes."

"Where do you go?"

"I don't, usually. But sometimes to Harvey's Lake."

"That's nice down there."

"Yes."

"You get the rich down there, don't you? They have beautiful cottages."

I recalled that Nip Stanton's father had a summer cottage at Harvey's Lake, about a dozen miles west of Wilkes-Barre. I wanted to see it, but the Nipper would never invite me, even though he did ask me to come, with everybody else in the class, to his birthday party.

"So you going to that party?"

"Which?" she said.

"The Nipper's."

Ellie sipped her drink and made a little grunt, which seemed to satisfy the need for an answer without actually giving me any notion of whether or not she was going. I knew that Ellie saw the Nipper at the Fox Hill Country Club, where her father was a member. Mr. Maynard didn't play golf, but he went to the parties, usually taking Ellie as his date. I would see Ellie with her father on the porch of the clubhouse. She was only a little motherless girl then, and I always felt sorry for her. It must have been boring to talk to so many adults. Last Christmas, when I got hired to help in the kitchen with the big Christmas party, I stood at the door and watched Ellie talking to Nip Stanton in a bright yellow party dress that made her yellow hair seem even brighter. That was the first time I knew I loved her, though I had to hide behind the swinging door. It would have been awful if she had seen me.

Now Ellie's smell, sweet as rain, crossed the table. I'd have recognized that smell anywhere. Everyone has a smell, of course, but Ellie's was so special, rich. It filled my nose and spread, like magic, through my body. I tingled all over, electric. I began to feel sexy myself, powerful.

"You ever go up to Hatchet Pond?" I asked her, feeling brazen.

"No," she said. "Never."

"Would you like to . . . with me, maybe?" Saying it, I

67

blushed. It was the next thing to an outright proposition to ask a girl up there.

"When?"

I had expected resistance but didn't get it. That could only mean one thing: *she liked me!*

It was hard to sleep that night, thinking about Ellie and me at Hatchet Pond the next morning. I lay beside the river, deep in my sleeping bag, but sat up when Will Denks banged some pots and pans.

He noticed I was alive. "You want fish? I got a couple fresh ones."

I rubbed the film from my eyes. Will had gone swimming and put on his underpants without drying himself, and his ass looked shiny. "What time is it?"

"Maybe nine," he said. It must have been much later than I imagined, since the dew had already burned off the ground, and the sun was high.

"Jeez . . ." I had agreed to meet Ellie in half an hour at the foot of Slocum Street by the Protestant chapel steps.

I stepped into the woods to piss. Pulling down my underpants in front, I pissed hard and yellow on the pine floor. It gave off an acid smell, piss and pine, which I liked.

"Here's fish," said Will, putting a bullhead in front of me on a tin plate.

"Thanks."

He watched me eat without a word.

"You going to try something?" he asked.

"With Ellie?"

"Ain't nobody else going to be with you?"

"I don't expect so," I said. "We're going to swim and maybe talk some."

He shouldn't have asked me such a thing. Even if I did try something, it would be a secret. Sex should be a secret between those who try it. I pulled tiny fishbones out of my teeth.

"Can I ask you something frank?" Will said.

"Sure. You're my best friend, aren't you?"

He hesitated. "You ever sleep with a girl?"

I stayed what you might call nonchalant. "Maybe."

Will said, "You can't answer *maybe* about that. You either did or didn't. It's like being pregnant—you are it or you ain't."

"All right, then. Nope, I didn't ever sleep with a girl."

Will's face shone like a small, lost sun; his hair seemed to frizz out further.

"How about you?" I asked.

"No, I never tried it. But I don't guess there is anything mystical about it. The idea is simple enough. In and out."

I pondered the concept of in and out for a moment. He had a good point. Nothing mystical about it. People tend to overestimate that kind of activity.

"You want a tip?" asked Will. "I read up on this once. There is something you ought to keep in mind."

I raised my eyebrows.

"If she wants it," he said, "don't rush in there. She ain't probably much more than a virgin herself, which means small and dry. You want to get her with your tongue first. Wet her up."

The notion did not appeal. "Really?"

"You got to."

"It sounds awful."

"Naw, it's okay. They say it tastes like grapes."

"Grapes?"

"Grapes."

I nearly changed my mind about sex on the spot. The thought of eating a woman's grapes like that gave me the shivers, but life was life. You couldn't remain ignorant forever. With no real joy, I set off for our meeting.

She sat on the chapel steps, holding her face to the sun for a tan. Her white skirt fluffed around her, and only her oxford shoes stuck out.

"Hey," I said.

"I thought you changed your mind."

"I was at the river. I overslept."

"You need a job, like me. It makes you dependable."

She had the day off, I said to myself, and had chosen to spend it with me.

"Feel like a swim?"

"Sure," she said, lifting her satchel.

It came to me that I didn't have a thing with me, a towel or suit. But I supposed I could get around this by swimming in my underwear, which looked something like a bathing suit. Ellie wasn't the type who would mind underpants.

We talked loud, climbing the mile or so to Hatchet Pond behind the patch. It was deserted up there most days, since the patch boys swam in the river. Hatchet Pond had too many waterweeds, lily pads, bugs, and snakes for some folks, but I loved it. It had warm, almost tepid, water. And the seclusion made it perfect for occasions like this one. I hoped Ellie wouldn't mind the sort of pussy, reeking water, which was fed by underground streams and spillage from a local mine. Some said it wasn't fit to swim in, but I'd been there a lot and never died.

"I haven't been here before," Ellie said, as we came through the trees to the pond, a yellow-green squint of water cupped among the trees, beautiful and still. "It doesn't look too healthy."

It did have a rank smell that morning, like your piss after you eat asparagus. "It's fine," I said. "I swim here all the time."

She looked at me funny. "Why's it so . . . yellow?"

"Frogs. The frogs churn up the bottom."

"Really?"

"Yep." As if to comply with me, a bullfrog squelched up the mudbank and gulped, a small grenade; its white throat pulsed.

"What an ugly frog," she said, looking like she was about to change her mind and go home.

"Frogs are a sure sign of good water," I said.

"Really?"

"Yep," I said. "They can't tolerate pollution."

Ellie put her towel down on a flat rock that overlooked the pond. She took her satchel and slipped behind a tree to change. I didn't want to seem to be trying to sneak a look, so I set my back to her and stared at the sun, which had grown fat as noon, hot and white. Waterbugs skimmed the pond, plucking rings on the smooth surface, while frogs went off at odd times like rusty springs. Bees zummed along in their way, landing on lily pads to suck at the big, white flowers.

"There's bugs all over the water," Ellie said, stepping from behind the tree in her fire-engine-red bathing suit.

"They won't bother you."

"What about the bees? I'm allergic."

"They're honeybees—no stingers."

She glanced at me, and I decided not to stretch the truth longer than I already had.

"Don't be scared of them," I said. "I come here all the time."

She said, "Why did you bring me up here? The swimming stinks."

I answered without thinking, too fast. "I like you, that's why."

"We could have gone to the river."

"Here it's more private." I searched her face for a reaction, but nothing happened. "We can talk better here, anyway. The river is too crowded."

She knew as well as I did that the Susquehanna was long enough so that one or two bends weren't crowded, but she accepted my explanation.

Meanwhile, I stole sideways glances at those legs of hers, which stuck out long and sexy from the red suit, which had little green bells on it. If you could swim at Christmas, this would be the suit to wear.

"I'm going in," she said, maybe to get out of my stare.

"Okay!" I called after her.

She stepped down the sloppy mudbank into the stagnant water, and her movement scared off a sleeping bullfrog, which belched angrily and plopped into the pond. It was fun having her back to me so that I could look to my heart's content, scanning her up and down. What a body!

"It stinks!" she said, wet to her knees. "Ugh . . . a dead fish!" She pushed the water to shove off a dead perch that had surfaced, belly-up, between her legs.

I was too entranced by her beauty to comment. I feasted on the soft backs of her knees, the little ass, the V of skin exposed on her back, the curly blond hair. It half sickened me, she was that perfect. I almost swooned off my rock.

Then *whoosh,* she was underwater, heading across the pond. It wasn't a big pond, and you could see a nice rock landing on the opposite bank; she was aiming for it. Her back being turned, I jumped out of my clothes, hoping she knew I'd want to skinny-dip out here. This place was famous for skinny-dipping. And there was the added fact that I wanted to get personal with her, and taking off my clothes was as good a way to start as any. It gets you going to see a naked body.

Soon I caught up to where she treaded water near a bay of lily pads.

"Hey," she said, seeing me, "here's a cool spot."

"Must be a spring."

I swam up to her, face-to-face. "I told you it was good water."

"I'm not drinking it," she said. "Too young to die."

"Who said you were supposed to drink it?"

She splashed and huffed. "How come the fish are all dead?"

"Fish are like people. They run out of juice and . . . *poof.* They die."

"Yuck," she said. "There's some kind of weeds underneath here. I can feel them."

"They can feel you, too."

I thought I made a good joke, but she immediately swam to the other shore. I followed, swimming with my eyes above the surface like a seal, watching her climb the bank and shake off the water and turn to sit in the sun.

I glided into the shallows, keeping low.

"Hey, come on out," she said after I didn't budge for maybe ten minutes.

"I like it here."

"I want to talk to you," she said.

"About what?"

She hesitated. "Airplanes."

"Airplanes?"

"That's what you read up on, isn't it?"

"Yeah, but—"

"Come on."

Why was she prodding me into the open? I knew I should have left on my underpants. It would have been more respectful to a lady. I hadn't even kissed her yet—which is normally the first step in a romance. I cursed myself for being so dumb. Here I was, not only butt-naked, but hard as pepperoni. I only just noticed it when I looked down and saw it bobbing in the water.

"Hey, come on up here! The sun's great."

Maybe she had seen me, after all. Maybe she wanted the full view. Why else would she prod me up there? If she was ready, then fine, I was too. If she wasn't, what could be better than for her to see me? She'd love it. And wasn't sex the whole point of Hatchet Pond? She hadn't come up here alone with me for her health, had she? Also, wasn't it time I lost my virginity? Louis lost his at twelve. Vincenzo you couldn't tell about, but I was sure he hadn't been pure at fifteen. And, God, hadn't Mike Torrentino got a girl pregnant already? Hadn't Billy Shawgo been laid before puberty? I didn't know about Nip Stanton, but he didn't act like a virgin. I suspected only me and Will Denks were left pure in the whole goddamn town. We gave the patch something of a bad name.

"Just wave your cock at a girl, and she'll do it," said Mike Torrentino to me one time in the schoolyard. He knew quite a bit about girls and sex, and his advice came to me in a flash.

But what if it did turn her on? What exactly would I do?

73

The basic notion seemed fairly easy—she had a hole, which would fit my pecker. I was to stick it up there and twist it around until it shot off. But did girls shoot off, too?

"What are you doing down there?" she asked.

What was she trying on me?

Okay, I said to myself. Go ahead. She's asking for it anyway. She wants it bad, probably. She needs it.

I stepped on weak knees out of the tepid pond water, pushing through camouflaging reeds until the waistline of water dropped, suddenly, first to my belly button, then to my knees. I stood in the bald sunlight, exposed, hard and huge, the skin pulled tight as could be and my whole organ curling upward toward the sky.

"Holy Simon!" she said in a soft astonished voice.

"Hi," I said.

"Jesus!" she said.

I couldn't see her well in the bright light, but her smile was too wide to mistake.

Then she started giggling. I'd half expected her to take fright and run, but I never counted on giggles.

I froze there, knee-deep in water.

"Hey," she said after a while, "I didn't mean to hurt your feelings, but . . ."

Blood rushed through my cheeks and temples, thumping and hot. It hadn't worked. I could see I hadn't turned her on.

Beet-red, I fell backward into the sloppy water and swam hard for the other shore. I grabbed my clothes in a heap and rushed through the prickerbush, the vetch and burdock, coughing as I ran. I was crying like a kid, sick and dizzy. Somewhere on the way home I stopped and dressed and fell on the ground facedown and let my tears soak the grass. I made an angel in the soft grass with my body, like you do in winter, in the snow.

8

Who needs a woman anyway? I thought, brushing the pine needles off my trousers and shirt. I got home about lunchtime. Mama was in the kitchen, kneading lumps of white dough into oblong loaves. They were laid out on the table on waxed paper and dusted with flour.

"Where you been, Sammy? Jesse wanted you."

"Nowhere."

"That's no answer for your mother."

"I've been swimming."

She pressed her knuckles into the dough. "Swim, swim, swim," she said. I couldn't tell what her opinion was.

I broke off a slab of uncooked dough.

"*Basta!*" Mama said, knocking me with one hand. "That'll make you sick. It ain't been cooked yet."

Gino came waltzing through with a mop. Mama had him waxing the wood floors with butcher's wax, and he hated this job. It was his one regular chore and it took him a whole afternoon every month because we had so many wood floors.

"You ain't going to tell me you done?" she said to Gino.

"I'm done."

"I'm going to check those floors close. If they don't shine like a new nickel, you got trouble."

Gino put up the mop and opened the icebox. He took out a leftover rabbit pie.

I sat down with Gino and took some pie for myself. It was good cold. The *Record* was on the table with Calvin Coolidge on the front page. He was in Philadelphia to celebrate the Fourth of July and stood on a train platform with his wife and the mayor, Kendrick. They gave him a forty-eight-gun salute, one for each state, and he made a speech about "inalienable rights" and "idealism" and "destiny."

"What are you reading about?" Gino asked me.

"Independence Day in Philly."

"What's that?"

"Fourth of July, that's what."

"Oh, that."

"The date when America said to hell with England. They were taxing us too heavy and ruled us with Redcoats. So we revolted."

"Yeah?"

"Yeah." Sometimes it wasn't worth talking to Gino. He was ignorant, to judge by what he said. I wondered how he'd ever turn out.

He ate quickly and ran off with an apple, leaving me to talk to Mama. She sat down opposite me, laying her red hands on the table.

"What you looking at me like that for?" I said.

"You got yourself in trouble?"

"Why do you ask me that?"

"I can tell when something is wrong."

I had nothing to say to her about Ellie Maynard. A mother doesn't need that kind of information. "Naw, you're dreaming up stuff."

"Okay, okay," she said, raising her hands. "Anyway, your neck is sunburnt." She went to a drawer by the sink and brought out some Zonite, which she spread into my neck and ears. It smelled like rabbit piss.

"That stinks," I said. "Anyway, I'm not really burned."

"Shut up."

I let her work it in deep with her fingers, and it felt good. Mama had a gardener's strong hands.

"Ouch," I said. "Don't rub so hard."

"It don't work if you don't rub it in hard."

I let her knead and pull, twist and wrench. She had always liked to rub my back, and I liked to let her. The smell of her above was a good thing—like wind in the woods. It came over you strong when she stood close, and your body tingled. You melted when she touched you, her fingertips hot and quick. They dug under your skin, deep, and found the hard knots that hurt, that needed relaxing. When she got done with you, it was like you had found a new body.

"Anyways," said Mama, "Lucy's been promised a job at the diner across from the biscuit company."

"She's really going to quit school?"

"Why shouldn't she? A girl don't need that much schooling, Sammy."

"A girl is the same as a boy. She has to make her way in the world just the same."

"A girl has to get married, that's all," she said.

"And what if her husband dies?"

Mama shrugged her shoulders. She hated arguments, since she always lost them. "She's going to marry Bonino."

"Bonino!"

"He's got money," she said. "That's good, huh?"

"He's a snake," I said. "And how do you know they're getting married?"

"I know."

"Did she say so?"

"No."

This relieved me. Mama was only jumping to conclusions.

If I knew Lucy, she had implied that Bonino was about to ask her to get married just so she could quit school.

"Why are things so crazy around here?" I said, more to myself than to Mama.

She started kneading and twisting again, pressing her apron into my shoulders.

"I got to see Father Francis today," I said, reminding myself. "He wants to see me at four."

"What for?"

"I don't know. He wants to see me."

"I knew you was in trouble."

"I'm not."

"Damn it, you're my only boy that don't cause trouble, and now here you go."

"Take it easy," I said. "You'll keel over."

"Don't I get enough with Louis in New York and Vincenzo in the union, and Lucy, my poor Lucy . . ." She trailed off, looking like despair.

I stood up and put my arms around her. "Mama, I am not in trouble. Listen to me."

"Don't you go and make worries for your mama," she said. "I got enough to worry without you."

"I think Father Francis wants me to mow the convent lawn or something. It's nothing serious."

This invention seemed to satisfy her. "You're my boy, Sammy."

"Thanks, Mama."

She lifted a fresh loaf from the oven and put it down on the counter. It steamed in the pan, the color of topsoil. "You want some fresh bread?"

"Sure."

"Let it cool a minute. Then *mangia, mangia*. Eat."

On the way to St. Anne's I went into Bo Wilson's for a root beer, and it was my luck Bonino sat next to Bo with a crocodile grin on his face like he just inherited a fleet of Buicks from that millionaire jailbird of a brother he had. You never saw Bonino except in a jacket, with a starched high collar and a fat tie with pictures. Today's tie had palm trees on it, beneath which girls did the hula dance on a white sandy beach. He put his thin fingers out for a handshake.

"Sammy, I been wanting for us to have a little heart-to-heart, hey boy?"

This wasn't my idea of a picnic. I tried to slink back, hoping he'd just go away.

"Bo here's been filling me in on you folks," said the snake, which made Bo Wilson's eyes blank out. He scuttled into the back room, where he kept bags of grain, tin cans, a mop and pail, some extra cases of soda, and stuff like that.

"What did you need to know?" I asked Bonino.

"I figure it don't hurt, the way I see it, to familiarize myself with the territory, if you follow my tune."

He offered me a Lucky Strike. "You got quite a gal there, ain't it?"

"Huh?" I accepted a light from his match.

"Ole Luce."

"Lucy?"

"A dame if there ever was a dame, if you follow my tune."

"I'm following your tune."

"Listen, Sam, may I call you Sam?"

"Sure."

"Just call me Bonino. You don't need no 'mister' with me, boy, if you follow my tune."

"I follow it fine."

"Great! We're pals, hey? Pals. I like pals. I got lots of pals down the line, where I come from. You ever come down the line?"

"No."

"I think you're right. I like it here better. This patch is nice. You folks sure got the place, though, ain't it? That yellow house. I don't think there's a patch in the Wyoming Valley with a house nice as that one. It's got class."

"Bonino," I said. "What do you do exactly for a living? You got a job somewhere?" I figured I had a duty to investigate some since my sister was so flipped out for the guy. You never know what a seventeen-year-old girl will do when her juices start to flow.

"I'm waiting on the funds, kid. There's funds coming my way, you know, from the family. I got this brother in Jersey, you see?"

"I follow your tune."

"You're a smart boy, Sam. You got my story figured out, don't you? You think like maybe I'm some kind of operator."

"I wouldn't say that."

"Between us, Sam, I'm totally legit. Legal as a Jesuit." He lifted his hand as if to swear something. "Listen," he said. "Step out back here. I want to show you something."

I followed him into the alley behind Bo's store, where his shiny Buick was pulled up to the door. It had a red leather interior and an ivory inlaid steering wheel. You could smell the rubber tires that heated in the sun. I put a hand on the hot blue hood.

"She's my dame," said Bonino. "A real lady."

"Lucy likes her," I said, trying to imply something that wouldn't just slip through Bonino's skull. I studied his face in the sun, the yellowy skin, the thin jaw coming to a point, the long bumpy nose with warts on one side. Hollywood would never beat down his door. But I had to admit, there was a charm about the man. What you saw was what you got, sort of like President Coolidge.

"I'd like to sell Buicks someday. Get myself a dealership. I'm a mechanic by trade, you know," Bonino went on.

"You ever work at a garage?"

"My whole life I worked," he said. "Quit school at twelve to work in my uncle's garage in Shamokin. Came back this way to work in Wilkes-Barre when the shop closed."

For the moment, Bonino didn't seem so bad. But he was definitely ugly. I still couldn't see what a beautiful girl like

80

Lucy could see in a man like this. A Buick isn't everything.

"You want to go for a drive?"

"Sure," I said. I didn't often get to ride in a Buick.

Bonino brightened. I watched him like you watch any curiosity as he revved the engine, let off the brake, and tore out through the patch down Exeter Avenue, driving me all the way to Bonser's Gas Station and back. As we drove, he talked up and down about brakes—brake linings, fluids, adjustments. I asked him to let me off at the church.

"The church?" he asked. "You religious or something?"

"Something," I said. "If you follow my tune."

His broken-toothed smile widened. He winked at me. "I get you, kid. You're some boy, you are. Lucy's got one helluva brother. Everything she said about you is true."

I don't know how he did it, but he made me feel kindly toward him. I half looked forward to seeing him again as he drove off down Balsom Street, the proudest man in Luzerne County.

At the church I stopped to listen as the tower bells rang with a tinny cheapness, and the pigeons squawked. It was four o'clock, but the flat brightness of the sun was more like noon, without shadows: pure radiation. The ground squeaked underfoot when you walked like with dry snow in January. I watched a lizard scramble under the church foundation and shuddered, imagining the basement full of ugly things like snakes and rats. On the doorstep a mound of red ants seethed, thousands of them, feeding on a bit of chocolate. Somebody must have thrown it away before going in to mass, where a mouthful of candy would make you feel guilty.

I pulled open the door, and it came easy. Too easy. Like a ghost had blown it open from inside. Ghosts, holy and otherwise, hung out in these buildings. I looked to either side of the dark church. Empty. The door shut behind me with a punky sound. I tried to stare into the main body of the church, toward the altar, but my eyes went blank. It was like a whale

81

had swallowed me. Dark, *so* dark . . . The nave didn't become visible for a bit, appearing first in windows—the glass streaked with color. Then came the cross over the altar, and the face of Christ—his thin, nailed hands and scrawny legs with the feet pegged. I crossed myself three times quickly to pay respects and show gratitude for what he'd done, his sacrifice for people he'd never even met. God wanted to make a connection with man, who was so far away and could not make contact. He created Jesus, a man who set himself up as an example of how men, at their best, could be. Jesus got himself killed, of course— the likely result of so much goodness in a bad world—but they couldn't kill God. He was still here, distant but close, saying nothing. He was the watcher, the Big Eye, staring off church walls, out of the sky at night.

Candles wavered in the dark: tiny points of light in the front chapel, an alcove where for a penny you could light a wick for somebody dead and St. Anne herself would intervene with God. I lit one here for Papa every day for six months after he got killed. Now I lit one every week for him, hoping that St. Anne was putting in good words for him all over the place.

It came down on me hard now about Papa; I got so weak I sat down on the nearest pew. It didn't seem fair how Papa was carried home mangled and unwashed like that and laid out on the porch, and how I'd been so hopeful about him, having prayed hour after hour that he was all right down there while they dug. I really thought God had said, "Okay, you can have your papa back." The news struck me dumb. I didn't cry for weeks. It wasn't real that he was dead, not Papa, who was so good to me and the family, so good to everybody in the patch. They all said so. They said so as I stood by the bier and they went past and shook my hand. I never believed it was him, my own papa, dead. I was dreaming, and the day would break shortly and I'd breathe a sigh and go down to breakfast, where he would fill my cup with coffee and warm milk. I would say, "Papa, I dreamed you were dead," and he would laugh. "Shut up and drink. Drink," he would say.

Now I knew he *was* dead. He was another Big Eye in heaven, staring through the clouds at me. He was in the million leaves that rattle in the wind, in the rocks by the river, underground. Which made me shudder when I realized he had actually seen me this morning, bare-ass, in front of Ellie Maynard! Papa, I said, I didn't mean anything by it! I wanted her, that's all. What about Adam and Eve? I saw pictures of them in a book once running naked in the woods.

My eyes watered, and my neck burned with the Zonite, which I must have touched with my fingers and accidentally rubbed into my eyes. Damn, I thought. Damn, damn, damn. I pounded a fist hard on the pew in front.

The thud startled me. I realized that I wasn't alone. Mrs. Montoro, the widow, hunched a few pews ahead of me, praying. I could hear her muttering through her rosary. She was dressed, as usual, in black shoes, black stockings, black dress, with a babushka on her head. Why hadn't she gone all the way and become a nun? She might as well, given that she came here every afternoon and never missed eight-o'clock morning mass. The saints were said to favor her requests, and for a small fee she would put in a good word for you.

Up front, and in alcoves dedicated to the saints, the candles burned, sometimes wavering in the dark, snuffing out like the body itself, which having spent the miserable length of itself, goes dark. Weirdly, I liked it here, so calm and damp and cool, like a tomb. The wicks burning around the room seemed to mirror each other. The world seemed caught here, doubled, multiplied in a cross-thatch of flames—a zillion little lights that flare, so briefly, against the barn-dark universe. Flash and fade.

"Hello, Sammy," a voice came. Father Francis was behind me, and his fingers touched the Zonite on my neck.

I jumped, shuddering.

"Come into my office, Sam."

"Yes, Father."

I followed him to the front, then turned right through his door.

"Sit down," he said, motioning to a cracked leather chair beside the bookcase.

It felt cold against my sweaty back.

I looked around the room, thinking how nice it was for a priest's office. It was nicer than Dr. Folario's, the dentist in Pittston, though smaller.

Jesus hung over the door. There was one big window with blue curtains that kept out the fresh air.

Father sat on the edge of the oak desk and scuffed his feet back and forth on the rug. He said, "How's everything at home?"

"Good."

"I bet your mother's glad your brother is home."

"Yeah, she hates hospitals as much as jails."

"I like your brother Vincenzo, even though he doesn't come to church."

"Me too."

"He stands up for what he believes in, which you don't see much in these times." He lit a cigar. His cheeks puffed like a bellows, and the sweat popped out on his forehead. His upper lip lathered, a moustache of sweat. The paunch bulged through his shirt above the belt. He wore the usual white socks.

"Sammy, you stand out among the patch boys," he said.

I thought, among the patch boys? Did he think Nip Stanton was any better?

"I was interested that you would attend your brother's meeting in Pittston," he went on. "Not many boys your age care about union politics."

True. I sure didn't, I thought.

"Not many care about anything at your age—except girls or baseball."

"Yup."

"Sammy," he said. "Have you by any chance thought about . . . a vocation?"

84

"A what?"

"You know, your future life."

"Oh." I paused to make a serious reply. "Yes."

"Well?"

"I might be a lawyer."

He stood up and paced the room, as if motion would help his process of thought. The cigar burned quickly as he sucked. He said, "Oh yes . . . that. Yes, it's a good profession. The law is very fine for those who do it. But as you know, Sam, it takes years of study at a good college to succeed as a lawyer. You'll need lots of money." He flicked white ash onto his desk, missing the ashtray by inches. "I asked your mother about this one day. She really thinks you are dreaming, not unless Louis comes through with a very generous offer."

I didn't say anything but looked away.

He shot me an irritated glance. "Your brother Louis would have been better off to live in Exeter."

"Why is that, Father?" I tried not to register emotion. Cold potatoes all the way.

He saw I had him. "Oh, you know. . . . One meets many temptations in the city that you don't get around here."

"I could get a scholarship, maybe," I said.

"Maybe you could," he said. "They don't give too many."

Father Francis went behind the desk, taking up his proper place. He folded his hands in front of him. "Sam," he said, "I admire your ambition about the law. But you know it's a long shot—a dream." He paused.

"I wonder if you ever read the Bible, Sam?"

"A bit," I said. "I read up on Jonah and the whale not long ago."

"Good."

"But it's those 'begats' that get me down."

"The . . . 'begats'?"

"You know. Abraham *begat* Isaac who *begat* somebody else."

This appeared to tickle him, and he smiled. "It's the women who do the *begetting*," he said, embarrassing himself by such a comment. He had a gold tooth on the left side, bottom row, and it shone with spit. He sombered up and said, "Do you believe in God, Sam?"

All right, I thought. What's he got on me? I looked at him and said, "Yep, I do."

"And do you want to serve Him above all else, like He wants you to?"

"If He wants it, yes."

He took on a serious look like I never saw on him before. "Sam, in which case, I wonder if you've ever thought about serving Him as a priest."

Jeez, I thought to myself. Father Samuel di Cantini. The notion had, many times, streaked through my brain. Often, at mass, I thought about myself in those robes, the center of a ceremony of importance to everybody. I understood how powerful a priest was, how they had control over the mystery of communion, the changing of bread and wine to flesh and blood. But there was that ban on girls. . . . It didn't seem possible to say, once and for all time, no. You would never have a family. You would live alone in a drafty house beside a chapel, with no one for real company but a nun or two. It chilled me a little. But then, now that I had ruined myself in front of Ellie Maynard and the eyes of Papa and God, all at once, maybe the priesthood was the thing. I'd guarantee a spot for myself in heaven, and I'd probably bring the whole di Cantini family behind me. A family with a son for a priest gets every break when God takes His final sum. Maybe I should say a prayer about this.

"I see you're meditating on this, Sam. That's good." He lurched back in his squeaky chair, then spread his knees apart. I could see his crotch, which had a hole in it below the zipper. He had on yellow cotton underpants, which shined through, and it struck me as a revelation that even a priest wore underpants. "But I should put another question to you," he said.

"What's that?"

He poured his eyes over me in a kindly way and said, "How do you feel about girls, Sam?"

"What do you mean, Father?"

"I mean, have you experienced physical desire for a girl?"

Just what I figured. He knew about Ellie Maynard all along. I said, "Yes, Father," and looked to the floor and tried to control my expression.

"You needn't be ashamed, Sam," he said.

"I'm not, Father," I said, but I began to sputter. "I just took my clothes off like anybody would have in the circumstances. They all go bare-ass up there. But the way she tempted me up out of the water like that, well you'd expect a boner in that situation, wouldn't you?"

The good Father stared at me. He shook his head. "I wouldn't know, Sam, I . . ." The ash on his cigar had gotten two inches long and it crumpled into sparks on his pants; he jumped to brush it off. Coming around again to the front, he laid his hand on my knee. "We are only human, Sam. But St. Paul warns us, he challenges us, to put God first, before everything. And that includes girls."

This conversation had gone on longer than seemed right for a summer afternoon, so I said, maybe too abruptly for his taste, "Can I go now, Father?"

"If you promise to think about what I've told you, Sam."

I quickly promised and stood up, face-to-face. My eyes turned to the door.

"Can I ask you one more question, Sam?"

I agreed by waiting.

"Have you ever been . . . *physical* . . . with a girl?"

"Nope," I said, catching his intent. "I haven't." I could say that plain as day without fear of getting struck dead by Our Father Who Art Up There.

"I'm very glad to hear that," he said. He put both his palms on my shoulders. "Remember, Sam. A priest has tremendous powers. God gives us the ability to transform bread and wine into flesh and blood. We are entrusted with the sacraments." His eyes widened. "I will pray for you, my son," he said. "I will ask God to speak to you about your vocation."

"Thanks," I said. "Can I go now, Father?"

"Of course." He seemed a bit annoyed. "And you should pray hard yourself about this," he added. "Will you do this for me?"

"Okay," I said, looking at him to say I meant it.

I stepped out into the afternoon light, which had begun to collect shadows. Wherever I looked, the world sank back. My legs badly wanted to move. Was I really going to be a priest? It would make more sense if Ellie Maynard were a Catholic. Imagine! I would get to hear her confessions!

God, God, I said to myself, make everything fall clear.

I climbed up behind Indian Rock, west of the patch, where Papa would take me to hunt arrowheads. The woods smelled hot and moist, and the leaves shone. The air was full of birdsong, squirrel noises, small animals stepping on twigs. Thinking about the future, you tended to drift away from reality. Here, the real world could be touched, felt, tasted. I put my tongue into the bark of a birch tree. It tasted bitter, the stuff of birch beer. The ground let off the ripe smell of last year's leaves, and my foot sunk into one soft spot, like shit, but I liked it, the fact that the earth wasn't hard everywhere; it had a million textures and colors. You could spend your entire life ten times over and never count the different things in one small patch of forest. Thinking of Papa, who could detect hidden things like an Indian, I looked for a bird's nest, but none showed itself. Because of Papa's secret sense for things, people asked to work beside him in the mines. They figured that if anybody could sense a cave-in, it would be Papa. He once led the whole shift out of the pits on a hunch. The foreman tried to get everyone to go back down, saying that Papa was crazy. Sure enough, an hour after they got out, it collapsed. A million tons of rock and dirt that crushed the pillars like saplings.

Something must have gone horribly wrong that day last summer when the roof gave and crushed Papa. He must have been asleep inside, his secret sense shut off. Who knows, maybe the foreman, Bruno Slazzi, refused to let him come out. Slazzi was killed with Papa; he was a tough, stupid guy from Palermo who lived in Bing Stanton's back pocket. He drove the miners crazy, keeping them right to the coal face till the whistle blew, cutting their pay if they reported to work a few minutes late or took extra breaks. Vincenzo said if Bruno Slazzi hadn't been killed last summer, the miners would have killed him anyway. A foreman in Hazleton had been murdered by his own men last April, and nobody got nailed for it. They found him several days after he was murdered, his head bashed in with a shovel. Everybody swore it must have been an accident, but nobody falls on a shovel like that. Bruno Slazzi would have gone that way long before if Papa hadn't defended him. Papa said that Slazzi couldn't help it if God didn't issue him brains at the beginning. He would help him fill out his reports and try to explain to him about the proper way to deal with people as human beings. Maybe Papa shouldn't have helped him. He should have refused to follow Slazzi into such a dangerous vein that day last summer.

Each time I remembered what happened at Hatchet Pond, I was glad Papa wasn't around to discuss what I'd done. Nobody else had ever seen me hard like that before, and I couldn't believe it happened with me in the water, my prick waving its nostril in the air like "how-do-you-do." I slumped back against a tree, thinking of Ellie Maynard and her beautiful body. I barely stopped myself from jerking off right there, in the woods. I had done it in the woods many times, but it seemed wrong to do such a thing no more than half an hour after talking to Father Francis about entering the priesthood. God would never understand.

I fell on a deep cushion of sleep and slept for God knows how long and woke startled by a train whistle in the distance. I got up and started walking, imagining that years, maybe decades, had passed since I'd been asleep—like Rip Van Winkle. I'd go back to the patch now, and the houses would be beautifully painted, the porches fresh with new boards. They'd be selling lovely fresh fruit—pineapples and things—in baskets in front of Bo Wilson's store. I'd rush home to find Mama at the door, an old lady with white hair, and she'd go wild for me. She'd kiss me all over. Later, Vincenzo would come home, himself a senator for Pennsylvania. He would have a tall, gorgeous wife. Lucy, he'd tell me, lived next door. She hadn't married Bonino after all. She had married a doctor from West Pittston, and he had set up practice in the patch. She had five sons, all with black eyes and black hair, all saying funny things and running in the yard. Louis, he would say, had replaced Bing Stanton as operator of #8. He lived in Bing's old house in West Pittston, married to a famous movie actress from New York City. Bing had gone bust and moved to Jersey, where he now sold seashells in Atlantic City. His son, the Nipper, was an assistant seashell seller. Gino, of all things, was now a famous lion tamer with Barnum and Bailey. Jesse had died, he said, in his sleep—very sad, of course, but not horrible. Everybody has to go sometime.

I ran down the hill through the woods and came out into a clearing from which you could see the Susquehanna Valley in green light. A coal train pulled by, gathering speed for the journey north. The huge ugly breaker was visible, and you faintly heard its whinnying sound, the cables grinding against each other as it drew hunks of raw anthracite along its belt. The breaker operated until nine o'clock, with all the boys who worked there sorting the garbage from the good stuff, their faces and hands black, their lungs full of dust. I'd had many a nightmare about that breaker, having seen men who worked there die off, one by one, at a young age. They'd employ you as soon as you turned fourteen. A lot of patch boys worked there now who had gone to junior high school with me. Billy Shanks, who played catch with me for years, was there at this moment. So was Hitch Lima's brother, Freddy, who'd been in the breaker since he was twelve, and nobody objected. At least the operators didn't let you go into the mines until you were sixteen.

90

Suddenly the light gouged my eyes, and I shaded my brow with one hand. Was that God prodding me with His light? Once I used to think that God sat inside the sun, which is why it burned so finely. I figured that the Devil sat in the moon, which is why night surrounded it. The stars, I reckoned, were tiny demons; the shooting stars were worse. But now that I had learned in school about astronomy and knew of planets and solar systems, I understood that light and dark were physical qualities having to do with energy. I also knew that God wasn't a simple ball of fire overhead in the sky. He kept pretty much out of sight, and it took some doing to smoke Him into the open. That's why folks hired Mrs. Montoro to do their praying for them. I also knew that the Devil hid himself pretty cleverly, too, and you had to keep an eye out or he'd fool you. That was the worst thing about living: right and wrong were so damnably close that you almost had to try them on to see which was which. I wondered, in fact, if you could ever tell anything until you fell dead and could peer back with a little distance on the things you'd done.

9

What drew me back to Hatchet Pond? I don't know, but I went back early each morning for a couple weeks after my papers were delivered. I liked early morning along Slocum Street, with the light fiery in the windows of Bo Wilson's store. At that hour, just after sunrise, the miners sipped their coffee as their wives dipped sleepy faces into basins of cold water. Dogs came out to piss, tilting sideways on three legs against trees or fences, watching the milk wagon clatter down the street, having finished with the patch by now, its tin barrels like beans in a split peapod. The driver sat on a high throne and reined in the horses. He was a big Hunky from Warsaw with a cannonball forehead and hairy arms bleached by the sun.

I would run straight down the middle of the street with my papers, sidestepping the fly-speckled horse turds, thinking that shit was real, and the pond was real, too: a warm body of water to enter, green and smelly.

I didn't swallow the water, of course, but floated, a human lily pad, on my back, arching my toes through the scum. Waterbugs stalled over the surface, millions of them, feeding on smaller, invisible bugs. Fish who were not yet dead from swallowing poisonous chemicals hopped into the sunlight and gulped the waterbugs that came too near the surface. I imagined a big dark fish, deep down, feeding on smaller fish who lived near the light. A hawk, high overhead, had made Hatchet Pond its private territory: It circled slowly, looking for God knows what. I watched it as I lay there, sometimes losing it in a flash of sunlight, wondering if maybe it might not dive into my heart. What a way to go! I wouldn't mind, except that they'd tell Mama I was swimming naked and alone at Hatchet Pond when I died. She'd never understand.

Vincenzo might understand. He and I had been getting closer. We would sit on the back porch at night and talk about things. He told me about his plans for a big strike that might happen at the end of the summer, a strike that would bring about the first real reforms in anthracite mining. Whether or not he lost his job didn't seem to worry him. He was smart enough to get better work anyway. He said that mining was only good work if you treated the job with respect; this meant that you avoided extreme risks for the sake of profit. Vincenzo was able to imagine a day—ten or twenty years off—when the miners would actually own the mines themselves. He explained to me about Russia and their great revolution, which had allowed the working classes to own a part of the factories or mines. America would have to change, or there would be a revolution. He said that so firmly that I believed him.

I didn't see Will Denks for the two weeks that I went to Hatchet Pond by myself, but I thought about him as I swam. The pond stank, but I preferred it to the river just now. The river was Will. No matter when in my life I'd see that river, I would think of him. If I ever came back in, say, 1970, a wealthy retired lawyer from New York City, I would go see that bend in the river where Will Denks once made his camp. It would be overgrown, with no sign of his beautifully crafted lean-to, the ring of stones where he cooked over an open fire, the engineered dock. But the trees would be the same, or similar. They'd be the tall children of the trees that lived there now. And Will Denks would be there, too, in the air, the water. He'd never really die so long as the Susquehanna poured below the patch through Luzerne County.

The two weeks at Hatchet Pond were the loneliest of the summer, I think. But I needed them. I had too many notions in my head that wanted a place to land. The buzz had to become silence before I could meet with people again. I didn't even go to church. Mama was furious, but I paid no attention. I said God wanted me elsewhere, which Jesse thought was terrific. He said God wanted him somewhere, too, and he disappeared from the house. We were lucky Gino didn't hear my remark, or God would have wanted him, too—probably to play marbles down the street.

It was near the end of my two quiet weeks that Lucy decided to run away and marry Bonino. "One thing after another," was the way Mama put it. She was actually pleased to have a married daughter, though she wished it had been done properly, in church. The neighbors would never shut up about our family now.

I heard about the wedding when I came home for lunch on a Saturday to find everybody gathered in the kitchen.

"What's going on?" I said.

"Read the letter," said Vincenzo. He passed me a note on yellow paper.

It was Lucy's hand, all right. It read: DEAR MAMA: I WILL BE GONE TOMORROW WHEN YOU WAKE UP. DON'T WORRY ABOUT ME. ME AND BONINO WENT TO NIAGARA FALLS TOGETHER IN HIS BUICK. WE GOT MARRIED BY A JUSTICE OF THE PEACE LAST NIGHT IN WILKES-BARRE. DON'T WORRY ABOUT NOTHING. I'LL SEND A CARD. YOUR DEAR DAUGHTER, LUCY.

"He must have knocked her up," said Gino. "Bang, bang, bang."

Mama figured this was a slur and said, "*Sie non voglia!*"

"I don't think she's pregnant," said Vincenzo. "She was in love with him. You could tell by the way she's been acting."

"I hope she enjoys the waterfall, anyways," said Jesse.

"Maybe Bonino will go over the falls in a barrel," said Gino.

"She's a married lady now," Vincenzo said. "We got to respect that. He didn't force her to do nothing. It's all her choice."

Mama said that she would have arranged a proper wedding if her daughter had only asked. Lucy's age didn't matter— Mama had herself been married to Papa a full year younger than Lucy, at sixteen. But Father Francis would be furious. A civil wedding wasn't a wedding in the eyes of God.

"Bang, bang, bang," said Gino.

Fortunately, Mama didn't exactly understand what Gino meant. She figured he was playing cowboys. For my part, I could hardly imagine my own sister, Lucy, naked in a distant hotel bed with that snake crawling over her, messing her up.

"The boy's got money, anyways," said Jesse. "His brother in Trenton is in the bootleg business. He's a gambler, too."

"Money like that we don't need," said Mama.

"He plans to open a garage or something," I said. "He told me. He knows everything about brakes—brake fluid, brake linings, adjustments." They all looked at me like I was nuts.

I didn't feel like eating anything and went up to my room to read *Ivanhoe* or write a letter to someone. It sometimes made me happier if I wrote my thoughts down in a letter. But who would I write? I sat at my desk, wondering, thinking of Lucy, Mama, Ellie Maynard.

Women were a puzzle, especially Mama. She was the first woman I knew well. But a puzzle has a solution, even though it might not be available at the moment. I gave up looking for Mama's solution long ago: She was my nag, my boss, my servant, my doctor. Each way of looking at her seemed equally true.

Lucy, on the other hand, puzzled me less. Older sisters fall into patterns. They fight with you, then expect allegiance. They curse you out for your habits—for the socks worn the third week in a row or underpants thrown on the bathroom floor and left—but what about their unspeakable habits? They rob you for petty cash and won't give you a dime back when you ask for it. But you tolerate them in spite of this, knowing how in the general mess and confusion of the world they're on your side. They won't let an outsider do you dirt. But today, Lucy had become as much a puzzle as Mama. More so. Though I half liked Bonino, he didn't seem like the sort anybody would really *marry*.

Which led me to thoughts of Ellie Maynard. Now if Bonino could with his reptile body and bony face contrive to marry my beautiful sister, why couldn't I work a similar magic on Ellie? I could win her with my eloquence, which Miss Turner had remarked on in front of the whole class on two specific occasions. Hadn't I written fine poems in rhyme since the second grade? I sat down to compose a poem instead of a letter:

If Only

How shall I win thy heart, my love,
When all around Thee others flock?
Not even our God who reigns above
Could turn Thy heart, that rock.

Not even God could make Thine eyes
Like glorious sunsets sit on me.
Not even God Himself, who tries
To daily make us see.

If I were a flower, and you, a bee,
I'd by the roadside sit content,
And oozing the nectar that is me,
O never with a lament.

If only Thy heart could know how I
Alone can make you happiest,
Then maybe we could together die,
Die happily, at rest.

I finished this one and buzzed all over, really tingled. It was beautiful! And true! I put it in the mail to Ellie the same afternoon, walking to the post office in West Pittston through the hot midday sun. Once I mailed it, I got cold feet and thought of trying to get it back. Will Denks knew where they kept the dynamite used for mining, and it occurred to me that we could blow up the box; but that seemed a little extreme to retrieve a poem. So I let it fly in the public mails—my heart in words.

The more I pondered, the more exciting it seemed to imagine Ellie Maynard in her bedroom, propped up against a pillow in her silky underwear or maybe naked, studying "If Only" by Samuel di Cantini, poet. I lost any thoughts of Lucy and Bonino, who by this time probably stood watching the big falls thunder and sparkle like all in a day's work.

Though a postcard came from Niagara Falls, full of chatty sentences in Lucy's hand, we didn't know when she would get back from her honeymoon. She'd been gone over a week when, on a wet weekday morning, with Vincenzo at work and Jesse asleep with his knee raised on a pillow in the living room, Bonino's Buick trundled up to our house. I was sitting on the porch, searching the *Record* for baseball scores. There was a big piece on Hornsby. The Babe was going crazy, too, slapping the ball into the stands every day. The Buick stopped so abruptly that Lucy was thrown forward, and her cloche fell off.

It had been rainy all week, the first full week of rain that summer, but today there was more mist than rain, though occasional drops swam through it like dew. Not the best sort of day for a homecoming, but I was happy to see Lucy. I didn't want to have to greet her and Bonino alone, so I rushed out back, where Mama was in the garden.

"They're here!" I said. "Lucy and Bonino!"

Mama sort of yelped, beagle-like, and raced around the house, her dress billowing.

Jesse was there because he had hurt his knee at work. A piece of rock fell on it and it swelled up, so the company doctor ordered him off work till it reduced itself to normal. Because he was such a hypochondriac, we didn't take it too seriously. He cried wolf maybe once too often, and nobody came running. He limped onto the front porch on his cane, wearing a yellow scarf and a straw hat. He was a very strange man.

Mama and Lucy cried into each other's arms. Lucy looked so different, her hair done fancy and her cheeks thick with rouge. She wore a print dress like you saw in the magazines but couldn't buy in Pittston or Wilkes-Barre or probably even Scranton. The outfit made her seem older and definitely married.

"Hi, Sammy!" she said to me. I let her hug me, though her perfume nearly knocked me down.

Bonino said nothing but hunched by the car, smoking. He looked terrific in a white suit, silver shirt and gold tie with ostriches racing over it. You had to hand it to Bonino: he was snappy.

I felt sorry for him. "Hi, Bonino," I said. "Welcome home." The word *home* was deliberate: I could have said *back*. He was family now, and there was no point in denying it. His Buick was now family, too.

Shifting from foot to foot, Bonino offered me a cigarette, which I turned down because Mama was there. She didn't want me to smoke because it stained the teeth.

"How was Niagara Falls?" I asked him.

"Real good. . . . Big."

"You buy anything there?"

"Yep."

I didn't press him.

Mama ushered us into the kitchen, where we sat around the table and heard their story: how Bonino had proposed unexpectedly, how Lucy couldn't resist such a nice offer and thought they might as well get married immediately. Bonino, she said, was ten years older than her and had waited long enough. We didn't press her on that one, but it rankled me to think of his pent-up desire loosed like a mad dog on my sister. Then again, it was her choice. Talking in turns, they told us about the hotels where they stayed, the sights along the way, the amazing people at Niagara Falls.

"Well, I got to tell you Father Francis was real mad," said Mama. "You go talk to him."

Lucy said she would. I knew Mama intended for them to get married all over again in the church, which seemed stupid to me. God couldn't possibly care about that. And Jesse said he didn't see why anyone would drive so far to see a waterfall. He would have gone to the Grand Canyon instead.

Lucy produced a bag of presents: a hat with "Niagara Falls" printed on it for Jesse, a scarf for Mama, an ashtray with a picture of the falls on it for me. It embarrassed me to get an ashtray, since it implied things about my character, but I thanked her.

Then we heard about their plans. One reason they got married was that Bonino had come into some money. His brother in Trenton sent him a packet, enough to buy the garage on Exeter Avenue just beyond the biscuit company. He would soon have enough to sell Buicks as well as service them. The money was the return on a small investment Bonino once made in his brother's business, and the risk had paid off. The garage, he said, was a small one, but he would specialize in brakes and mufflers.

"That's going to put you out of business in six months," said Jesse. "Ain't enough people got cars for that."

Bonino said he had facts and figures. His brother in Trenton supported him a hundred percent; he would pump gas, too, which would assure an income.

Mama looked on with a glow like the Rose of Sharon. She had her daughter home, a married lady, and her son-in-law would be in business for himself. The nightmare had turned into a pleasant daydream. *Marriage*, for her, was the magic word.

Furthermore, Bonino had rented half of a duplex in the patch. He and Lucy could move in in a week. Meanwhile, they expected to stay with us—in Lucy's bedroom!

I didn't like the idea of Bonino in the room next to me, but Mama quickly said they could stay as long as they liked. Family was family, even if they did elope.

I hoped they wouldn't try anything sexy while I was in the next room. I decided to sleep at the river that week, just in case. It would kill me to hear it. My heart would ache for Ellie Maynard.

Gino came crashing home for lunch, as usual: Meals always drew him in.

"Gino!" Lucy shrieked. She'd never shown much interest in her little brother before, but she was married now and needed to act like it.

"Look what the wind blew in," Gino said.

"Behave, Gino," said Mama.

"You don't act nice, I'll slap your mouth," said Jesse, who occasionally felt obliged to make a remark like that, since he was the oldest man around.

"Easy does it, Gramps," said Gino.

"Look what we brought you from Niagara Falls," said Lucy, holding up a small stuffed alligator. A banner saying "Welcome to the Falls" was stitched to its horny skin.

"A dinosaur!" he said.

"It's a lizard," she said.

"It's an alligator," I said.

"We had alligators in Italy," said Jesse. "I had a cousin in Rimini got eat by one."

This prompted Bonino to tell a story about his brother, who frequently went to Miami on business, where he once saw a man wrestle an alligator for six hours straight. The man was a Creole Indian, said Bonino, which amazed me. I hadn't realized how well informed Bonino was.

As we sat there, eating lunch, I felt good all over, warm and cozy. I could never live like Will Denks—alone on the river, with nobody but Hark Wood for a relative.

After lunch, the rest of them drove in Bonino's Buick to see the duplex down the street. I stayed behind because the mailman had come with two letters for me. I didn't have much in the way of correspondence, so this surprised me. I wanted to read them privately in my bedroom, alone. One was stamped from New York City; it was in Louis's hand, a fancy scrawl in black ink on a thick white envelope. The other was local, and it gave no return address: a mystery letter. I saved it for last, opening the one from Louis immediately. "Dear Sammy," it ran:

> Hey, boy! What's happening in the patch? Got some girl on the hook, heh? No? Just don't get nobody knocked up. . . . That's the worst you can do, though. It ain't so bad, they say. Ha, ha, ha. Anyways, remember I said you could come and see me in New York some time? I was thinking about you last night, so I said to myself, *Hey, get him down here!* Why not? Here's some dough—don't lose it, heh?—fifteen bucks. Get the train from Scranton—it goes regular. And pick a week that seems okay, if Mama says you can come. If she don't want you to go then PUT THE MONEY BACK IN THE MAIL.
>
> Your brother,
Louis

That note summed up my brother in short space. He was not the smartest guy you'd ever meet, but he had a good heart. He thought hard about people. Everybody liked Louis and said he would make out fine if nobody arrested him first.

The other letter made me nervous. Who would write me from Exeter? Why didn't they simply cross the street and knock on the door? Why waste a stamp and good paper? The envelope wasn't high-quality like the one Louis sent, but it wasn't bad. The postmark suggested it had taken two days to cross the street. I slit open the letter with my penknife.

Dear Sammy,
Your poem was beautiful. When did you learn to write poems? The rhymes were very accurate. Thank you for it. And hello.

Ellie

And hello! Hadn't she added that, it would have crushed me. She might as well kiss me good-bye with so much polite talk. But *And hello* said more. Much more. It meant she loved me in her heart, but quietly, in secret, the way I loved her. She wasn't the type to make a big deal out of love. It was more fun this way, swelling inside you, fed by every little daily thing: starlight, sunrise, flowers, the way the dirt smells after rain. If you say your love out loud, it fizzles like a Goodyear sprung on a rusty nail. Love needs pressure—like a good rubber tire. It needs to be blown up, tight. *And hello!* Could you believe it! She probably didn't know how smart I was until my poem arrived. Or know how deep I loved her. Now she knew it, and had answered me back with something of her own: *And hello!* That was her true voice, the voice of love, sprung loose by the eloquence of my pen. Poetry worked. Today I understood why people wrote books and plays and poems: they were secret messages to someone.

I lay back quietly on my bed, my feet up and bare, and let my heart take me high as a kite. I stretched out my arms and floated, thinking only of the present moment, the sweet stillness, the ease of wanting really nothing more.

10

Vincenzo came home more exhausted every day. It was hard for him to go to the mines at six, work all day, and then go to meetings, which seemed to happen every night now that the strike drew closer. He had endless talks with Nick Maroni, who Mama said was not being a decent father to his three sons to waste so much time on politics. Vincenzo and Maroni huddled in the living room each night, drinking espresso and making lists of God knows what. And Grandpa Jesse egged them on. He sat there with his leg on a pillow, drinking wine, saying that the class system was America's downfall, while Maroni and Vincenzo ate that up.

I had been told in school that we didn't have a class system in America because everybody comes under the same law. The Constitution insists on it. Still, I really couldn't argue back with Vincenzo, especially when he came home from the mines so tired. When he got home late, I worried that something had gone wrong. At least the mines were a little safer now than when the miners had nothing for light but open flames fed by whale oil, which sometimes set off gas pockets. *Ka-boom.* The carbide lamps weren't much better. We had one in the basement, and I sometimes would take it up to Indian Rock to scout inside the cave for arrowheads. All you worried about in the mines these days was methane gas, firedamp, smoke, carbon dioxide, soot, and falling rock.

Vincenzo was pretty sure now the strike would happen. An operator near Pottsville had just been shot by a miner, and it was all over the papers. Blew his head off in front of his own house. Grandpa Jesse figured he deserved it, but Mama said that wasn't Christian and he should shut his mouth. She would turn away, saying, "*Magari fosse ancora in vita.*" She thought Papa's death had brought on all this trouble, which of course, it had, for us.

"There isn't nobody deserves being murdered," said Vincenzo. "Violence solves nothing."

Jesse commented that Vincenzo would never go anywhere as a union leader if he didn't have guts.

"You have to trust somebody sometime," Maroni said.

"They had to bring in the army in 1922," said Jesse, reminding everybody of the obvious. "That was a hot one, went through spring and summer. Harding promised the miners everything they asked for, so they stopped the strike, but he was a liar. Your papa was mad as hell, Vince." His eyeballs darted back and forth, and he gestured with both hands. He could remember every detail of the strike of '23, a short one, and the strike of '20, which the president put a stop to. "That goddamn Wilson sold us down the creek," said Jesse. "Some Democrat *he* was!"

"Never trust a politician," I said.

Jesse went on, as usual, to retell the stories of Sugarloaf and Lattimer, the two famous massacres. At Lattimer, eighteen men were shot by the police for assembling to strike—a direct contradiction of American law. The miners still called it Black Day. At Sugarloaf, near Hazleton, a similar thing occurred. It was history, although you didn't get this kind of history in school. Schools told you the nicer stuff, like the story of Columbus and how nobody would finance his exploration until one day the king of Spain called him to the palace and said, "Okay, Columbus: Here are three ships. If the world is really flat, it's your ass."

"The real struggle in the world is between owners of property and them without it," said Vincenzo, aloud to himself. He had been reading up on socialism, which usually set Jesse off on stories about Togliatti, the Italian Socialist hero that got a Russian town named after him. Togliattigrad.

I liked the *idea* of socialism myself, but I also wanted to be rich. You don't have to explain or justify yourself if you have enough cash. Bing Stanton was hardly ever questioned to his face in this valley, for instance. I remembered how people gawked at Mr. Samuel D. Warriner, chairman of the Anthracite Operators, with awe when he motored into Exeter to address an assembly of miners for the Fourth of July last year. He wore a light silk suit and a Panama hat. His white cane glinted in the sun. He had a limo with a chauffeur who wore gloves.

I could never tell anyone that I wanted to be rich. Especially not these Socialists. Under socialism, everyone is equal. It's like democracy, only this time you mean it.

"We got to strike once and for all," Maroni said. "We can't have no new strike every year."

Jesse nodded excitedly. Poor Grandpa Jesse. His knee got worse each day now and the doctor didn't know why. His foot was going blue because the circulation had been interrupted at the knee, and if things didn't improve, they might have to chop it off. The prospect of a peg-leg Jesse around the house twenty-four hours a day was enough to force Mama to pay Mrs. Montoro an extra fifty cents a month for intercessions with God. This was money we didn't have, since Jesse's salary was gone. They didn't pay you a cent in the mines if you didn't show up.

One afternoon, on a Friday after work, a special conversation took place between me and my brother. Vincenzo had come home tired, as usual, with a mountain of union work to do. But Mama's speakeasy needed to be cleaned for the weekend, and Vincenzo saw it as his duty to help Mama whenever he could. He enlisted me in the kitchen. We said nothing to each other, but I followed him down into the cellar. The close damp walls had a wormy smell to them, and my eyes adjusted slowly to the light. I walked behind Vincenzo down the stairs with my right hand on his shoulder, using him as a guide.

"How you doing?" he said and sat down on the bottom step as I pulled out a stool.

"Okay."

"A lot on your mind these days, Sam?"

"Not really."

"Something's eating you a little, no?"

"Naw."

"Just checking," he said. "I'm sorry I don't have time to pitch to you. You'd probably like to get more practice."

We lit kerosene lamps and set to work arranging tables and chairs.

"The union stuff keeps me so damn busy," he said. "I wish we could spend more time together, Sammy."

I felt sorry for Vince. He tried so hard to be perfect. But there's no point in perfection. It wears you down. "Take it easy some," I said. "You work too hard."

"Thanks, Sam." He rubbed his hands through his hair. "I'm tired these days. You're right," he said. "The union work is like ramming your head into a brick wall." He folded his arms to his chest. "I hope we can work together soon—on some union things. You could go to Pittsburgh with me next year."

"Really?"

"Sure. Why not? You'll be nearly seventeen then."

I pretended like going to Pittsburgh sounded terrific, when in truth Pittsburgh had never been a dream of mine. Miami Beach, now, I could see.

He bit his lip like he was pissed I had nothing more to say to him. But what could I say? I stood there with a tray of glasses needing to be washed.

"Does all this stuff about the strike get you worried? I know Mama goes nuts about it," he said.

I shrugged.

"Sam, it's important what I got to do, and you got to try to understand. You're the only one I can count on in the family to appreciate what I'm doing."

The blood gushed through my cheeks.

"Are you with me on this, Sammy?"

"I am, Vince." I wondered if I sounded convincing.

"Good," he said. "That makes me happy." He leaned against my cheek and hugged me with one arm, scraping my ear against his coarse face. He smelled like turpentine.

"Thanks, Vince."

"Come on upstairs—you ought to get some sleep. It's almost eleven."

"What about you? You got to get up at five."

He said, "I don't need much sleep."

I said, "Bullshit. We all need sleep."

He messed my hair with one hand before going upstairs, which I both liked and hated. It made me feel about six, but it showed his affection for me. Why did everything come so mixed, so complicated? When he shut the door, I couldn't stop myself from slobbering. I rinsed out the glasses in the basin, set them up to dry on the bar, and went upstairs. On the back porch, I let the night rush in at me, hot and noisy with the crickets. I wiped more tears from my eyes, not sure why everything had to be so damned emotional, since nothing in particular had happened. I guess it was knowing that Vincenzo had been thinking about me like that, like a brother.

Lucy was around the house every day now, playing at being Mrs. Bonino. Thank God I had the river and Will to escape to once in a while. As for Bonino, he was busy at the garage

107

that he was going to open soon. I found myself too often with nothing to do except talk to Lucy, who would sit in front of her mirror for hours. She was an artist of the face, drawing her long lashes out like licorice. Each one looked like it had come individually wrapped. But she took a certain interest in me, especially my relations with Ellie Maynard, which I had stupidly mentioned to her. Sisters have a way of getting you to spill your private beans.

"Do you love her?" she asked me, knowing only a tenth of the full story.

"What is love?"

"It's when you don't think your life can go on without somebody—like Ellie."

"Then I'm in love." That sounded nice but didn't feel quite as true as I'd have liked.

But my answer pleased Lucy and she turned to me, flapping her eyelids. "Is this the first time, Sammy?"

"I guess so." What happened between me and Mildred Prodner in the seventh grade didn't really count. We had kissed by the Exeter Municipal Dump one day after school. The smell ruined it for me, and Mildred Prodner moved away the next year anyway.

Lucy closed the bedroom door and sat down beside me on the bed, wearing only her thin slip. The fresh skin of her neck fairly glowed.

"Sammy," she said. "Have you screwed her yet?"

"Yet!" I said. It disgusted me to hear my own flesh-and-blood sister say *screwed*. And her a married lady!

"Aha . . ." she said. "I thought you had been screwing somebody. You can tell."

This startled me. How could she tell? It wasn't even true. Was it because the big pimple on my chin had disappeared? Will Denks told me I'd get no more of them suckers when my sex life started.

"I haven't screwed nobody," I said.

"Not Ellie?" she said.

"Of course not."

"I heard from a little bird that you and Ellie were seen together at the chapel. They said you took her off into the woods."

"We went swimming." I felt my cheeks heat up like fry pans on the stove. "Nothing more."

"Where?"

"Hatchet Pond."

This sent her nuts. "You *did* screw her, you *did*! Nobody takes a girl up there and don't screw her."

"Well, *I* didn't." I felt indignant now. "But I would have if she let me."

Lucy had a way of dragging stuff out of me. She got me to tell her the whole story, though I didn't let on about the boner. I just said Ellie didn't show the right kind of interest.

"Next time, you *screw* her!" she said, pointing a finger.

"What makes you think there will be a next time?" I yelled. I guess I had her there. I went to my room, lay down, and slept to escape my loneliness for the love of Ellie Maynard.

The next morning I cut through the open field at the base of the patch and on past the colliery to the river. It had been so crazy at home lately, my plans for spending the whole summer with Will Denks had been messed up pretty nicely. I hardly saw Will except on weekends or once in a while when I broke away for the night. Nearing the lean-to, I almost shouted for Will. Instead, I peeped into the lean-to, thinking he might be asleep or reading, but nobody was home. I was about to shout for him when I heard voices. Laughter in the woods. It carried across the air like bells in winter.

Guessing I shouldn't be there, I listened closer. Laughter tinkled in the leaves. I should have gone home then, but I had come down to the river many times when there were other people with Will. So I tiptoed to the river, where the sounds came from, and saw them. Will Denks and a girl.

I didn't want to get too close or I'd be discovered, so I

circled around the point, from where I knew I could watch them unseen. My heart pumped like a butterfly in a jar.

On a raised bit of land, I squinted at them from maybe fifty yards away. At first I thought it was Ellie, which would have done me in. I'd have leaped off the Fort Jenkins Bridge, for sure. But it wasn't her. It was someone like her—a skinny girl, fair-haired and taller than Will, with long legs like only a girl can have. I didn't recognize her but wondered where in hell Will met her. Who was she? And why hadn't he mentioned this to me before?

They stood knee-deep in the river, talking, holding hands. Then they climbed back on the rocks, where they sat talking. Will Denks kissed her and caressed her hair; he ran his hands along her legs and touched her stomach. He put his own legs between the two of hers, and they rolled across the flat rock, after which he pulled her to her feet and held her to his chest, close, his arms around her. They kissed, like angels, and walked back into the trees.

I was lost there, wondering what new thing in the world would happen next.

11

I buttoned a starchy white shirt to the collar and tied a fat knot in my tie, a yellow one with purple tulips across it. Blood seeped from my razor-nicked upper lip, and I kept ruining white handkerchiefs and making it bleed worse by daubing. It was four, and Nip Stanton's party started at five, so I had to rush. Looking into the oblong mirror, I worked my hair from one side to the other, parting it dead center. Like all the di Cantinis, I had coarse black hair that I slicked down with oil.

In the bathroom, still bleeding, I brushed my teeth with Dr. West and gave the mirror one last mean Jack Dempsey grin. To hell with the blood! I had the whiskers to shave, which was more than Nip Stanton could say for himself at sixteen.

Why was I going to the Nipper's party anyway? It wasn't right, especially since we heard by the grapevine that pretty quick Bing Stanton was going to fire my brother. He had to do it subtle, so as not to provoke the unions. That wouldn't do him any good. But he was soon going to have plenty of reason to fire Vincenzo, who didn't have his heart in the actual job of mining anymore. I had decided *not* to attend this party, and here I was, dressed to kill, ready to step out like a cock in the barnyard on Mother's Day.

I wanted to leave by four, but there I was at 4:15 with Vincenzo already home from work. If he saw me, I was finished. He would never understand. So I slipped down the back stairs into the kitchen, where Mama stood by the stove. She understood about my not being seen.

"He's downstairs washing," she whispered.

Vincenzo always went into the basement to wash up before coming into the house.

"I better run."

"Okay," she said. "But Jesse ain't good. Don't let him see you neither."

Jesse had been driving everybody nuts with complaining about his leg, which he said had been ruined by the bum knee. He made me examine a series of splotches running from the kneecap to the groin, but I couldn't see much of anything except some freckles. Jesse was such a hypochondriac you couldn't panic too quickly. Once back in Italy they brought him home with what he swore was a heart attack; he was laid up in bed for two months and couldn't catch his breath. But it passed. He also claimed to have a gut ulcer, which nowadays surfaced whenever Mama cooked liver. And there were his piles. He didn't talk about them much, but Lucy explained to me what they were. I saw blood in the toilet one day and figured it had something to do with Jesse, judging from the way he hollered whenever he sat down to business. The shrieks rang up and down the plumbing like he was giving birth to triplets with every plop. I knew six good jokes about piles, but I didn't say them in the house out of respect. As for the gut ulcers, Jesse took cold tea-bag enemas once a week to soothe them. You didn't dare approach the bathroom when he was at work on it, what with the noises—*slop, whoosh,* and *yeow!* He kept cold tea in the icebox for this purpose; it must have stung his butt something awful. Anyway, the gut ulcer didn't squelch Jesse's appetite for garlic soup, fried peppers, tripe, or salami. He ate like Mr. Coolidge was about to declare rationing.

I guess I waited too long to get out of the house, for in stomped Vincenzo. He looked at me crosswise.

"Hi, Vince."

"Where you going, all dolled up?"

"A party."

"Whose?"

I looked sideways to Mama, who was ignoring me in a time of need. "The library," I said. "Mrs. Dietrich is the librarian."

"So what?"

"She's having a get-together for some of us who use the library kind of . . . regular."

That was so left-field that Vincenzo couldn't quite tuck it through his brain. He let it pass. But I felt bad for having lied. A lie sours the day. It "fathers a hundred children," as Jesse often said—quoting some Italian proverb.

The sun stood high, though it was near suppertime in the patch. It had been a fine day with only a few high wispy clouds. I sucked in short breaths, partly because I felt scared, but also because it was suckable—sweet and slightly damp with the late afternoon. I went through the patch and across the Exeter town line into West Pittston, taking a roundabout way so nobody important would see me. Being too dressed up is as uncomfortable as being naked.

The houses got richer as I walked, not so much because they were better houses, but they were kept up like the rich tend to, with painted clapboards and no broken railings. Also, the rich hang their clothing to dry in the basement, even in summer, so you can't see their underwear. Mothers in the patch hung the works from a line on the front porch or in the yard. There's nothing so nice in midsummer as squeaky-fresh underwear full of wind.

All the way to Nip's house I wondered what being rich

was like and what the difference was between the rich and poor. The di Cantinis were not poor, according to my calculations. Absolutely not. We ate as well as anybody, especially on Sundays. We had a bigger house than most, which we owned. The rumors of Louis's wealth had been so exaggerated that some thought we must be rich as Cornelius Vanderbilt himself. My sister had spread a lot of these rumors, trying to impress the boys. She had a lot to learn about discretion.

When you look at it, wealth only means you've got more cash than somebody else, though obviously the rich get more attention than most of us. More hatred, too. People fear them and say dumb things and put on airs in their presence. I vowed not to act any different at this party. *Be yourself,* I shouted in my head. That was always Papa's advice. I had nothing to be ashamed of; in fact, the di Cantini family had respect in the whole region. We paid our bills. We attended church—except for Vincenzo and Jesse. Louis had succeeded in New York. Vincenzo had his union work, and was making his mark. I had gotten A in everything in school except arithmetic since the fourth grade, when I first realized how smart I was. I would graduate valedictorian and nobody doubted it. On top of which, Lucy was seventeen years old and had even got married without being pregnant, which spoke well for her. I had to search for something good to say about Gino, who had distinguished himself in school last spring by calling his teacher a "damned moongoose," but Gino would come out fine, even if he couldn't tell a mongoose from a moongoose.

Elms began to replace the scrub oak of the patch, and the lawns, many of which I mowed myself to make a little cash, became smoother, greener. The sidewalks went from dirt to slate, and motorcars appeared along the curbs. The houses got whiter and whiter, too, chalk-white and smack-fresh. The windows acquired shutters, all spread open to let in the air. I could hear a wireless blasting away—the baritone voice of Nelson Eddy as mellow as the wind—the faint smell of mint from somebody's garden. Old ladies sat on porches, their hair bunched up like haystacks, their faces talcum-powder pale. I recognized only one person, old Salvatore Pastonini, who worked as gardener for a doctor. His head was a big, uneven loaf of bread dough, lightly dusted with a film of clay. He was spreading manure in a flower bed, and when he saw me he stopped, straightened his back, and yelled some Sicilian phrase, which I acknowledged by nodding, since I didn't talk Sicilian. He grinned back toothlessly and returned to his digging.

I made my way to the river, where the Stantons lived on Susquehanna Avenue, the grandest street I'd ever seen. They had a fancy corner house, white and brown, surrounded by wide lawns and flowery gardens. From their front porch they overlooked the avenue and a park that went along the river. The steeples and rooftops of Pittston shone across the river. The Fort Jenkins Bridge was only two blocks away. I caught a whiff of fresh-cut grass as I approached their house, the huge weeping willow in the backyard green against the sky. I went up the front stairs of the house, which was proper (although many were gathered in the backyard already), holding on to the black wrought-iron railing as I mounted the porch, step by step, like walking up to the altar for your first holy communion. I held my back stiff to look taller, since the rich are usually tall. I licked the cut lip with my tongue and cleared my throat a few times so I wouldn't croak when introducing myself to Mrs. Stanton.

I looked through the screen door nervously to see that quite a few of my schoolmates were waiting in the dark hallway to say something polite to Mrs. Stanton. I decided against pounding on the frame and calling attention to myself and just walked in, like you do at the dentist's, and stood behind others in line.

"Hello. I'm Nip's mother, Mrs. Stanton," said Mrs. Stanton, an old-looking big titty woman. The rich *are* tall, I thought. Even the ladies. It puzzled me why she was so old, more like somebody's grandma than mother. "I'm so glad you could come," she added, hitting the *so* like an organ's bass pedal.

"I'm Sammy di Cantini," I said.

115

"Yes, Nip has mentioned you, Sammy. He's out back. Why don't you go along there? We have plenty of lemonade." She said this like a recital, looking over my shoulder while she spoke. Which is another thing about the rich: they look over your shoulder while they talk; the poor look you dead.

My eye slipped sideways to a beautiful room, the main living room. I stepped inside for a quick eyeball, noticing a velvety blue sofa by a brick fireplace, surrounded on either side by matching chairs. A grand piano had its hood up on a stake and was pushed to one corner of the room. There were quite a few old books in a cherry bookcase with glass windows. A deep rose rug on the floor had a peacock frozen in the center with its tail spread; I caught its eye and shivered. It knew I was not supposed to be poking around there, yet I loved that room, especially the bookcase, and decided that someday I'd have one like it. I would parade leather sets of lawbooks around my living room and sit by the fire in winter and read. People would wonder if I had really read all those books, but I wouldn't tell them. It's wrong to show off.

"And who might you be?" asked somebody in a deep voice. A man was sitting in a chair near the wall, but I hadn't seen him.

"Excuse me, sir."

"Don't excuse yourself. Tell me your name."

"I'm Sammy di Cantini, from the patch," I said and regretted adding the patch business. What did it matter?

"I'm Mr. Stanton."

Now that my eyes had adjusted to the dimness, I recognized him. "I was just looking at . . . the books."

"They were my father's," he said and took a drink from a large tumbler, which he held like a crystal ball in both hands. "Your brother is something of a revolutionary, isn't he?" he said. "A troublemaker."

It seemed that talk always turned to Vincenzo. But just because Vincenzo was my brother didn't mean I was to be held responsible for his opinions.

"Vincenzo can sometimes go a little far," I said.

Mr. Stanton smiled funny. "Really? He seems to have the ear of my men."

"He doesn't understand that you have to make a profit."

"I certainly do. We don't operate for the fun of it."

"If the miners go on strike, it's the miners who will suffer most." I realized what a hole I had dug for myself, trying to impress him. "But the operators have probably asked for this trouble. The mines are dangerous."

Bing Stanton stood up, putting a hand on my shoulder. "Nipper told me how smart you were, Sam."

"Thanks."

"You and I should talk again sometime."

He held out his hand to shake. I shook it squarely and felt as though I'd entered into a conspiracy.

"Hey Sam!" called somebody. "Come on out!"

It was the Nipper himself, standing in the doorway, decked out like a young prince in white trousers with high loose cuffs, a white shirt with thin stripes, and a navy blue blazer. He wore a red tie with a stickpin probably borrowed from his father. His hair looked brassy, lank and slicked back. It was the slickest hair in town. He stood tall and vain, as though having a birthday was an accomplishment.

I never knew what to say to Nip Stanton, who never knew what to say to me. So we gawked together, hemming and hawing. Then I followed him outside, where we stood for a moment on the porch to watch the crowd on the lawn cluster in little talk-groups or blink into the shade of the big willow, absorbed in their own versions of the party.

It didn't seem possible Nip had brought in so many people I never saw before. He had a lot of friends down at Fox Hill— the golfing boys, who came from Wilkes-Barre and Scranton— but I never imagined myself standing among them. The boys all had the same lanky hair, like the Nipper, brushed back slick along the sides. They smelled strongly of after-shave, which I'd never worn. We used plain alcohol in the patch. There were

117

strange girls here, too, with hair full of ribbons. Their necklaces sparkled. You could tell most of them had been kissed more than once by their brassy smiles. These boys didn't scare them one bit.

At the center of it all was Ellie Maynard, who had four boys clucking around her, bug-eyed and spitless. It disgusted me to see this: such prettiness swallowed up by a mob that didn't deserve the sight of her, let alone her conversation. I got goose pimples on my arms that made the hairs stand up, thinking of her wonderful letter. *And hello!*

The bunch broke into cackles around her. What had she said that was so cute? She wasn't normally what you'd call funny. They were playing up to her.

"Ellie's here," said Nip behind me. I had forgotten about him.

They say ignorance is bliss, so I ignored him. I walked down the steps, aiming for the table that was laid out with cold meats, cheese, and vanilla cookies. "The lemonade bucket on the left is hootched up," Nip said. He seemed to gloat as though he'd stolen a dollar bill from the collection plate at high mass for the burial of the dead. "It's got gin in it."

"I don't drink."

"Then you better dip into the other barrel." He grinned like a sardine can.

I made straight for the right side of the table, taking a glass and dipping it into the barrel. Who could resist real lemonade with sliced lemon floating in it? I tried one or two goodies, taking care not to lick my fingers as I'd have done at home, keeping one eye on Ellie Maynard. I didn't want to be too obvious, so I started toward the porch—beyond her—gradually noticing a very familiar face. It was Will Denks, the lover-boy himself. Will Denks, who "didn't go to parties," as he said, but who rolled girls over rocks by the river—in public view! He was here to look at more than the architecture.

He had found some party clothes, too—a white straw hat, a rumpled old jacket, some ridiculous cream-colored pants.

Maybe that sexy mysterious dame of his borrowed some duds from her old man.

Nipper whispered to him, nodding in my direction, and before I could spit sideways they were walking my way. I planned to stay cool, the best way to deal with surprises.

"Hey, Willy," I said, bowing like a gentleman.

"Hey." He was jumpy, you could tell. Embarrassed.

"You boys know each other, I take it," said Nip. He liked to say things like that.

"Your lady's here, I see," said Will, like he was announcing the weather. He flung a glance at Ellie Maynard in case anyone mistook what he meant.

My lady! How could Will Denks say such a thing to me, and in public? I damn near said, "What about *your* lady, Romeo?"

Nip went red, but he was clearly delighted. His ears twitched. He dug his blue eyes into me, like nails. The two of them stood together, blond and thin, both taller than me by several inches.

"She *is* your lady, ain't she?" Will said.

"Ellie?"

"Ellie Maynard."

"Yeah . . . well. No, she isn't. Not at all, and you know it."

Will and Nip exchanged a conspiratorial look.

"I hear you went swimming with her," Nip said. "At the pond."

"Well, maybe I did and maybe I didn't."

"Willy here says you did."

Will looked over my shoulder, like a millionaire.

"I also hear you showed her your pecker," said Nip, cool as lettuce. He could have been saying, "I hear you two played tennis."

"Did Will tell you that, too?"

"No. Somebody else did."

"Well, you heard wrong," I said.

"Really?"

119

"That's what I'm telling you."

"Okay, okay. Don't get huffy about it."

Eyes swarmed like bees around me, and I had to fight to hold back tears. I'd have pissed tears all over the ground if Bing Stanton hadn't appeared on the back porch, drawing attention away from me.

Bing had one hand resting on the banister, and his yellow sports jacket glowed like an exotic flower. His cheeks flushed pink with booze, and he smoked a pipe. The ashes in the barrel glowed when he sucked in, and his rimless glasses glowed, too. So did his blond-gray hair and the fluffed, matching eyebrows that needed trimming. A garnet stickpin in his wide white tie showed from where I stood, giving the signal to anybody who didn't know it that this was a rich man, maybe the richest man in Luzerne County. He had a wealthy way of standing, tall but not stiff, confident. His dark linen trousers blended with the dusky porch, so that he disappeared from the waist down. He seemed to float behind the balustrade, a ghost in air. I blew a wad of snot to one side in the grass to clear my head.

"There's the old man," Will said to me in a whisper.

"I know."

Nip left to speak to his father while I stood beside Will Denks. You can't trust anyone, I thought. Now Will had all the cards to play against me, and I couldn't say anything about *his* escapades or I would look like a Peeping Tom. A chill fell between me and Will Denks right then, and I knew it would last a long time—maybe forever. He probably wanted to be on the inside with the Nipper. But hadn't I done the same thing myself with Bing, only minutes before? Why the hell did I come here anyway? Was there any point to my tricking Vincenzo? He damn near exhausts himself fighting against Bing Stanton while his own brother gets cozy in the man's own parlor. . . . I should have walked out right then. Or before I had to listen to them talk about my pecker. Was it even possible Ellie told Nip about that? My friend? My love? Without Will and Ellie, I felt marooned and miserable. Like I was alone against the sky, the last man on earth. I closed my eyes and half prayed, "Vincenzo, I'm so sorry." If only I had his integrity. He never got himself in these situations. Nobody ever screwed him, and he screwed nobody. He had no secrets, no private aims. Everything with him seemed open, public, honest—but tough. *Shit*, I said to myself. *Shit, shit, shit.*

"You meet his mother?" asked Will.

"Lady Big Tits?"

"Ain't they something?"

We both smiled. I wanted so bad to forgive Will Denks.

"Why'd you say that, Will?" I asked. It popped out of me.

"What?"

"I can't believe you told that to somebody . . . about me and Ellie."

He growled, like he had done nothing and I shouldn't harp on it. "Come on, Sam. What's it matter?"

"It does, that's all."

"Well, that's too bad then." He looked at me hard. "You got to grow up someday."

Will Denks turned on his heels in Ellie's direction, joining the fancy gang who were barbed on her green eyes, her fan club. I got a hollow feeling inside, big as a watermelon, almost too big to carry; to calm my nerves, I made straight for that lightning punch. I filled a tall glass and drank. It burned my gut, and my cheeks blazed. But I felt better in ten minutes, after two glasses of Nip's special hootch.

The sight of so many handsome young ladies had its effect on me. It struck me that Ellie Maynard wasn't the only girl at this party with long legs and fetching eyes. I developed something like supernatural vision, enabling me to penetrate calico, cotton, silk, and linen. I could really *see* Missie Sovanelli's fourteen-year-old breasts through her blue silk blouse, hard and crunchy as popcorn. I could see through Helen Carnovsky's party dress to her panties, lacy and smelling like ripe avocado. In the haze of my hootched-up world, I did not object to Miranda Nardo's acne, which seemed to fizz and pop when she got excited—the Carbonated Woman.

More than the girls from the patch, a few of the daisies from the country-club set attracted my inner eye. One of them was the tallest girl I ever saw, maybe six feet of her, a brunette with no breasts and legs like bean poles. Her rosebud mouth seemed to invite kisses, the way she puckered. One glimpse of her seared a picture in my brain that would stay there for years, I could tell. I would imagine her in bed with me sometimes, long and hot, the fur between her legs like a possum. When I was rich, I would call her up for sure. We would marry and have a houseful of tall kids with rosebud lips. She began to laugh, and her voice crackled through the air. Her laugh was the kind that swells the Fox Hill Country Club at their annual Christmas party. When she turned, I saw her shoulder blades stick out, like wedges, like wings. They were beautiful shoulder blades. The girls in the patch just never had them, it seemed. They had big breasts, which had no style.

I felt a bit wobbly but I circled through the pastel clouds of swishy girls and fawning boys. I hardly knew where I was or what I was saying till I rounded a big oak and saw the Nipper alone with Ellie Maynard. He had her backed up against the picket fence, and she had a shitty grin on her face. It dazed me, but I pulled my thoughts together and launched myself in their direction.

"Nipper!" I said, loud.

He swung around in confusion, like I had woke him up. "Hey, Sammy," he said. "What's up, boy?" The puzzlement fizzled, and he slid me a sneer in the shape of a grin.

It didn't fool me. "I want to talk to Ellie," I said.

He drew himself up half an inch extra, totaling maybe five foot ten. His grin blew off in the serious breeze I brought with me. "Well, I happen to be talking to her at the moment, thank you. And since it's my birthday, maybe I'll just keep on talking to her as long as I like."

He had never spoken tough to my face before, and it threw

me. But I came back hard: "Why don't we ask her who she'd rather talk to, then?"

Nipper showed no sign of budging.

I turned to Ellie. "So which of us would you like to talk to?"

Her mouth drooped at either side, and she looked away, embarrassed. It flabbergasted me. Then her letter flashed into my head. I sidled up close to her and, with a slight smile and cocked head, said, "*And hello!*"

"If she wanted to talk to you, di Cantini, she'd talk," said the Nipper.

"Oh yeah?" I said.

"Oh yeah."

We had come to a point in our conversation where phrases become shuttlecocks, bouncing back and forth over an invisible net. So I turned to Ellie. "Is he right?" I asked. "You want *him* instead of me?"

She looked at me awkward, then turned from us both, leaning over the picket fence with her arms between the whitewashed palings.

Nip bit his lip, and said, "Get out of my party."

"Get stuffed," I said.

"I said, get out!"

"Okay," I responded. "I know when I'm not welcome. But . . ." I half thought Ellie would swing around and say, "I'm leaving too, Nip Stanton, and with him," but she didn't. She never moved. "Okay," I repeated. "Okay, okay, okay."

The Nipper glared at me, and a few who noticed that trouble was brewing stood vulturing at the sidelines. "Get out!" Nip said. But this time I didn't like his tone or care for the audience.

I swung hard from the hips, an uppercut that landed bone-flush on the tip of his nose. The crack was pitiful, but worse was the blood spurting out of his noseholes like tomato puree. The event—if you can rightly call my popping Nipper's nose an event—happened like in a slow-motion movie. My fist flew, a wild bird, right into his face, uncommanded. And *crack*. My hand stung like the dickens, beginning at the knuckles and tingling to the elbow. But I didn't doubt Nip's nose stung worse; it was terrible to see him run like that, right through the middle of his own party, up past his father, into the house.

Ellie swung my way, deadly, and said, "You . . . you bully!"

"Ellie, I—"

"Bully, bully, bully," she said.

The crowd didn't speak or budge for fear of doing the wrong thing. At least they weren't staring at me. I took advantage of the moment and slipped, neatly, through a side gate behind a rosebush, then broke into a run down the wide street. The neighborhoods whizzed by one after the other, though I kept my eyes straight ahead. I ran maybe five or six miles, some of it in circles, then slowed to a cool sweaty walk. The exercise helped drain the fury from my body. I hated that bastard, Nip Stanton, and I hated Ellie Maynard, who had deserted me in more ways than one, and I could not see how Will Denks could have done what he did.

At home, the cellar was filled with miners, Mama's weekend crowd. They shouted and clapped, singing "Un Mozzetino di Fiore," but I shut out the noise with my hands, clapped them over both ears like muffs. Sweat soaked my shirt. As the singing died off, I took up a fountain pen. I dug the letters of Will Denks's name into the top of the desk that once belonged to Papa. The fresh letters gleamed in the wood. It just wasn't right that Will Denks had done that to me. Not right at all. The unfairness went through me like a knife blade. How could you trust anybody if your best friend could do you in to your face?

Once I dug Will's name into my desk at school but not because I hated him, like tonight. I dug it for friendship, to remind me of Will when I looked down during geometry class. I dug it illegibly, in a way only I could read, since there was a certain faction who might think it unnatural that I should be digging boy-names into the desk instead of girl-names. They couldn't understand a friendship like ours.

Now I sat there, redigging the letters, reading them, then I gouged out the whole name in a couple of hard strokes, leaving a gopher hole in the desk.

Jesus was frowning at me from the wall in his beard and halo, the picture-glass flickering in the red light of dusk. I don't know how he caught my eye like he did, but he caught it severely, knowing I had hatred nesting in me deep.

Out on the lawn, some miners stumbled away and shouted to each other. I leaned on the window jamb to watch them, and they seemed like creatures from another planet. It was still pretty early, but I needed to sleep. I got in bed and pulled the sheets up to my chin, shivering; my voice began somewhere far away, praying. It said, "Jesus, I don't really hate Will. No I don't. And I'm sorry I gave such an impression. I know all the stories Father Francis told in catechism and in confessions about your enemy and how he is your responsibility. 'Turn a cheek,' he said. Your enemy can't know what he's doing or he wouldn't do it, so you've got to forgive him, even though it doesn't seem fair."

I never did get to the *amen* but fell into iron sleep, the kind that locks out light and sound.

12

I arranged with Gino to take over my paper route and got my neighbor, Hitch Lima, to mow the lawns in West Pittston. Both of them agreed to give me a small commission on these jobs, since I had gone through the work of getting them in the first place. The caddying would have to suffer. Though I was one of the best caddies at Fox Hill, plenty of other boys could do the same work. I knew that whenever I came back I'd be in demand again at Fox Hill, since I almost never lost a ball and could give advice about which clubs worked best in which situations. I also could keep score, which a lot of the boys couldn't. They lost track too easily.

The telegram went out to Louis in New York only two days before. ROLL OUT THE RED CARPET, I wired. I'M ON MY WAY. It occurred to me that maybe I would *never* come home again.

Before leaving, I made a quick trip to Pittston to buy clothes for the journey. My own finances were still okay, especially since Lucy had paid me back the money she borrowed. Bonino must have given it to her, to keep on my good side. I took Grandpa Jesse's tie with the waterfalls from his closet, since he didn't care, and dusted off Papa's old Panama. What I bought in Pittston, at the dry goods, was a nice brown suit, double-breasted. I figured that, dressed so, no one could keep me down.

Mama saw me off in tears, as usual. *"Che tu sia benedetto,"* was her blessing as she helped me onto the train, the local Laurel Line from Pittston to Scranton, where you'd catch the express to New York. I glanced backward through the window at her, and she was still muttering to herself, probably more Italian stuff. I kept wishing she would cut the Italian. This was America, and we had our own language. It seemed stupid to hang on to an old one, one that nobody liked to use except the old ladies, mostly widows, and the men playing dominoes in the park. I used to hate it when Mama and Papa talked in bed at night, their language bubbling up in their sheets like a foreign broth, a stew that none of us wanted to feed on. I made a point never to speak Italian back to Mama or Papa, even when they addressed me in their language. It was not *my* language. I figured that so long as I now belonged to the American race, I should speak their tongue.

Scranton always excited me, set low in a valley with green mountains surrounding it steeply. Penn Avenue was beautiful, with its wide storefronts, the National Bank Building rising high, maybe a dozen stories, with the tree-lined courthouse square looking so fresh and clean. I bought the morning *Scrantonian* in a drug store across from the station. The Lackawanna Station looked like something out of ancient Greece or Rome, with marble pillars and many steps. The lobby was full of plants, a green marble floor and walls making an echo chamber out of everything. The high, painted ceiling brought to mind a cathedral or museum. Negroes in uniform kept the floor slick as ice, so I had to walk gingerly in my leather-soled shoes. I left my suitcase at the baggage counter, tipping my Panama to the fat lady behind the desk, whose neck rose up like a surf beneath her chin. A triple chin, I figured. She was the fattest lady I ever saw without buying a ticket.

There was a cafeteria in the lobby like the ones you hear about in Paris, the little tables and cane chairs out on the main floor, where people could watch you eating as they passed. I bought a cup of coffee and sat down to read my paper. A front-page story about the United Mine Workers straightened my back immediately. There it was, my brother's name in black and white—Vincenzo di Cantini! We were famous! I liked knowing I was not just anybody hanging around the station. *And* it pleased me to keep my fame to myself. Why should I go around bragging? I took a pencil from my suit jacket and underlined my brother's name. It was there on the same page with a story about President Coolidge and Henry Ford. Coolidge was lazy as a mule. He did nothing in the White House, although many folks said this was exactly what a president ought to do. Will Denks agreed with this line of talk whenever you mentioned Coolidge. "Presidents get us in trouble when they set out to achieve things," said Will Denks. "Look at Wilson. He got us into a war just because we weren't doing nothing."

Nobody minds a lazy man except his wife, and even there Coolidge got off easy: His wife took a long nap with him each afternoon. Grandpa Jesse said they were sex fiends, but I doubted it. Coolidge didn't have a sexy way about him. He was old and ugly. His usual statement, as reported by the *Wilkes-Barre Record*, was "I have no comment on that." This strategy prevented him from saying stupid things, and it seemed to work. You didn't hear much talk against him. He was lots better than Harding—"Silent Cal," as they called him, who slept even more than Coolidge. His personal secretary, C. Bascom Slemp, ran the country; they called him "The Fixer." Jesse knew the gossip about presidents, and I enjoyed hearing it. One day I figured I might run for the president myself, in which case

Jesse's gossip would come in handy. One thing I was sure of: I would never comment on anything.

Having finished my coffee, I made some notes to myself in a pad, then tipped a porter to carry my bag to the platform. This was to show everybody in the station I was not just nobody.

"New York City train," I said loudly to the porter so he would know where to take me. He wheezed and limped along on a bum leg, which ruined much of the pleasure for me. I gave him another quarter, which is twice what I should have paid in the first place.

The train rumbled and steamed in place as a queer lady sat next to me in the carriage. She had holes in her stockings and wore a black dress like the widows from the old country. Her front teeth were separated by a quarter-inch, and when she bit on her sandwich her teeth poked holes in the soft bread. This came as a disappointment, since I'd hoped to sit beside somebody famous on the way to New York City, like Clara Bow, or at least a fashionable lady. I knew a little bit about women's clothes because of Lucy. She had taken me with her to buy a dress after she came back from Niagara Falls; it had cost $15.95— a pleated taffeta dress—more than Mama ever paid for three dresses, Lucy said. Bonino really had the cash.

"Where you headed, boy?" asked the lady, talking with food in her mouth.

I did not crave her conversation. "New York City."

"To see the Yanks, huh?"

"I intend to go to the theater," I said, and lit a cigarette.

"Ain't never been to no theater myself," she said, rhyming *theater* with *creator*. "How old are you?"

"Sixteen, almost seventeen," I said, figuring you get a year's leeway.

"You don't look but fifteen," she said.

This made me mad.

"Don't mean to offend you," she said. "I got a boy your age. I'm used to boys. I got five boys in all."

"Five!"

"Five still living."

"I'm sorry about that."

"About what?"

"The dead ones."

"Oh . . . there's only one dead one. Slim."

"How'd he get killed?"

"Trucking accident."

"He get run over?"

She nodded her head yes, then got up to go to the bathroom. Ladies go to the bathroom more than men in general, but on trains they go nuts that way.

I hoped she wouldn't come back, and she didn't. My conversation seemed to finish her off, which was all right by me. I wanted either a conversation with somebody famous or nothing.

Arriving at Penn Station, I went looking for the subway to where Louis rented his apartment. He had explained to me about how to get the subway, and it wasn't simple.

I think I walked for a while in circles before somebody, a nice-looking old man in a suit, showed me where to get the subway. He could see I was a bit strange here and led me to the entrance. "Thank you, sir," I said, and he patted my shoulder. All through I felt oozy and warm. New York was tops, I thought, as I went underground. My eyes went blind, and I remembered the terrible day I went into the mineshaft near the ball field. But my sight returned quickly.

The subway came rattling through the dark, stopped, and I got on facing backward. Across from me, on the yellow wicker seat, a beautiful lady faced me with her ankles crossed and her broad hat tipped sideways. She had a ruby mouth that puckered up. In the next seat, a tall man twirled a toothpick in his teeth, his hat pulled forward over his brow. I noticed his fancy leather brogues and the overstuffed briefcase beside him. I cleared my throat loud to attract their attention, then tipped my Panama to each in turn. They did not respond, so I felt relieved when we arrived at Fourth Street, my stop. I came up into the bright sunlight dazzled. When my eyes came back to focus, I could see the Loew's movie house, a real palace, with *Sally of the Sawdust* advertised on the marquee. I wondered how many famous stars of stage and screen stood there with me, even now, on the crowded sidewalk. A Franklin passed me, with a well-dressed lady riding proud in the back in a pink cloche. Who could she be? Mrs. Rockefeller or Mrs. Vanderbilt?

The traffic and crowds took me aback, even though I had prepared myself for both. To stand with buildings rising around you like dinosaurs and a thousand faces flying past in fifty different makes of cars could make you spin. I leaned against a building to catch my breath, watching a trolley car go by, a foreign limo, then a Packard, a Cadillac, and a brand-new Willys-Knight with the driver up front in uniform. I couldn't make out some of the cars, which were foreign—maybe German. The English ones I knew. I can't say how long I stood there, kind of dazed and palpitating inside.

It was hot, but I didn't mind, as the white sun reflected off the windows of the high buildings, and sea gulls flashed their wings. I kept thinking of ancient Egypt, which we had studied this year under Miss Wandalewsky; not even the pyramids could match New York City. Egypt never had so many different kinds of vehicles; I gawked as a Metz went by, followed by a Winton. A beautiful old Pierce-Arrow was parked by the curb, its headlights sticking out weird as a beetle's eyes. A blue Dodge turned the corner, followed by a long white Maxwell in which an old lady wore a hat like an ostrich landing on her head. Then a Chinaman pedaled by on a bike. You couldn't know what you'd see next in New York City.

Having bought a hot dog from an Italian vendor, I swung around to West Eleventh, where the apartment was. Though I told Louis in my telegram I'd be there about six, it was only 3:30. He might not be home from his office yet, if he had an office. It surprised me how, when you got right down to it,

I didn't know a damn thing about my brother's occupation. Maybe he was a barber or a shoe salesman. Think of all the hair and shoes in New York City. You could get rich at anything here.

Where Louis lived was not what I'd expected. But, as Louis later said, there weren't any rats. A rat-free building was something you paid handsomely for in New York City. I walked up to the fifth floor, the highest one, where Louis had his apartment. The dark steps smelled of garlic and onions. Some lady was yelling in Italian, and her voice echoed in the stairwell. A baby screamed its head off, maybe two or three babies.

I stood for a moment at the door to read the nice brass plate: MR. LOUIS N. DI CANTINI. The *N* stood for Nuncio, which Louis inherited from Papa's father, Nuncio di Cantini, now dead. My middle name is Dominic, so it looked weird in my name if you used the initial: Mr. Samuel D. di Cantini. It sounded like a stutter. I wanted to change it to something fancy, like a *W*. Mr. Samuel W. di Cantini. The *W* could stand for Worthington.

I knocked three times.

A lady with black hair and deep almond-shaped eyes opened the door. She was skinny except for her breasts, which stuck out like you'd expect for New York City. I swallowed the wrong way and choked.

"You okay?" she said, clapping me hard on the back. "You got to be little Sammy. Heh? Come in. I'll get you a soda."

Little Sammy? What a raw deal, I thought. Five foot six inches didn't make up a *little* Sammy. Louis still had me pegged at four foot eleven, where I got stuck for a year or two when I was much younger.

I followed her into the sticky-hot apartment, and she gave me a glass of soda that I gulped to ease the choking. We sat down to introduce ourselves properly.

The place was decent. The walls needed paint, but the curtains looked new and pressed. A red velvet couch took up one side of the room, and a cracked leather chair stood in one

132

corner beside a painted table, which supported a tall pink lamp with a medallion landscape of shepherds. A drop table by the windows had two cane chairs at either side of it. A rope rug on the floor covered just enough wood so the place didn't seem too bare. The kitchen was off to one side, around a corner; with the bedroom door partly open, I could make out the edge of a mahogany dresser.

"You okay now?"

"Yeah. I swallowed my spit wrong."

She made big eyes and said, "I'm Franca, a friend of your brother's. He said you was coming today, so I hung around."

"Where is he?"

"At work. He works a lot, that Louis. Always a hard worker. I tell him, Louis, you work that hard all your life it will kill you. You got to take it easy. The money ain't worth it." She spoke in an accent something like Mrs. Montoro's. I guessed she was Sicilian, like Bonino. You can tell Sicily by the high cheekbones and deep, almond eyes. I liked her features.

"You want some coffee?"

"Yes, thank you," I said.

She brought espresso and offered me a cigarette, taking one herself. Then she explained how her family had come from near Palermo. Her brother, Nicolo, had a cheese shop on West Sixth; he knew Louis and had introduced them. She was a singer by profession, and Louis was trying to get her a job at a speakeasy where he knew the owner. She said there was nobody like Louis. Everybody in New York City loved Louis, in spite of some recent setbacks in which he got swindled. He was going somewhere in this world, she said. Even Maccerio loved him. When I asked her who was Maccerio, she looked at me as if I had just got off the boat, and explained that Maccerio was the ward captain of the Democratic Party. His power ran from Second up to Twenty-third, and if Louis continued as Maccerio's close buddy, nothing could stop him.

I told her I never knew that Louis was a politician as well as a businessman, and she said, "Well now you learn something." She gave me more espresso, then said she owed a lot to Louis; she could tell I was his brother by my eyes, which were as pretty as a girl's. I liked this talk, especially about my eyes, which had never struck me as pretty before. She noticed right away the waterfalls on my tie, complimenting my taste; she liked my white shoes, too, which were unusual. I thanked her and said her dress was decent, too. I wasn't convinced that *unusual* was the word for my shoes; but a compliment was a compliment. A warm curdling occurred in my belly and a glow warmed my neck and cheeks; I told her that Louis sure had good taste in ladies. She winked and said she hoped I'd hang around for a while and pulled some Italian cookies, the white glazed ones, from the cupboard and spread them out on waxed paper.

We ate the cookies, maybe a dozen of them, while she told me her story. I heard about the war, which was terrible, and how her papa got killed. He had been in the trenches, she said. She told me how her mama had gotten the typhoid and shriveled up and died, which left her alone to raise the *bambini* when she was herself only thirteen. Now she was thirty-one, a bit old for a singer. She had never remarried since her husband, a sailor, was drowned at sea. I told her I'd never heard so much calamity in one life before, and she agreed. I thought *we* had it hard because Papa was crushed in the mines. We had it easy compared to Franca.

She had such a way of talking that I could well have sat there listening all week. Though it was hot and I sweated like a hog, Franca smelled like cut grass. Her hair, as black as anthracite, looked like she'd washed it only a minute before I arrived.

Three hours passed before Louis walked in to find me happy as a tick in a dog's ear. His gold fillings lit up the room, and he grabbed me like he hadn't seen me in twenty years, scrambling my hair with one hand and jabbing my belly with the other. He'd played the rough guy since childhood, so this was just his way to say hello. I was glad to see him, too, but not so glad as to mess his silk suit or scramble his hairdo. That slicked-back hair would have cost him forty minutes in front of a mirror.

To celebrate that I had made it there without falling off the train, Louis brought out a fancy bottle of hootch and three glasses. We drank up and went in a taxi to a place called Mario's, where they served cold veal in tuna sauce. Then Louis took us down the street for gelato, the watery ice cream they ate in the old country. New York made me think again I would go to Italy when I was famous and rich. They roll out the carpet for any Son of Italy who has made it big in America. I realized that the famous and rich don't generally like it when they're recognized in public, but I knew in my heart I wouldn't mind.

After a full night of talk and food, we went back to Louis's. I had never seen him so happy—telling jokes, teasing everybody. New York City brought out the best in him. But what I hadn't known till we got home was that Franca actually lived there with my brother. He'd never referred to it in his letters. I saw only one bed in his bedroom, and it wasn't a big bed, which made me wonder how they got comfortable. And they weren't married! Now it's one thing to have intercourse of a sexual nature with a lady not your wife; but Louis seemed to live here with Franca like man and wife. In the bathroom her toothbrush hung beside his. Her lady stuff filled the windowsill, blue and pink bottles of lotion and cream. God would not appreciate this arrangement.

I put up on the red couch, which was so short you had to sleep sideways with your legs hitched over one end. It wasn't terrible, since the couch was covered with cushy velvet, but the sheets reeked of perfume, filling me with sexy visions. Added to this was the noise drifting in from the bedroom. It began with a rustling of sheet, giggles, whispering, and increased slowly to a shriek or two, followed by grunts and snorts and loud breathing that didn't even sound human. I pictured a snorting beast above them, one that tore them apart

135

while they slept. But they settled down, I can't say how late. Then there was only the swirling surf of traffic below the window; I sank finally into a thick sleep and dreamt of Franca: nude and running through the waves.

For a couple days I went on my own around New York City, visiting the Statue of Liberty one afternoon and the Brooklyn Bridge the next; in both cases, I realized why God believed He was boss. You felt like you owned the planet seeing so much of it at one glance. You thought if only you had the mind to, you could step off into the air and fly. The sun blasted overhead, a high summer wind flapping the Stars and Stripes like fresh sheets on a clothesline. I made a secret promise to myself that when the time was right, I would live in New York City by myself. You couldn't live in the patch forever and be a success. The patch suggested failure, a lack of nerve. This was the big world.

I loved the millions of people here—even the bums—who poured into the streets every day on Fifth Avenue and Broadway and Madison. I loved the long-nosed cars that drove up to the Plaza, the ladies in taffeta dresses, tiered in the new style, the men with pastel-colored suits—greens, yellows, blues. You could feel the money stashed away in the banks here—more dollars than drops of water in the sea. America was money, big money, cars, clothes, and power. For the first time in history, we ran the world. Our brains were the hottest, full of brand-new ideas that would change everything. In New York City there was intelligence everywhere: in the wind, in the light that flashed off high windows, in the quick looks and swift pace of people on the streets. I wanted to join this city. What better place could there be for a lawyer? "Attorney Samuel di Cantini for the defense," they would say.

Franca took me to see the newest pictures: Bebe Daniels in *The Wild Susan*, which tickled us both; Lon Chaney in *The Unholy Three* (in which he played a ventriloquist who turns into a grandmother), which stretched it a bit. We ate chocolate peanuts, giggled, and made wild jokes afterward. Franca thought Lon Chaney as the grandmother looked like me, and—unfortunately—she or he did.

On my fourth day in New York City, Louis took me to work with him.

"I got faith in you, Sammy," he said at breakfast. "You say you maybe want to come to live in New York someday?"

"Maybe."

"He likes it here," said Franca, who was burning toast for us.

"I'm taking you to meet Maccerio," said Louis. "I told him my brother was in town and he said to bring you in." He drank a cup of coffee in one gulp. "Maccerio is the ward captain. We're in business together."

"I didn't know you were in politics," I said.

He looked at me straight and grinned. "You don't know a lot of things, do you?"

I shrugged. That was not a nice question.

"What did you think I did?"

"Mama thought you were in business. Maybe in the olive-oil business or something."

He laughed. "Everybody is in olives. This goddamn town runs on olive oil." He laughed harder. "You get yourself ready. Put on one of *my* ties."

This meant he didn't like my waterfalls. I was hurt but said nothing and found a regular dull polka-dot one in his closet. It went well with the suit. My shoes got a fresh lick of white polish. Maybe this Maccerio could get me a job here, which would tide me over till I got my law degree. I put this to Louis as we walked toward Maccerio's, having taken a short taxi ride across town.

"You want to come here, eh?" His arm slipped around my shoulder. "You want to come into business with your brother Louis?"

I hated his arm around my shoulder. "I guess you've done okay in business," I said.

137

"You got to understand about business, Sammy," he said. "It takes capital to make money. Capital is money in the bank. I made a little investment recently that wasn't too smart. I took a nose dive. But my friend Maccerio helped me out. I'm back on solid ground now, and I'm going to be richer than ever. Mama ain't going to want for nothing."

I figured I should be blunt with Louis. "What about my college money? You once said you'd help me."

"What do you need college for?" he said. "I never got no college, and I'm doing great."

"You can't be a lawyer without college."

"You don't need to be a lawyer. Lawyers work for the people who got money. They're like . . . servants."

"But what if I want to be one?"

Louis offered me a Fatima to calm me down. "Listen. You hang around here a bit. Watch how I live. You won't want no college." He lit the cigarette for me.

I could see it would be murder to get money for college out of Louis. Maybe the priesthood was my only chance after all.

"You wait and see, Sammy. I'm going to be rich," he said. "And you can be rich, too."

"Yeah?"

"You bet your ass." The idea of the money fired him up and he started to walk faster. He took his arm off my shoulder and plunged ahead like a general aiming into battle. His lower lip stuck out.

"I'm going to make more money, Sammy, than anybody in the patch even knows is out there." Louis was talking more to himself now than to me. He never even looked sideways. Then he noticed me again. "You really want to work here?"

"Yes."

"How old are you anyways?"

I said sixteen, almost seventeen. He didn't know any better. I could have said twenty and he wouldn't have known better.

"That's too young. You're just a goddamn kid."

"I'm not either."

He said, "Listen, you tag along with me. See if you like my type of work, okay? We'll talk to Maccerio. You could join us when you're eighteen. If he asks your age today, say eighteen."

I didn't understand about politics, but I sensed that Maccerio was not a level operator. We went into a place called Lorenzo's on First Avenue, a long dark room crowded with little tables and jammed with people for the lunch hour. I'd forgotten how late it was, since we got up at ten and sat around the kitchen eating toast for two hours. The room smelled like garlic and basil. I got hungry just sniffing, though the food odors mingled strangely with cigar smoke. Men sat smoking cigars in every corner, blowing smoke clouds above their bald heads.

"Who's that?" I asked as we passed the bust of somebody famous. It looked like Julius Caesar.

"Caruso," said Louis. "Don't you know Caruso?"

We climbed stairs at the back to where Maccerio lorded it over a private dining room. His dark bull neck slopped around a starched collar. His black silk tie was stuck with a diamond pin the size of a knuckle, and he wore rings on his puffy fingers. Oil slicked his forehead, dimpled in two places. His smile did not seem welcoming or happy: it was more like a grimace.

Maccerio squeezed my hand hard, and I stared for probably too long at the matted hair on the back of his hand. More hairs sprang out of a loose buttonhole in his shirt.

"Sammy wants to move to New York," said Louis. "He's a good boy. Eighteen years old."

Maccerio looked me over like a piece of meat.

"*Bene*, good, good—I like a young boy," he said hoarsely. Every word he spoke seemed to fight its way through a curtain of mucous.

We sat down together. Three other men sat at the table, in nice summer jackets. They did not look Italian.

"Give the boy a glass," Maccerio said to the waiter. "*Io*

139

offro." He poured a full portion of grappa, a strong alcohol drink that Jesse brought out for special occasions. He kept it in his bedroom closet, year-round. We drank a toast; it was harsh to swallow, but I didn't react. I could drink anything if I had to.

"What kind of work you want, then?" Maccerio said to me.

My brother looked away.

"I want to be a lawyer here—after I go to college. But I'll need to make money some other way, for a while. I don't know how."

Eyebrows lifted around the table.

"He's a smart kid in school," Louis said. "He gets straight A on his report card."

Maccerio looked at me like he had seen an ostrich. He said, "I like a smart boy."

"Smart ain't the word for him, he's genius," my brother went on. "You never know what he'll say."

"We could maybe use some brains around here," said Maccerio. "You like money, Sam?"

"Money is time," I said, taking a swig of the grappa.

"What else is there?" he asked, chuckling. Everybody laughed. "You got a good boy here, Lou," he said. "He's a sharp one, like you say." He tapped his skull.

When the waiter came Maccerio ordered for everyone: tortellini al sugo, arrosto di pollo. The menu was typed on a single sheet of paper with no prices.

"You got a girl back home in Pennsylvania?" Maccerio asked, pronouncing *Pennsylvania* like it had ten syllables.

"There's a girl I like," I said. "Ellie Maynard."

"Maynard," he said. "Not Mayannardo?"

His troops broke into giggles like small boys, but I saw nothing funny.

"Her papa's a big deal," said Louis. "Runs a school."

Maccerio nodded. I don't think he was impressed, but didn't matter.

"She's the prettiest girl in our school," I said. "They're all after her, even Nip Stanton."

Louis said, "He's the son of Bing Stanton, who operates shafts in Luzerne County."

Maccerio nodded gravely. "She don't fall at your feet, huh?" I shook my head.

"But she falls down in front of Stanton, no?"

I hesitated. "Well, not exactly 'falls down'—"

"But she likes him more than she likes you," he said. "No?"

It was awful but maybe true. She always seemed to sit by him in school.

"Then maybe you ought to see that money can buy more than *time* for a young boy like you." As he said that, his teeth bared.

"I guess so," I said. But it occurred to me that if a girl wouldn't take you broke and as you were, maybe you ought to drop her. Love should flow back and forth between people. If it didn't, both sides would end up unsatisfied. This came as a revelation to me, and a small lid rose in the back of my head, allowing me to breathe more easily.

A big antipasto appeared before us: prosciutto, olives, celery, peppers, bits of sausage.

"This boy can work for me anytime he wants," said Maccerio.

Louis sweated like a horse, gobbling up the prosciutto.

Some others joined us, and the attention shifted away from me. I got lost in the food and, later, stumbled down to the bathroom, located near the kitchen—a hot little room in the basement where half a dozen cooks hollered at each other in Italian. I felt woozy and leaned against the wall, watching pots of boiling water fizz and steam. A rich smell of sauce sweetened the air. One fat cook sliced onions as I stood there, working the knife like a miraculous device. I lost track of time. When I finally made it back upstairs, everybody but Louis was gone.

"Where'd they all go?"

"They had to leave on business," Louis said. "We got to go, too. Maccerio said to bring you on an assignment."

"What's that?"

Louis patted me on the back and showed me out the door.

We took the uptown subway to Thirty-third and walked west to a high gray building with a revolving door on the sidewalk.

"What are we supposed to do?" I asked.

"Don't ask so many questions, Sammy. Do what I tell you."

You could feel the resolution in Louis. He didn't want distractions, so I shut up. We got into a brassy elevator, where an old Negro on a stool asked what floor we wanted. Twenty-ninth, Louis told him, the highest number on the board; we had a long ride ahead of us. The machine ground its gears, cables clacking and whinnying, as if the whole machine needed oil. The Negro, whose close-shaven white hair looked like baby powder on his black scalp, never looked at us once.

"Twenty-nine," he said.

Louis gave him two bits as we stepped out into a hall of shiny floor tiles with a potted plant in one corner beside a leather couch. A dark oil painting of a horse and wagon rolling through the countryside hung on the wall. Of the many doors, only one said ENTRANCE; below that it said ATLANTIC-UNION CREDIT COMPANY, and below that was the name C. P. WARBURTON, PRESIDENT. You couldn't see through the snowy glass.

"Sammy," he said to me, "put this in the right-hand pocket of your jacket." He handed me a revolver.

"What's this for?"

"Shooting people."

"I mean, why did you give it to me?"

"When I nod to you, point it *carefully* at Mr. Warburton."

I was flabbergasted. "But Lou, I—"

"And whatever you do, don't kill nobody. It's loaded."

"Kill nobody," I said. "Listen, Lou, I wonder if—"

"Sammy, you do exactly like I tell you." He said it in a

way that didn't allow for argument and threw open the door and walked in.

I followed with the gun in my jacket, terrified it would accidentally go off and kill me—in front of everyone. Lou didn't turn around but strode past a row of secretaries whose job it was to protect the road to Mr. Warburton's private office.

"Excuse me, sir!"

"Your name, sir!"

All typewriters in the room stopped clacking. A dozen ladies stared at us popeyed. I tried to look like nothing was wrong and that they shouldn't worry, smiling and waving as I passed them. Louis rapped hard on the door and walked straight in.

C. P. Warburton was not as big as his name. He was tiny, in fact: a middle-aged man in a blue suit who wore wire-rimmed glasses and sported a thin moustache; his thinning hair stuck close to his head with strong-smelling tonic. He stood firmly behind his desk.

"What do you want, Mr. Cantini?"

"Mr. *di* Cantini," Louis said. His jaw froze forward. "We got to have that money today, I'm afraid. *Now*, to be exact."

"I told Maccerio I'd have it in two weeks. We talked only yesterday on the phone." He leaned on pudgy fingers spread out on the desktop like tripods.

"I'm sorry, but he asked me to come for it now." Louis lit up a cigarette. "We had lunch with him not half an hour ago. He said today was payday."

Mr. Warburton scowled like a junkyard dog. "Mr. *di* Cantini, I'm going to have to ask you to leave. I will not have you . . . Italians . . . just walking in here without an appointment." He picked up the phone. "Miss Giles, will you come and escort Mr. *di* Cantini to the door?"

The remark about Italians bothered me. He was treating us like crooks. And Louis was upset, too. You could tell by the furrows deepening in his brow. He flicked the big door shut behind him without even turning around. But Mr. Warburton looked at us fierce, like he wasn't going to stand for any Italian slamming his fancy door.

"I'm sorry to appear rude," said Louis, calm and precise, "but a job is a job. I'm afraid we must have that money now."

"Well, that's impossible," he said. "Tell Maccerio I will have it in two weeks like I said, and that he can stop sending his thugs around here like this. It creates a dreadful disturbance in the office." As he spoke, his eyeballs twitched and his moustache quivered.

Louis nodded my way. It was the moment I'd feared, but sometimes you have to drive along the shoulder of a road; if you jerk back onto the main drag too quickly, you spill the car. You have to drive through a crisis. So I pulled the revolver.

I aimed straight at Mr. Warburton's nose. His eyeballs stopped twitching.

Louis said, "It would make a more dreadful scene if you wound up dead on the floor of your own office, all because of five thousand silly dollars."

"You goddamn wops," Warburton said, going to a safe hidden behind a picture, from which he took out a metal box and counted five thousand in hundreds. He slipped the money into a manila envelope and handed it over. "Tell Maccerio to shove this up his ass," he said. It surprised me that a distinguished-looking man of his position would talk like that.

"Thank you very much, Mr. Warburton," said Louis, polite to the end. He put the envelope in his pocket and nodded to me again.

I lowered the gun into my pocket and Louis opened the door. He put his hand out to say, "After you." I led the way back through the secretaries, who gaped at us like we had no clothes on.

In the hall, waiting for the elevator, Louis said, "Give me the gun back, Sammy. You did beautiful."

"Thanks." I just didn't have more to say at this point. My guts were tapioca pudding.

The Negro let us into the elevator, bored as ever. We rode

down in silence, and Louis gave him another two bits, which he didn't acknowledge. I felt bad about him and gave him another quarter, which he took.

Outside, I said, "Jeezus . . . is this what you do every day, Louis?"

"Naw. This was unusual. I do a lot of accounting, mostly. Some politics. You talk people into seeing things your way. It's a lot of fun."

I didn't question him about *how* he brought folks to his point of view. It was clear that I wasn't built for politics. Maybe I wasn't even built to be a lawyer.

13

Louis didn't ask me to go to work with him again after I got frank and said I wasn't interested. He told me I would change my mind one day and left it there. I was too young yet anyway, he added. For my part, I liked staying home with Franca; she told me stories about distant places she had been: Rome, Napoli, Genoa, Washington, D.C. I saw that Louis didn't appreciate her, not like she deserved; at night, when she came home late from shopping, he accused her of seeing Luigi, whoever Luigi was. She would say who in hell wants a Luigi when she's got a Louis, and this usually convinced him. It happened like this three nights in a row, but on the third night he lost his temper and slapped her around the bedroom with the door closed so I wouldn't directly see it. She screamed like he had taken a knife to her, and her mouth bled a little when she came out. She said nothing the rest of the evening but read a magazine in Italian. I was nervous and drank wine. Louis didn't seem bothered, filling out racing forms in the kitchen. I don't know why, but I got to thinking about Ellie Maynard again that night. It came on me hard. Did she prefer Nip Stanton over me? Anger inflated my body; I could not reconcile Nip Stanton and Ellie Maynard together, and wished one of them would drop dead. That would be better than this.

I fell asleep after drinking too much wine, curled up in the sofa; I dreamed I had wandered down to a wharf by the Hudson River. It was after midnight. I wandered out along the shaky wooden pier, noticing a shadowy figure at the end with his arms raised up. He was hooded, but I found myself heading straight for him—but not scared like I should have been. I sensed who it was. I screamed "Papa! Papa!" and ran wildly into his open arms, but as they closed around me I saw into the ice-blue eyes. It was Bing Stanton. He smiled a weasel's snaggletoothed grin. He was laughing, loud, but it wasn't a man's laugh but an animal's. He asked me if I had seen Maccerio, and I said no. He called me a liar and said that the di Cantinis were all liars and deserved what they got. Then I felt a revolver under his armpit as he pressed me closer to him, and I knew he would try to shoot me. I resolved not to let him kill me and gathered my strength and heaved, breaking his bear hug. I knocked him backward and he fell head over heels for what seemed like minutes. He splashed into the dark river, but the howling didn't stop. It grew louder and louder, so loud I couldn't stand it and leaned over and screamed, "*Shut up! Shut up!*" But I felt myself falling as well, blown forward off the pier by a big wind, sucked downward into the water. "*Shut up!*" I kept yelling. "*Shut up!*"

I woke into the warm arms of Franca, who'd heard me screaming and came out to see if I was all right.

"You had a real bad dream," she said. "Shush now. It's okay. You're okay now. Go to sleep."

"I was dreaming."

"I know, I know," she whispered close to me. I could smell her breath. "You go back to sleep, Sammy."

I touched her forehead. It was damp and hot. I reached around the back of her head to touch her hair, so long and soft; it smelled like sleep. I pulled a few strands to my face and breathed them.

"Go back to sleep," she said. "Everything's okay."

"You're beautiful, Franca," I said.

"Shush."

"It's true."

"You go to sleep like you're supposed." She pulled away and was gone. The door to their bedroom closed softly. I was on my own again, afraid to dream, staring at the weird yellow lights that crossed the ceiling and walls.

I planned to stay awake till morning, but I fell asleep near dawn and slept through until ten. Louis was gone by then. I knew he had an important lunch appointment that day and would not be home till later. He said he would take us to a Yankee ballgame that afternoon, and I could hardly wait. I wanted so bad to see Babe Ruth in person, and Sad Sam Jones was pitching that day against Boston.

I saw Franca go from the bedroom into the shower and heard the water pick against the tiles. I imagined the hot needles stinging her face, running down her back and bare legs. I wanted one like her, a sexy one, who would take showers and walk naked around the house. Her long hair would touch her shoulders and shine. It might be blond or black. I began to think maybe I preferred black hair after all. Black was like the earth, the ground where all life started. But blond was air, clouds, and fire. . . .

The shower shut off, and Franca stepped into the room with a towel around her, nothing else. Nothing else! I was still debating the difference between blond and black hair when black stood directly in front of me. The very idea of blond leaped out the window. It could not compete with the real black thing.

"You feeling better now?" she asked. "I was worried about you last night. You screamed like a robber come through the window."

"We're too high for a robber to come through any window," I said. "Five stories."

"Oh, you . . . you're too smart for a boy." She winked at me. "*Ragazzo.*"

I screwed up my face in protest, sitting up straight.

"What's the matter?" she said, heading straight toward me in her towel. She sat on the edge of the couch. "You don't like me to say you're a boy? Is that it?"

I smiled and told her I'd had a terrible dream.

"What did you dream?"

"Nothing . . . stuff about home."

"I don't dream," she said. "Never."

"Why not?"

"No imagination," she said. "Is your oldest brother cute as you and Louis?"

This tickled me. "Vince doesn't go in for girls. He's in love with his union."

"More politics?"

"Yep. He takes it very serious. Louis doesn't take anything to heart the way Vincenzo does. Louis wants to make money."

"Vincenzo don't want money?"

"Not at all. That sounds crazy, but it's true."

"What's he want, then?"

I said, without having to think it over too long, "He wants justice."

She suddenly lifted the sheet that clothed my body to the chest. The idea of justice was over her head.

"What are you doing, Franca?"

"Can't I take a peek at you?"

I wasn't wearing pajamas, just underpants, which embarrassed me. But she wasn't asking, she was doing. She was the type who went ahead, so I had no choice but to peer down her towel, which came loose as she bent forward. Her breasts dangled, full as water balloons, with nipples like red poppies.

"Louis wouldn't go for this," I said. "He really wouldn't."

"He ain't here, is he?" She sat up and sort of pushed me back. The sheet came off completely. She let her towel fall to

149

the floor as well, and bent down and kissed my belly. My underpants stood up like a circus tent.

"You got hair on your belly," she said. "How old are you?"

"Twenty," I said.

"You ain't no twenty. Fifteen or fourteen?"

"Okay . . . nineteen."

"That's what I like . . . the truth." She sucked her cheeks in. "Lift up," she said. "Your hips, lift."

I did, and she rolled back my underpants to midthigh. I was bare bone, pure hard salami.

"That's good," she said. "That's *real* good." She was impressed by what I had to offer a woman.

Reaching down, she touched my balls, then lifted and squeezed them in her palm. With her other hand, she grabbed me and began to jerk, hard. She hurt me, but the pain was tolerable. She had a concentrated look on her face, while my head spun like a lazy susan. My heart beat in my wrists and temples, and I felt a peculiar, distant pounding at the back of my head. Then I came, sputtering a white smear across my stomach, which Franca stirred slowly with one finger while kissing my chest.

We hadn't noticed the footsteps outside, nor heard the door open. Our private commotion had deafened us. But there stood Louis di Cantini himself in the doorway with a cigarette crooked in the corner of his half-grin. I was sure he would shoot us both dead.

He didn't say a word as he blew smoke rings toward us, his mouth round as a fish's.

Franca skipped bare-ass from the couch into the bedroom and slammed the door.

"Don't kill me, Lou," I said. "I didn't mean it, I didn't mean anything." I spoke quietly, terrified, embarrassed to be seen there in that condition. "Please, Lou, you got to let me explain this. You got—" I choked off the sentence. Sobs started up in me, and I was soon a mess.

I'm depraved, I thought. I'd go straight to Father Francis

150

when I got home and confess the whole business. I would ask to be sent to a monastery, as soon as possible. There are places for people like me—bare cells, where you pray twenty out of twenty-four hours a day. You wear burlap sacks and eat stale bread three meals a day.

Without speaking, Louis gathered his briefcase from the kitchen table, where he had left it by accident, and went back out the door. He didn't even slam it.

All was ruined. But at least he had decided not to shoot me dead; I felt a bit calmer. The Yanks were definitely out the window now. The Babe would have to swing without us. Good-bye New York City. Good-bye law-school. Good-bye everything.

Still sobbing, I went to the bathroom and sponged myself clean. I put on my clothes, packed whatever I'd brought, and took myself to Pennsylvania Station. I didn't say anything to Franca. She was crying behind the bedroom door when I left, and I hoped I would never see her again. I even hoped I would never see New York City or my brother again.

14

The train sat forever in Pennsylvania Station, with sunlight washing the carriage floorboards. The heat was the heat of hell: unforgiving, choking. It wanted me to sweat, to feel the grittiness of myself, the filth and rot of my soul. I tried to blot out Franca and Louis, New York, Maccerio, everything. I closed my eyes and leaned my head back on the warm, itchy cushion. A coal-black Negro porter swept the aisle, slowly, as if we would be here for good. He eyeballed me close. Could he read my mind? I had a hot dog on my lap, but the smell sickened me. My stomach felt too full, the idea of appetite itself disgusting.

I kept shuffling pictures in my head, trying to keep out the horrible image of Louis in the doorway, the cigarette crooked in his mouth. The image of Franca, naked. The image of my own ridiculous body. But the worst pictures flashed again and again, sharp, painful. I knew they would forever creep into my sleep, lighting my dreams with their sickly sepia glow. Memory is a prison with endless cells. Mostly you can forget what is locked in the darkest corridors, the faces and deeds you want to banish, but unexpectedly, in dreams, at supper, in the middle of a good time, anywhere, the lights can be thrown on, and the cells click open. The white teeth gleam at you, the resentful stares, the miserable snickers. You see that everything you ever said or did goes with you to the end.

At long last we pulled out of the station, barely chugging. The engine stopped, started, stopped. The brakes wheezed. The carriage jerked, then swayed from side to side. Unaware of my sin and shame, the conductor took my ticket, clipped it, and handed it back.

I wanted to keep my eyes closed, to shut out the world and then fall asleep, and by some miracle I succeeded, drowsing for two hours. But as the air grew fresher and I smelled the Pocono pines, my eyes opened on a whoosh of greenness, the blue lakes and sky. I peered out the window, sucking in breaths of sweet air, pressing my nose to the glass. Birds lit from tree to tree, and I noticed the pinpoint of a red-tail hawk on the edge of a cloud. I could smell the ground, the big woods, the wild mountain flowers. Once I spotted a doe in a brief clearing; it seemed to wonder what the fuss was and why anyone bothered to hurl themselves at such a speed from place to place. The doe's moist stare stayed in my head as I closed my eyes again and tried to get back to sleep.

Tears salted my cheeks. I was mulling over Louis. What would he think of me? How could I ever talk to him again? What kind of girl was that Franca?

"Shit," I said aloud. The word floated like a balloon in the carriage and startled an old man, who had been quietly muttering to himself in the seat across from me. He looked like a minister or undertaker, in a dark suit with white socks.

The train churned through the Poconos, wheeling past the deep woods like a Mississippi steamboat. Its whistle left bright exclamation marks in the blue sky, the noise startling rabbits from the brush at either side of the tracks. Half an hour from Scranton, I saw the first coal breaker rear its head in the distance. The mining country started up, with little towns clustered around shafts, the familiar patches with their shabby triplexes and company stores. It was broken country, the sides of mountains torn out, the woods leveled and patchwork buildings stumbling down the hills. Not like New York City, where everything seemed fixed and sure of itself. But I breathed easier here.

At the Pittston Laurel Line Station, a long green building on a back road east of Main Street, I got off in a hurry; the embarrassment, the misery of myself, would disappear at home. Soon New York would exist only as a name in my head, not a real place where I was guilty of a genuine crime. I wanted to see all the little sights along the way to the patch, to smell the reek of culm dumps, sewage, the black dust of the coal train as it hunkered past. I wanted to see the black-faced miners going past me like dark ghosts, the patch boys at their games, the skinny girls, and to hear the rumors, the family squabbles. I wanted Lucy's nonsense, even Bonino's. I wanted the river and Will Denks. I could hardly wait to look out my bedroom window at midnight when the moon swelled over the valley, shining on the river, making the leaves in the woods behind our house seem to burn. I would love the weird coughing of the mules at night, Grandpa Jesse grunting in his sleep or yelling as he shit, Mama snapping at Gino. To hell with New York City and that stinking Franca. Maybe in twenty years Louis would talk to me again. Maybe.

Main Street hummed quietly—an ordinary business day. The Brown-Wright milk wagon clattered to the barn, and there were horses and cars in the road, the past and the future side by side, seeming wary of each other. Now that the county was paving all the roads, it was clear which would win out. I stopped to watch Sal Minetti, who used to live in the patch,

154

as he loaded a Ford pickup with crated bananas. He nodded to me and I smiled back.

I dropped into Ketchum's Candy Store and bought my favorites: chocolate ants and hard rock candy. Mrs. Ketchum knew what I liked and didn't ask what I wanted but only how much. I took a quarter's worth and went back into the sun, which had settled into place firmly above the horizon. The daylight seemed fixed forever, banana-colored, warm.

In front of Lily's Corner Drug, I stared at several tubes of Ipana toothpaste in the window. Below the toothpaste was a display of Rapid Shave, with an array of straight razors for sale with leather strops. The shaving gear reminded me of Papa. I used to stand, a small boy, between his legs while he shaved. He swirled hot water into the dry soap in a bowl, and it would foam up, and he would dollop the sudsy mixture on my cheeks and chin and say, "You better get a razor, too, you want to be big like me." He stood in his long-johns, giving off the strong smell of himself, a smell I could never forget. How I loved him, his squat legs and grumbly voice. He would strop the razor to a fierce keenness and make long slow sweeps lengthwise down his cheeks, leaving the moustache for last. The darkness of sleep, having grown thick on his face through night, was swept away. Then he powdered his face generously, whitening it, and would kiss me hard, leaving some of the powder on my face, which always made me mad, and I would run to Mama to complain. By evening, after work, the white face of morning would be dark again, dusted with coal, blackface like the minstrels.

"Hey, Sammy!" said the waitress, Maud Muncy, waving me inside the drugstore. She usually gave me the second ice-cream soda free, so I went in.

"Hello, Maudie," I said. "How you been?"

"Okay. Nobody wants to eat today, so I'm bored."

"I just came in from New York City," I said, pulling up a stool. I wished I hadn't mentioned my trip. There wasn't much to brag about. She'd faint if I told her what happened to me on the red velvet couch. "How about a soda? Cherry ice cream."

"Sure thing."

I watched her open the shiny compartments where the ice cream was kept on dry ice; the steam swirled up.

"There," she said, setting the large soda in front of me. "So you been away somewheres?"

"Yeah." I picked off the cherry to eat separately and licked cream from around the rim, wishing I had kept my fat mouth shut.

"Just get back?"

I nodded, sucking on the straw.

"So maybe you didn't hear what's happened?"

"What?"

"Somebody shot Nick Maroni," she said. "He's dead."

Nick Maroni was *dead?* I couldn't take it in.

"Look," Maud said, putting a day-old newspaper on the counter. The front page told the whole story. He was shot coming out of the union hall in Exeter. Nobody knew who shot him or why. He was the "real man" behind the UMW in this area, the paper said; my brother was just the spokesman, the speechmaker. Maroni was shot dead at noon in broad daylight, and the police couldn't even locate a suspect. Were the cops involved in this? I could believe that the C&I were paid off by Bing Stanton, but the state and local police had to be independent of the operators. Didn't they? "There are no suspects," said the article. "A funeral will be held at Lucca Funeral Home in Exeter on Tuesday." It ended: "Mr. Maroni is survived by a wife, the former Anne Rocchio, and three sons."

"They say there'll be a protest," Maud Muncy said. "Vincenzo is in charge. He's getting everybody organized."

I siphoned off the ice-cream soda in silence, frozen to the bone inside.

"You liked Nick Maroni." Maud Muncy said.

"He came to the house a lot." So many pictures of him came to mind: Nick with Jesse, Nick standing in the garden beside Mama; the times he came up to my room and we talked about baseball.

"Want another soda? Free . . . on me?"

"No, thanks, Maudie. I better go."

That I hadn't seen Will Denks for so long, not talked to him since the party, rankled me something fierce, and before I went home I knew I had to stop by the river. The thought that I'd see Will with that girl of his upset me, but I was already so sick from hearing what happened to poor Nick Maroni that New York City and all my silly quarrels with the Nipper and Will Denks seemed ridiculous.

When I came up on him, from behind, he stood by the table he'd got at a junkyard last summer, cutting up a bullhead for supper. The guts were laid out on the table. Will Denks didn't stop working to greet me, but he never went overboard with the greetings. He turned with a big grin, like he'd expected me.

"There's a protest rally at the shaft Tuesday, after Maroni's funeral," he said. "They say the C&I killed him and that Stanton was behind it."

"That's murder!" I said, a bit surprised that, after so long, we made no small talk.

"Of course it's murder."

Will distinctly ignored all that had passed between us. He seemed more interested in politics than usual. As he cooked, he told me about the last few days in Exeter. "Vincenzo has got the men organized," he explained. "They're planning to march in protest on the mines when the six o'clock shift gets out. There's nobody ain't supposed to work because of the funeral, but some will anyways. It's going to be crazy." He stirred the bullhead in hot butter. "They're bringing guns. I heard about all this stuff at Tommy Carlo's."

"*Who* is bringing guns? Not Vincenzo."

"No, but the C&I are moving in like an army. They got reinforcements coming from Philadelphia. Pinchot might come himself. He don't want any national news against him. Not now. It could ruin his reelection."

I said nothing. This was hardly the homecoming I'd expected. I didn't even know how to feel.

"So what about New York?" Will asked, at last. He had a way of not bringing up some topics until the end. I wondered if he might be jealous, since he had never been anywhere. "You didn't stay long."

"It's okay. Nothing much. You know, lots of people and high buildings."

"So you ain't moving down there tomorrow?"

"No," I said, annoyed with him. "Not for a while."

Will looked at me blankly. He hardly ever let on much interest in life beyond his camp—not even downriver. New York City, for him, was as real as Alaska or the moon.

"You know, I'm kind of sorry we didn't talk before I left. That business at Nipper's place didn't sit well with me. I was goddamn mad at you."

You could see Will Denks hated personal talk. He preferred machines because they responded in a cool, logical fashion to the way you tuned them. People can't be trusted that way. They go fickle, strange, and sour.

"That punch kind of went to my head, I suppose." He gave a half-grin.

That amounted, in Will's book, to a confession. He would have made a lousy Catholic. The priests would wring his neck. But I felt better now. Will had given, a little.

We sat by the water and ate the fish together and it seemed like old times, like Will Denks and I would sit here and cook and swim and the world would never turn into the dark empty space ahead of us, and we would always be the same best friends.

Slocum Street swarmed with strangers; the porches were jammed. I passed Hitch Lima and Billy Shawgo, who grinned as though aware of something I couldn't possibly know about. My brown suit didn't go over with the patch boys, who never dressed up in summer. Catholics hardly ever put on good clothes, even for church, once school got out. I drew queer looks from the porches, people guessing I must have turned Baptist or something. Baptists were always dressing up at weird times.

Not far from home I met Gino. He jumped from behind a hedge, barking like a dog. "Get lost, Gino," I said.

"It ain't worth going home. The place is a zoo."

"What do you mean?"

He was sweaty and old-looking for a boy. "They've all gone nuts. It ain't worth going home." He puffed hard. "Jesse's a mad dog, Vincenzo don't say nothing, and Mama keeps talking Italian. She thinks Maroni got what he asked for, and she don't want more trouble. She told Vincenzo to quit the union now."

"Is she home?"

"She ain't been home since the news about Maroni. Went to Lucy's, and she ain't coming back till the strike is over. I'm staying there, too. The C&I got our house staked out day and night."

That didn't sound possible. They couldn't simply stake out your house when you hadn't committed a crime. This was America! I told Gino to tell Mama I was back from New York City and would come to see her soon. I intended to stay at the river with Will Denks, so she could rest her mind. Who would have guessed the summer would bring this twist: Mama *wanting* me to sleep somewhere other than in my own bed at home!

I slipped in the back door of our house to see things for myself. The kitchen was empty, but I heard Vincenzo in the living room making a speech to some of the leaders of the local union—what they called the "strike committee." Nothing unusual for him; he seemed to be saying that the time was ripe. They must seize their opportunity. How many more miners had to be crushed or maimed? He cited Papa, who was dead because Bing Stanton let them rob the pillars; he cited Jesse's knee, which had become so bad he might never work again; he cited Maroni, of course, harping on the poor widow left wihout a pension and the three sons without a father. He read

159

from a list of maimed or killed miners going back ten years, which he followed by more case histories. I hung back behind the door. My brother had an angel's tongue. You couldn't *not* listen to him. He could have been an actor on Broadway, except that this was no play.

Vincenzo had no interest in making himself famous. I was sure he would step aside if another man, a better leader, stood up. He was a loner, not at all like Louis, who really enjoyed being in a crowd. But he had made himself care about the miners. It mattered to him about Maroni's widow and her three sons, about the conditions his friends had to work under in the mines. It mattered enough for him to give up baseball, where he could have been a star. Even coal itself mattered to him.

Coal was nothing more than a million years of living cells compressed in a vein, weighed down by centuries and by tons of dirt. It was dinosaurs, lizards, prehistoric birds with wide kite-wings and toothy beaks. It was crabs, worms, fish, chickens, and men, all cramped in the narrow seams, what used to be their life turning into hard anthracite coal, blazing in America's furnaces and stoves.

I wondered if I could ever care about the miners like Vincenzo did. Maybe. I felt bad about Nick Maroni, and as angry as I was sad about Papa's death. I hadn't really let myself get angry before, since there was nothing you could do about an accident. My whole nature tended to let things slide, to assume that nothing you ever did changed anything. Sometimes I didn't even answer what I knew perfectly well at school; it felt so useless. The world was ignorant, and the ignorance was so deep that no single voice mattered. The same problem was worse in a democracy, where one vote alone seemed stupid, piddling. The "masses" were not something I understood. I never liked people in crowds—except maybe on Broadway or Fifth Avenue, where the spectacle itself fired me up. But I usually felt insignificant among people. On the other hand, I considered the private world in my head—what I said in my own brain—everything. Nothing outside my own feelings counted. Other people hardly existed, or they existed only because I needed them—like props in a play. If I closed my eyes, they disappeared.

I began to wonder who the hell was this Sammy di Cantini? The body in the kitchen, crouched, slinking behind a door, listening to Vincenzo? Was I *real*?

I opened the door and stood in full view of my brother and his friends. Vincenzo paused, caught my eye, and continued with his speech. He seemed glad I was there.

You could trust him like you could trust a priest. In fact, you could trust him more. Vincenzo was inspiring. He made injustice appear physical, a poison circulating in your veins. You could taste it on your tongue.

Jesse sat with his bum leg on a stool, grinning. The meeting probably reminded him of the old country, where the men of the village met in parks or on street corners to argue politics every night after supper. When Vincenzo finished, Jesse wanted everybody to stay for coffee, but most left quickly to avoid his conversation. It's awful to be old, I thought. It's worse to be old and boring.

"I'll be there with you on Tuesday," I said to Vincenzo when he came into the kitchen.

"I'm glad you want to," he said, grabbing my forearm in his powerful grip. "I was hoping you'd be back. I figured you'd never come back once you seen New York."

"To hell with New York," I said, turning aside with embarrassment.

"You didn't like it?"

"I'd rather be in Exeter."

Vincenzo liked this. "You live here, Sammy." He stated this as a simple fact. Vincenzo had a knack for laying down facts. He could say, "The sky is blue" and make it sound like a revelation.

"How was Louis?"

"Okay," I said, not elaborating. "Let me help you pass out coffee."

161

"Thanks. There's only a couple men staying."

After shaking the hands of Vincenzo's friends, I listened to their last preparations for the Tuesday walkout. Then I went upstairs to get out of my clothes, which disgusted me, especially the tie with the waterfalls and my scuffed white shoes. My Panama was crushed to one side.

I dumped everything on the floor in a heap, even my underwear, and stood in front of the mirror on my closet door. I examined my chest, which had begun to sprout dark hair; my strong, square hips; my private parts—man-size and dark in the early evening light. My legs were solid as my shoulders. I was firm and tight, a tough human animal who should fear nobody, nothing, with brains enough in my head to understand this planet and my place on its wild, sad surface. The time had come to begin where I was, from what I was: myself, Sammy, me, alone.

15

"Where the hell you been?" Mama said without even so much as hello as I stepped into Lucy's house. "*Mi fanno male i piedi,*" she complained, rubbing her feet.

"I only got back this afternoon."

"You went up to the house?"

"I had to change my clothes," I said.

"They gone nuts—*pazzo.* Stay away from there, Sammy. I told Vincenzo he has ruined my life, ruined the family. Here I am, my age, and nowheres to sleep. Thrown out of my own house." She gestured like an orchestra conductor. "*Dio non voglia.*"

"You're sleeping here, ain't you?" asked Lucy, who sat with a box of chocolate nuggets on her lap. Now that she was married, it was time to get fat. "Bonino don't mind," she continued. "Fact is, he said he likes you to stay here, didn't he, Mama?"

163

It looked like nobody would ever call Bonino anything but Bonino, not even his wife.

Mama scratched the threadbare arms of the sofa. Her eyes looked hollow, the life flickering in them like a candle at the end of a cave. The red strands of her hair spun loose and wild. She looked witchlike, nervous. I sat beside her and put my arm around her shoulders. She was right to stay here, since the C&I had the house staked out. Men from out of town poked in and out of the woods behind our house. You felt they were watching you from the leaves, from the air itself.

"So how was my Louis?" Mama asked. "Is he rich?"

"He's not broke," I said. "He made a bad investment. But he's getting it back."

"Him. . . ." she said.

"He's got a nice apartment, and he took me to lunch with his boss, Maccerio."

Mama didn't like the idea of a boss who would have lunch with you. A boss, she said, should have lunch with other bosses. "So does he cook for himself?" she asked.

"Mostly."

"How does he do it?"

"He's got a book. It tells you step by step."

Mama and Lucy lit up. "What was the taste?" Mama asked, fairly gloating. She thought nobody could cook like her.

"Lousy taste," I said. "I couldn't stay there any longer because I was starving." More laughs. "Jeez . . . he gave me ice cream for breakfast."

"Ice cream?"

"With hot chocolate and peanuts."

Everybody said it was ridiculous to eat ice cream with chocolate and peanuts for breakfast; they wondered if this was something Louis ate himself, which led them into questions about life in New York City. I was happy I managed to get them off the subject of the C&I. It wasn't easy to stay cheerful in Bonino's house, so small, dim, and stuffy. The air clung to you, reaching into your lungs when you breathed like a hot

164

rubber glove. Lucy had bought the furniture at a junk sale in Shamokin, and it looked junky. The couch had springs poking up that you had to try to sit between. Its brocaded pattern had long since been worn to a threadbare surface. Lampshades barely hung on the rims. The rug had holes in it. Since there was only one bedroom, Mama and Gino slept on the living-room floor on quilts.

"Sammy!"

"Hi," I said, turning.

It was old snake-oil himself. Bonino. He came through the door all toothy and pleasant, dressed in a mechanic's overalls.

"How was New York?"

"Good."

He insisted on being friendly, like a man running for sheriff, and clasped me with both hands, shook me, then offered a cold soda, which I accepted. Thirst is not picky.

"Bonino has signed the papers for his garage," said Lucy. There was brag in her voice.

"Good," I said. "It doesn't pay to be out of work for too long. You get used to it."

"He's going to hire another mechanic. They'll fix and re-build brakes."

I said that brakes always needed fixing or rebuilding, just to sound cheerful.

Mama kept bringing the conversation back to the walkout and Vincenzo. Vincenzo had been a quiet boy, she told us. He was made for the priesthood. Now he didn't even go to mass.

I listened till the ants of numbness crept to my ears before announcing that I would sleep by the river, which nobody minded, since Lucy's floor was taken. I said I'd come back for breakfast every day, so long as it wasn't ice cream.

Free of Lucy's house, I stopped by a hedge to smell the unseen garden on the other side of it. The aroma swirled in the night air, sweetly, and a breeze slid off from the river. I shook the hedge to hear the leaves make their tinny rattle, looking up at the fine spray of stars across the Milky Way and thinking that every small fact of the universe, when properly noticed, was a kind of prayer.

The sun rose through a mist across the river and Will Denks was still asleep in his bag, his face turned my way; I leaned close to him. Sleep drained all the cleverness from him. He looked like a child now, a boy with crumpled blond hair and one cheek puffed against the pillow. His lips were redder than usual, and he smelled of pine, river water, woodsmoke, and Hark Wood's whiskey.

I lay back to think over the past few days, brooding about New York City and how I had shamed myself in front of Louis. I thought about Franca, too, the beautiful Franca, so naughty with her long legs, her red lips and large breasts. I got her out of my mind with a sharp twist of the neck. I had to feel my way through sins in my own time and way, work through them slowly, like walking through a briar patch. But forgiveness was there, waiting to be taken. It sat on the river like the mist at dawn, mine to breathe in when I got there, scratched and bleeding, to the water's edge.

I brooded on Bing Stanton, too, the man who had killed Papa, indirectly, and had brought Nipper into the world. He was ruining Jesse, Vincenzo, and me without knowing it. It was selfishness that made him take a position against the union and its reasonable reforms. Why did I ever let myself get sucked into talking to him that day at his house? The miners didn't want much, after all. Didn't they go underground each day, risking their lives? If mining could be made safer, it should be. The debate should be closed.

At the river, I took off my underpants and got in ankle-deep. The water was warm as piss; by power of suggestion, I let fly a yellow jet into the stream. The minnows edged up close, wondering what in hell. I waded in further, letting the water rise around my balls and the air turn slowly to liquid till the river was lush around me, and time seemed continuous and close, surrounding. Not the *clickety-click* of seconds. Time was the world's body. I let go all the way, falling into the current, which carried me a quarter-hour before I breaststroked back to the landing below Will's camp. Morning was strange on the river, and you didn't want to miss it by swimming underwater. The bugs plucked tiny rings on the surface, and a faint smoke glided along, white, just above it. You smelled moss and mud as you nosed forward like a salmon, upstream. This was life, I said to myself. Death was downstream, moving toward the sea; life was upstream, cross-grain, fought.

"Don't you want no breakfast or what?" hollered Will Denks from the bank.

"What?" I came on shore, bare-ass.

"You would make a good priest, Sammy. You've got the head for it. You've even got morals," he said, probably to tease.

"Thanks loads." It was just like a Protestant to push one of his best friends into the priesthood. He didn't understand what celibate meant. It wasn't like giving up cigars.

"You going to that rally today?" Will asked.

"Of course I am."

"We could hitch up a tree behind the mule barn," he said. "Get ourselves a good view."

"I should stand with the men, don't you think?"

"Why? You ain't no miner, Sammy. They might not appreciate it."

"Vincenzo will. I'd like to show him my support, anyway." I spat in the loose dirt, a hunky glob. "You could stand with me. The more men we got, the better. Who knows if anybody will even come?"

Will Denks hated to be put on the spot and shrank back, bending over to wash grounds from the coffee pot. "Hey, I forgot to tell you something," he said. "Somebody came to see you when you was gone."

"Who?" I was skeptical. Will wanted to change the subject, and this was a trick.

"Ellie Maynard, she said her name was. You know somebody by that name? A girl?"

"What'd she want?"

"She came to see you, that's all. I said you were out of town for a bit. Come see her whenever you got back. That was the message."

"Really?"

"Cross my heart and hope to evaporate."

I went back to the camp for breakfast with my heart thumping, thinking of Ellie. Hark Wood hunched by the fire with a pan of fried sausages. He must have come out of the woods while I was swimming, to put in one of his rare appearances.

"Hey, boys, I brung you some them hot dogs," he said. The juice drizzled down his chin, and he smelled like cowshit.

"Have a hot dog, Sammy," said Will.

I took one, unsure of how they'd settle. Hark's dogs barked back at you all day.

"We're heading up to that walkout," said Will Denks to Hark. "Later on."

"No you ain't," said Hark. "Don't you go near that, you hear?"

Will Denks chomped on a dog.

"They got guns, even nerve gas, I heard. Cops up and down the valley, goddamn bastards." He grinned, almost toothless. His hair was a wire brush, white and stiff.

"My brother says it'll be peaceful," I said. "He's giving the speech, so he ought to know."

"He don't know nothing," said Hark, spitting his words. Hark often pretended to be in a foul mood, but we didn't take it personally. "You listen here, boy," he said pointing to Will. "You 'tend to that meeting and your ass is hay."

Will Denks merely grinned.

Hark spat.

"I don't care for politics noways. It's stupid," Will said.

Hark grunted approval. He figured he had taught the boy well. Neither of them felt they owed anything to society, which clearly didn't feel it owed anything to them. They lived on the edge of things.

"You better go alone today," said Will, looking straight at me. With the eye that Hark couldn't see, he winked.

168

I'd seen Will Denks lie to Hark Wood many times, and it always upset me. Hark had raised Will by hand; Will owed him some allegiance.

"How'd you take to New York, Sam?" asked Hark. "Will here says you went to see Lou."

"I liked it okay, but I like it here better."

Hark Wood scoffed. "Then you don't know your own asshole," he said. "Anybody who don't like New York don't know his own asshole."

"I ain't never been nowhere," said Will Denks. "Don't expect to, neither."

Whenever Will got around Hark, his grammar seemed to collapse even further, just to make Hark Wood feel comfortable. Hark sometimes teased me for trying to talk like a lawyer.

"Have you been to New York?" I asked Hark.

"Hell, yes, back in '08." He pronounced the zero like *ought*. "Saw Pete Wilson pitch against Boston for the Yanks. Shut them out, his first time throwing in the majors."

Hark Wood had talked baseball to Will Denks since he was a baby. He was a Yankee fan from the old days.

"What's happening this summer?" I asked Hark. "I haven't been reading the papers like usual."

"Earle Combs," he said. "He's a rookie, better than the Babe."

"Really?"

"He's knocking over .300, *way* over. Another Heinie Manush." Heinie Manush played for Detroit two years before, batting .334 as a rookie. "You mean you went to New York and didn't never see the Yanks?"

I had indeed missed the Yanks. Hadn't I been yanked off, I'd have seen them, I said it myself—not the sort of thing you said out loud.

"You boys ain't up to much this summer," said Hark. "Why don't you get a couple them young girls down here. You're both the age for it. Or maybe hop yourself a train to Buffalo."

Will Denks smiled and gave Hark Wood two more sausages. He was good to Hark. In fact, Will Denks loved Hark Wood like a father, though Hark didn't deserve it.

I could not get my mind off Ellie Maynard, that she would come down to the river camp to find me. That had to mean something. No girl went that far without a reason, especially to a place where boys swam bare-ass.

"More hot dogs?" asked Will, two links sizzling in the pan, brown and oily.

"I got to go," I said.

"Where?"

"None of your business."

Will Denks grinned. "Give her hell for me," he said. "About time you brought her into line."

Me? Bring Ellie Maynard into line? It was not my way to bring women into line, now or ever. I hurried to the West Pittston library, secretly hoping that somehow a miraculous change had come over her, that she would fling open her arms and beg for my favors.

But maybe Ellie wasn't even working today. Didn't she work the afternoon shift? I nearly turned back, but the lure was too great. *You shouldn't bother to look for her,* said a little birdie in my head. Possibility opened before me like a wide, new land. *Don't waste your time.* But soon I stood bang in front of the West Pittston Public Library, my nose into the screen door, shading my eyes to see through the dim mesh.

"Sammy!" she said, behind me. Her voice tinkled like goat bells.

"Ellie!"

"I was just coming to work. How'd you know when my hours were?"

"Luck, I guess."

"Good luck, then. Come on inside."

I followed her into the long reading room, which was powerful with the smell of old books and polished wood. The tables shone waxy and bare, except for one stacked high with copies of the *Saturday Evening Post* and *Collier's*. Mrs. Dietrich was on duty, as ever, and lowered her eyes at us. You sensed she didn't approve of Ellie Maynard as an assistant. She would have preferred a dried-up powderhead like herself.

"Let's go back into the map room," said Ellie, casual, like she was asking me to pass the sugar.

The map room! Imagine me and Ellie tucked away in the map room—a dark little niche off the reference alcove. My heart clapped, and sweat dribbled down the insides of my forearms like it did on the way to the dentist. The map room!

Africa hung with its big green bulge along the wall, its dainty toe dipping into the ocean. South America hung as its mate beside it, lean at the waist and puff-chested. Its bright shin was called Argentina, and it caught my eye.

"Would you like to go to Argentina with me, Ellie?"

She looked at me queerly. "What?"

"Would you like to visit Argentina—with me?"

"That's what I thought you said." She opened the door of a narrow broom closet, her ass like a melon, her shoulders pretty in a white blouse. What was on her mind?

She turned around. "Here is a special book on airplanes," she said. "It came in while you were away, and I asked Mrs. Dietrich if I could put it aside for you."

Airplanes? I held the book like a slab of granite. "Thanks," I said. "I guess I never expected you'd give me a book on airplanes."

"You said you wanted to read up on them." Her sidelong smile was not to be believed.

After a pause I said, "You ever been to New York City?"

"No."

"I just got back. My brother lives there."

"How's he like it?"

"Good. He's in business."

"I heard that."

We bobbed like dinghies in high water. It didn't appear that our conversation would ever reach the shore.

171

"Well, I suppose I'll go back home and read this," I said, holding up the book. "Thanks."

She led me out into the reference alcove and toward the reading room. We stopped at the screen door.

I held out my hand to shake.

Her hand was limp as a dead carp. "When are we going to Argentina, then?"

"You really want to go?"

"Why not?"

Mrs. Dietrich looked like she was about to give birth to a hippopotamus.

Ellie had to zip her mouth shut; she shushed me with one finger, touching my lips. I loved her finger on my lips, it was so sexy.

"You ever been to Argentina?" I asked.

"Will you please!" said Mrs. Dietrich, on her feet.

There was nobody in the library but us, so we weren't exactly putting the damper on scholarship.

"You'll get me fired," said Ellie in a soft voice.

"This girl has never been to Argentina, Mrs. Dietrich!" I said in a loud voice. "And now she expects that I should take her."

Mrs. Dietrich's face was a purple-red blotch.

"Go," said Ellie, hiding a smile.

"Can I come see you here again?" I held the book about airplanes to my chest.

"If you want. You can do what you want—it's a free country."

The screen door came between us, and I leaped down the steps and ran off at high speed down Exeter Avenue. I ran, ran, ran, wanting to rip out the pages of my book and toss them into the air like flowers. I could have run all the way to Argentina.

16

At 5:00 P.M. by the river, a bar of sunlight dragged itself across the dirt and pulled the wall of Will's lean-to into shadows. The leaves turned pale yellow; the fat web-fingered oak leaves, the spears of elms, and the rustling poplar. The air smelled damp and minty, like in April, when the possibilities of a new summer lie ahead of you, fresh and countless. Time would hold at this point until the sun couldn't stand the pressure any longer and would plunge. The sky would turn dusky blue.

I finished a thick ham steak, which Will Denks got from the butcher. He occasionally splurged on store-bought meat, though I liked the stuff he shot himself better. Since tonight was a big night, he figured it was as good a time as any to eat a slice of ham, fried in butter over the fire. He got hold of some bootleg gin, too. The gin had come down from Canada in a fleet of cars with hollow fenders and doors, all perfectly illegal. Louis himself used to drive these cars for Nino "The

Nook," the Pittston bootlegger. It was Nino who fixed Louis up with his job in New York. Nino still came once a month to fill Mama's gin barrel in the cellar—for special occasions. It was lousy to drink, but it was gin. It tasted like Gulf Motor Oil, so we poured huckleberry juice into it for flavor.

"Don't gag," said Will. I gargled—then let it slip down the hatch and blaze a trail to my gut. "I should be a sword swallower," I said.

Will swished the booze around in his mouth, letting it stain his teeth. "Hope it goes smooth tonight," he said. "I seen a battalion of cops uptown."

The fact was that operators—and the cops they hired, the C&I—didn't play around with strikes. They lost too much money on them, though a walkout wasn't exactly a strike. Vincenzo had printed up leaflets saying that in memory of Nick Maroni all miners with a conscience should stay away from work to attend the funeral. After the funeral, there would be a brief rally at #8 shaft in Exeter, where Maroni had worked. The leaflets specifically told the miners that this should all be done peacefully. No violence. One death was one too many, it said. I could tell it had been written by Vincenzo, who often ended his speeches talking about peace. This set him apart from the Pittsburgh people, who were out for blood and believed you had to crush the operators first, then negotiate from strength.

It didn't seem fair that the C&I could tote guns but not the miners. David and Goliath was one thing, reality another. You shouldn't have to stand there and let them blow you away when the situation was their fault in the first place. I'd never met a greedy miner. What interested them was meat, bread, coffee, and clothes for their families. Maybe a little booze. They wanted decent houses, too . . . the basic needs. They felt no thrill in being fancier than their neighbors. Papa once said that people who cared too much about possessions were bored with life. Life, for him, was the family he had made, the family and the new land, America, where everyone had a chance to invent

174

himself as he saw fit. Papa would have admired Vincenzo, today. He admired men with strong principles. Louis was another matter. When Louis took up with Nino "The Nook" in bootlegging, Papa hit the roof. He told Louis outright to stop it, though Louis never listened to anyone. Papa would have hated Mama's cellar speakeasy, the spectacle of drunk miners in his own house. But Mama was too practical for scruples. "There ain't no law in heaven against booze," she said. "The Lord himself changed water into hootch." So that was that: *benvenuto a tutti.*

We drained off another glass each of huckleberry hootch, ignoring the taste, then smoked two cigars. It was almost 5:30 by the time we started up the steep bank toward the shaft. I skipped Maroni's funeral altogether, thinking I'd be out of place there. It would have brought Papa's funeral back to mind, too, which I wanted to avoid. But I felt a little weird going to the rally when I hadn't been to the funeral. It was like going to a reception but not the wedding.

"You're really going to sit up in a tree?" I said.

"I suppose. Ain't no miner, am I?"

"You could show support."

He kicked the dirt. "What's it matter?"

"It does," I said.

Will Denks got that "lay off" look, so I didn't press him. He had swallowed Hark Wood's attitudes hook, line, and sinker.

We didn't have far to go, but the ground was mushy behind the high trees, culmy. Our tracks followed us to the foot of a tall and easily climbable oak.

"You first," I said to Will.

Climbing took the tension out of us. My hands gripped the rough bark and hurt, and my knees were skinned as we crept out on a low limb. From where we sat you saw the river cut through dense woods and the shaft entrance below. The breaker worked beyond it, the charcoal walls glinting at the edges, the long shoots rolling. Raw coal trundled up the belt from a stationary car, rattling on the belt, while a loud gas engine drove the works. The mining office and mule barn stood adjacent to the shaft entrance, with a few outbuildings straggling behind them. One large culm dump burned invisibly along the road to Exeter Avenue, which you couldn't see from our perch, and the patch itself, built into a nearby hillside, poked its chimneys through the summer foliage. The white chapel spire spiked the sky.

We had made it just on time. Already the C&I and Staties had formed lines along the gravel road, and half a dozen of them stood at the shaft entrance. They carried rifles, with clubs hanging from their belts.

The air crackled like dry ice, and a dry wind blew up from the nearby culmy fields.

"Jeez," said Will Denks. "Ain't this history?"

A few white-eyed miners with dusty faces stood beside the colliery entrance, stunned and stupid with the commotion. They leaned on picks and shovels. Mules brayed as they drew fresh carloads from the shaft. Then the 5:50 whistle blew, the end of the day's last shift. Men put down their tools when they heard it and began their ascent into the real world of light and talk, of families and houses. Smoke shrieked from the whistle stack, dwindling to a ghost. It left a queer aftersound: a hole in the air. My forearms rippled with gooseflesh.

We heard the marchers singing in the blind distance. Heard them before we saw them. Then they appeared: the UMW and those in sympathy with them. Some were just friends of Nick Maroni, with no politics whatsoever. Gravel sputtered under their feet. I didn't recognize their song, which was like a funeral march but more inspiring. The cops braced for trouble, some locking arms. Others clicked the safeties off their rifles. The captains signaled this way or that, excited. Nobody spoke.

"I'm going down," I said. "I got to go down there."

"Okay," Will Denks said. "Me, too." He could smell the action.

I trembled inside as we shimmied down the tree so fast it tore our trousers. My palms burned against the bark.

A wide-plank porch, which Vincenzo planned to use for a platform, stuck out like a dock from the business office beside the colliery. Staties stood by the steps, coolly threatening, but when Vincenzo and half a dozen UMW officials from the western side of the state approached them, they parted ranks. I wondered if this meant the cops were all bluff. Or could it be a trap?

The miners came singing into the main shaft area, an unlikely choir, and were still singing as Vincenzo arranged everyone on the porch. He walked directly up to the railing to rest his hands on it. It was very dignified, like he was about to recite the Gettysburg Address. Maybe sixty miners were below him, now drawn into a neat pack. Another forty or so who could not resist the temptation to hear what he'd say hung back behind them. I didn't see anyone leave. You don't walk out on history, which doesn't present itself so obviously many times in a life.

I was shaky with a deep thrill that started in my heart and went out from there, radiating like rings from a stone dropped in water. My knees were useless as we made our way through cops and miners to the front of the crowd, where we stood so Vincenzo could see us.

He caught my eye, and I gave a little wave. I wished I had worn a white shirt and black armband like the rest of his supporters. Something in me never agreed with dressing up like other people: it was one reason I would never make a priest. Vincenzo saw me and nodded, which sent a zing through my body.

Somebody handed him a bullhorn, which he didn't need: his voice was naturally loud. He used it anyway—for the effect, holding it to his lips and raising his other hand over his head, to bring the singing to a halt. The pause stung the air. You heard nothing but mules coughing in the barn.

"My friends," Vincenzo said. "*My* friends, and *Nick Maroni's* friends." He let that sink in. We were all friends. It was friendship that brought us together now, not any hatred or bitterness. "That was a sad ceremony for us all, I know. Nick is dead. He'll never come to work at this shaft again. Never." Pause. "We will miss him." Pause. "It is more sad that a man in his prime should be taken from us, killed for no reason. Nick Maroni was a man with something to offer, and he gave us all he had. He understood that we as miners work underground in a dangerous world." He stopped to let the poetry sink in, aware that people appreciated his way with words.

"Mining will always be dangerous work. There's no way around that, but we accept it. We are coal miners. What we don't need on top of this is bad lighting, pillar robbing, bad ventilation, and poor wages. 'We are workers, not slaves.' Nick Maroni said that often. But he's dead now, and we got to take it up for him. We got to press through his reforms. Don't we?" This question was a command, too.

His supporters understood this, and cheered. The crowd began to rumble and seethe, and the shouting and clapping lasted for several minutes, growing louder instead of softer until Vincenzo raised his free hand for silence. The rough sea fell still.

"We are here tonight because our good friend, Nick Maroni, is dead. But we are also here to make sure that as few of us as possible ever come into a tragedy like his. Think of your families—your mothers and wives, your children. We demand that the operators treat us like men, men who expect to work hard for what they get. But who expect to get something for their work, too."

This excited everyone; the crowd's single voice rose in the clear hard sky, burst open like a bright umbrella. They could hardly believe my brother's speech. I had heard him practicing it in the bathroom to make the words sound natural; you could hear him anywhere in the house, like thunder.

"Our demands are simple," Vincenzo went on. "There are leaflets being passed out right now." He signaled to some union men in the crowd. "The safety precautions we insist on, and the wage scale we propose, including benefits, are carefully outlined for Mr. Bing Stanton. It's there in black and white."

Shouts cut the air. Vincenzo had the right words, all right. They loved it.

"Bing Stanton has got to stop profiteering on our backs," he said. "He can reduce his margin of profit by ten or fifteen percent in order to increase our safety margin by ten or fifteen *hundred* percent."

Again, shouts and cheers rippled across the broad field. The cops looked tense now, scared.

"That doesn't sound feasible," said Will Denks, the party pooper.

I jerked my ear away from him. Leave it to Will Denks to support a fat cat, I thought.

"The United Mine Workers cares about you and your family. We stand with the working men of this country and around the world. Remember: we can't improve *nothing* unless we risk something, too; unless we are willing to work *together*." The words split like kingpins on a solid strike.

As Vincenzo talked, a lone car churned up the road, crackling over the red gravel. A backward glance confirmed what somehow I had already guessed: Bing Stanton was here. He arrived in his new Buick, a top-of-the-line model—the sort of car Bonino would have killed for. And you sensed a startling in the crowd, the silent chatter in a hundred hearts. What did he think he was doing?

"We must stand together!" Vincenzo shouted again, having a hard time concentrating after he recognized Bing Stanton in the driver's seat. Heads turned away from Vincenzo as Bing Stanton came to a dead halt behind the crowd and got out. He customarily appeared at this time each afternoon to close the shift, but nobody imagined he'd turn up today.

Stanton looked handsome in his blue suit. Long and silky, he stood beside his car and studied the crowd. They turned away from his stare, sheepish, as though he'd caught them at something. It disgusted me to see them. They felt ashamed and would have denied all association with my brother in a second if you asked them.

"Pardon, gentlemen," said Bing Stanton, walking casually

around the crowd toward the steps to his office as the cops straightened like soldiers under review. He maneuvered himself onto the porch right next to Vincenzo, calm as a green bean, and asked if he might say a few words to the men. It was, after all, his porch anyway. That was my guess at what he said. My brother seemed hesitant to let him talk and argued back. Then some of Bing's men came out of the office and filtered among the union people, who looked very nervous. Vincenzo had no choice, finally. He could not simply continue his speech. The momentum was lost.

"I'd like to say a few words to all of you," Bing Stanton said. You could tell he hadn't spoken to a large audience on many occasions because his voice was reedy and the words hung back, full of spit. His blondish-gray hair was slicked back, lank, along his head. His angular jaw lifted high in the sun, which burned at a fierce angle just above the trees. "I want you all to know I had nothing, I repeat—*nothing*—to do with Nick Maroni's murder. A pack of lies has been circulating this valley. Lies, plain and simple. That's my first and main point, and you have my word it's true."

"Some word," I said to Will Denks.

"You know most of you were missing from your job today. You were absent without permission. And you don't even belong to this so-called . . . union. Most of you don't. Well, I could do otherwise than I am going to do. But the fact is I am going to ignore everyone's absence today and pretend it didn't even happen. You were all here and working as far as I am concerned, and the payroll will reflect such."

The crowd murmured. This was a peculiar turn for events to take, and they weren't sure what to think.

"Furthermore," said Bing Stanton, his voice getting more resonant with each word, "I have studied the safety demands made by some of you, and they are not unjustified. What I want to say is that we, the anthracite operators of northeastern Pennsylvania, have called a special meeting to discuss all reasonable demands. The meeting will take place in Carbondale next Saturday morning. I will be there, I assure you, and will do everything in my power to see that this mining operation is as safe as can be."

"Nothing in there about salaries," I said.

"You're a goddamn liar, Stanton!" shouted somebody in the crowd. "A damn son of a bitch and a liar!" It was Jed Tanusky, who worked with Vincenzo. A loud-mouthed Pole sometimes comes in handy.

But this turned everything the wrong way around. Tanusky kept screaming that Bing Stanton was this or that, his friends trying to hold him down. Then the whole back row broke into an argument, provoking a young cop to club one miner on the head. The blood streamed down his face, shiny and bright, and he fell over. Two of his friends jumped the cop, and this drew a swarm of Staties.

"Let's get out of here, Will," I said. He nodded, and we scrambled sideways through the mob. There was no point in getting your head bashed in for nothing. We wanted to *see* the action, not *be* it.

But the C&I drew themselves now into a tight ring around the miners. We were stuck.

"Over here!" Will shouted, darting between two cops who seemed preoccupied. But they caught him before I could do more than start in his direction. Next thing, I saw Will kicking at one, with the other behind him. When they knocked him down hard, his face flat into the gravel, I dove for the three of them, blindly.

There was so much commotion, and my face hurt so bad from the way I caught it on a cop's boot, that I didn't even hear the shot. It must have been quick and pretty much silent, more like a hollow thud. But somebody near me—a cop, I think—shouted, "They shot Bing Stanton! Stanton is down!"

The cops let us go and ran toward the porch. The C&I began to close ranks, cooler-headed than the Staties, better-trained. They had worked at riots before and moved slowly, scanning the scene to figure out exactly what had happened.

When the shouting didn't die down, they fired several warning shots in the air.

The message that Bing Stanton had been shot circulated quickly, passing like nerve gas over the mob, and when each man heard the news he stopped short of whatever he was doing, saying, or about to say. The crowd became a still photograph going yellow at the edges, fading. History had thrown its varnish over the life around us, staining every surface.

I don't know how I knew, exactly, but the next wave of information came more like a confirmation than fresh news: It was Vincenzo who was shot.

"It's Vincenzo! He's shot!" a man up front yelled. The relay system had the words echoing around me, tearing at my eardrums.

Now the crowd was rumbling again, and a dogfight broke out just behind me. I used the confusion to break sideways past a cop, weaving like a halfback through the enemy team and crossing the goal line before anybody knew I was trying for it. I was suddenly on the porch, pushing through the hunched, bewildered bodies. "Let me through," I said. "Let me through!"

Vincenzo lay on his back, staring up with fear glittery in his eyes. His face white, he was clutching his right shoulder. His tongue and teeth were bloody.

"Vince," I said. "You're going to be okay. We'll take you to the hospital."

He never moved his eyes, looking past me. It was like he couldn't hear me or see me, like he'd lost a whole world in a single, stupid moment.

Bing Stanton bent over beside me. He wasn't saying a word, just looking, dazed by what was going on. He shook his head back and forth, moving his lips without sound, like he was praying.

I said, "Help me carry him to your car. He's losing blood."

He nodded but he didn't make a move.

"Grab his legs!" I said. I pulled him along with one hand till he lifted my brother's legs. Somebody else helped me with

182

the rest of him, while another cleared the way through cops and the mob to Bing Stanton's Buick, where we laid Vincenzo across the broad backseat.

He was quiet in the dark seat behind us, the blood gobbing from his mouth. I wondered where he could be shot to make blood come out of his mouth like that. His eyes had closed.

Bing Stanton pulled himself together with a small shudder and a deep breath, and threw the car into first. We moved by a series of jolts and stutters, Bing's foot trembling against the clutch. He waved directions to several of his men, who signaled to the cops at the far end of the crowd. The mob bristled and screamed, but the cops maintained a loose ring around them. We gathered speed quickly as we left the colliery grounds, popping the gravel under our tires.

Bing Stanton's knuckles went white around the wheel, his right foot hard to the floor, as we sprayed dirt at every corner through West Pittston. People stared from the sidewalks, wondering what was going on. You didn't expect to see me and Bing Stanton speeding along Exeter Avenue in the same car. I leaned back over the seat to hold my brother's hand, gone limp and cool. His shirt was bloody down the front, a sop rag, and his eyes never opened once. He seemed in no pain, though you couldn't tell with Vincenzo. He was capable of holding it inside. I heard myself saying, "Don't die, Vincy," over and over.

17

It was 8:32 by the clock above the nurses's station. Vincenzo went into the operating room at seven. In the hour and a half that passed, nobody said a word to me about his condition.

Vince's eyes had been open before he went down, and it seemed that he could hear me. Once he mumbled something, but it made no sense. I squeezed his hand and told him to be quiet, that he was a hero. He was the hero of all miners, and my hero. He had taught me something important, that you've got to stand behind what you think. Most people don't have the courage for this, so the world gets steadily worse instead of better. They're gagged by fear, a giant timidity that lets everything slide. Vincenzo lay there without blinking, strapped to a narrow table on wheels and covered to the neck by a sheet; the nurse had put a compress to his shoulder to stop the bleeding, and the smell of alcohol was strong. Downstairs, they were preparing the operating room, which gave me a little extra time with Vincenzo by myself. I didn't want to see them roll him away and squeezed his hand hard. He'd be fixed up in no time, the nurse said. A bullet in the shoulder was nothing serious.

Talk stumbled out of my mouth, and not much of it made sense, but it seemed to help Vincenzo, who stared calmly at the ceiling. A kind of peace had settled over him, a strange mist. I wished he would blink his eyes like the living, but he didn't. "You'll be back making speeches soon," I said to him. And when they had to roll him away, I got close and said I loved him and pressed his hand even harder.

I wished he would squeeze back. There is nothing worse than saying what you feel strongly without a response, not a flicker. I felt hollow as they wheeled him down the hallway, the nurses clucking around him like pigeons.

"Why don't you sit down, son," said the nurse at the station. "Your brother may be quite a while."

That helped me. A while was okay. She definitely didn't say for good. I sat on the cane chair by the wall and picked up the *Saturday Evening Post* and stared at pictures of beautiful cars and Miami hotels. I couldn't stop myself from hurting inside and rubbed my eyes. I was never sadder, maybe not even for Papa. I kept telling myself it was silly to be sad when Vincenzo would be all right. A bullet in the shoulder was no big deal. Men in the war got much worse than that and lived to tell.

The Pittston Hospital was a square, red brick building on the riverbank, south of the Fort Jenkins Bridge. Will and I often swam by it, bare-ass, wondering if the nurses liked to peek at us from the windows. I had never been in a hospital before tonight. The halls smelled awful and their bareness echoed every cough or cry. It seemed weird that the sick and dying came together in these walls, tended by nurses and orderlies instead of their families. As if nobody wanted them. The sick and dying didn't belong anymore, so they were brought here, where the sight of them—no matter how ugly—seemed normal. This was a reverse world, a place where sickness was ordinary, where health was oddness.

I paced the hall near the black lung ward, where miners sometimes died from breathing in anthracite dust. I saw a young man spit blood in a pan and an older man without a leg, on crutches. I knew him well and was glad he didn't notice me when I walked past. That would be Jesse, soon, I thought. The gangrene would be setting in if he didn't heal.

It was dark, with only a few lights lit in the hallways; people began to look like shadows. I felt I was dead now, one of the shadows in the darkened world.

I don't know how much time passed before I saw Bing Stanton out of the corner of my eye. He was slump-shouldered, knocking his pipe on the heel of his shoe and leaning, sagging, on the window ledge. He blew smoke in slow, blue draughts. Why was he here? I felt hate flood through me. If Bing Stanton had never been born, even if he had been shot himself years ago, my Papa would be alive; Vincenzo would be well today. I hated him, and if somebody had put a gun in my hand that minute, I'd have shot him. His life had caused more misery for other people than one life was worth.

The thought of Vincenzo in the operating room set my head spinning. I was soon unaware of Bing Stanton at all. A sadness for Vincenzo kept surging up in me, a fear and sadness. The future lit up in my brain. What would Mama think or do if anything happened to Vincenzo? Would we have the money to live on without his salary? Now that Jesse couldn't work, we were in trouble. Would Louis's money be enough? After the scene between me and Franca, Louis, of course, hated me. He would say it was my turn to go into the mines and make some money.

I went up to the nurse's station, feeling like I had to know *something*. "Is there news yet, ma'am?"

"The Doctor will tell you when there is," the nurse said. Her cold response shocked me. She went right back to typing a letter.

186

"I want to know," I said. "Please."

She took off her rimless glasses and glared at me as if to say, "Buzz off."

"He's my brother, and I got a right to know what is going on."

"Son, there is no way I can answer you without going down to the operating room myself. If you'll take a seat, I'll let you know something as soon as I can."

It seemed my heart was going to burst. Nobody had ever treated me like this before, not even in New York City.

"The boy is just asking a question," said Bing Stanton over my shoulder.

The nurse's face went paler than her uniform; she stood at attention. "Excuse me, Mr. Stanton, I—"

"Find out what's going on," he said.

"Yes, Mr. Stanton, I'll ask Dr. Molinari."

"Fine."

She went charging toward the elevator.

I felt my stomach sour. *This man has a goddamn nerve,* I said inside, *a goddamn nerve.* I went to the lavatory, where I stood in front of the toilet with the seat raised, but nothing came up. You can't puke up emptiness. I spit into the ammonia-smelling bowl, flushed, then stared into the bathroom mirror; I couldn't stand my looks: the thick lips, the greasy black hair. A pimple reddened my chin, though my face was olive overall, like army-surplus tent canvas. I wished I looked different, any way but this. Mirrors often left me feeling small, damp, and ugly. They had no way to register the Sammy I could feel inside me.

I had fifty cents in my pocket and took the back stairs to the second-floor cafeteria. With a cup of black coffee and a doughnut untouched in front of me, I sat looking out the window. If only there were stars, a familiar constellation, or the moon, I'd have felt better. But the night was cloudy. I knew there would be no stars or moon that night.

"Please, God," I prayed. "Let my brother be all right. If

you will heal him, I'll do anything you say. You name it—
I'll be a priest, a missionary in the jungles, a doctor in Alaska.
Think about Mama, God! It was bad enough that you took
Papa, wasn't it? We need Vincenzo. He's a good man, God. I
know he doesn't go to church or anything, but he follows the
Bible like he'd written it himself. He's good to everybody." I
whispered in a soft voice, the only person in the room except
for the lady behind the counter. She was probably used to
people who prayed quietly in the cafeteria. There must have
often been folks here making promises to God, ones they would
forget if God did a miracle for them. If God didn't work the
cure, they'd spite Him and do opposite. But I meant what I
said. I'd have gone off the next day to Alaska or the Amazon.
I'd have gone into the biggest Catholic library in the world,
if that's what God asked of me, and sat down to read every
single book.

The cafeteria looked across the river through big sliding
windows, and I got up to stare back at the world I had left
behind this evening. It was strange how different things seemed
on this side of the Susquehanna, almost foreign, like suddenly
being grown up. At this time of night, the river turned black
well before the sky did, and the little towns along it were
squeezed between two massive pincers of dark, gradually, until
just a row of sparks was left. These embers flickered in the
black water. They grew narrow, sometimes, like threads of
fire, and when a boat would pass upriver it would drag those
lines in its wake like stars in a net.

I took a swig of the coffee and stuffed the doughnut into
myself like tasteless fuel. When I got downstairs the nurse told
me Vincenzo was still in surgery.

"But how *is* he?" I asked.

"It's too early to tell," she said. A certain satisfaction at
having been sent on a needless trip bobbed up and down not
too deeply under her comment. She went back to her typing
and soon the dim clacking sound filled the hallway.

I kept thinking about the bullet in my brother. He would

be under some kind of chloroform now. I had been under this once at the dentist's, and it made me puke all the way home. Worse, it had filled my head with visions like the end of the world might bring.

"Sammy, do you know what you'll do when you get out of school?" asked Bing Stanton out of the blue. He stood next to me like it was his duty.

"Huh?"

"I was wondering, you know, about your future. Maybe I could help in some way, perhaps . . ." His voice trailed off.

Perhaps! I said the word to myself. What did he want? To give me money? To offer me a job in the mines? I didn't know what to say to him. I couldn't take this in. I felt sick and knew that if I didn't get to the lavatory soon, the floor would be messed up beautiful. "Excuse me," I said.

This time I was able to spew up hunks of green-and-yellow garbage that seemed no relation to the powdered doughnut I had eaten. It was like evil had solidified in my guts and needed to be puked out. My whole chest ached from the heaving.

When I came out of the stall, Bing Stanton was hanging by the sinks. "Here's my handkerchief," he said.

"I don't need it." There were hand towels on a metal bar.

At the nurses' station, Dr. Molinari leaned on the chest-high counter, writing. His mask was pushed up on his forehead.

"Can you step into my office?" he said.

I nodded and followed, though each step hurt. My legs didn't want to go where they were going.

"I'm Dr. Molinari," he said. "And you are . . .?"

"Sammy. I'm his brother."

"Will you have a seat?"

My head was suddenly light, maybe from the puking, and I could hardly keep my eyes on the doctor. "How is he then?"

"Well, I am afraid that he has passed away. We did everything we could. There just wasn't much for it." He continued in the way doctors do, explaining the details of what happened

189

and why it couldn't be fixed. But I had stopped listening. Vincenzo was dead.

Dr. Molinari was old enough that the hair around his ears was silver. I wondered why God would let Dr. Molinari get to his age, and Vincenzo had to die so young. Vincenzo should have lived to three times his age. He did good things for people.

The doctor said he was sorry and left the room so I could pull myself together. After a blow like this, you need time to collect your breath and feelings. You feel the world whipped from under your legs. But it's surprising how quickly you begin to make adjustments, accepting the new condition of things, no matter how different. You think, maybe you hope, that the world will stay put this way for a bit. But it doesn't. The world never stays put. Life has no set number of innings and is never over till the game is called on account of darkness.

Vincenzo was dead: that was the fact I'd have to swallow. I remembered Vincenzo as a young boy at the swimming hole and diving from the highest rock or swinging from a tall tree. The quiet one, the oldest, but braver than me or Louis. Papa would scold him: "You'll break your neck!" But Vincenzo did whatever was his for doing. Ran, leaped, swung—in his own independent way. I recalled Vincenzo on the mound, his arm like a steel band, his strange windup, his fastball sizzling in your mitt. Your hand smoked for an hour afterward. And there was Vincenzo the miner, black-faced when the whistle blew. No matter how tired, he came home full of ideas for reform, filling the kitchen with his notions while Mama cooked at the Roper Range and Gino shadowboxed in the corner and Grandpa Jesse worked the Italian crossword from *Il Popolo*. Papa's death had pushed Vincenzo into a silent fury, and you knew he'd never stop till he had what he wanted. He had everything to offer the world, but there was no world left to him.

Dr. Molinari came back for me and led me out into the hall; he patted my back and said a few things and disappeared. You could tell he was upset, and that it was easier to let me go.

190

Bing Stanton was still standing in the hallway, and when I came out of the office his face tightened and he asked if I needed a ride home. I said no, and he dawdled a moment. Not till he was gone did I notice Will Denks.

"Sammy," he said. "I heard what happened."

Will's arm was in a sling.

"The bastards broke my arm. I been down in the cast room," he said, holding up his injured wing. "Or I'd have been here sooner."

"Yeah." My mouth didn't fill with language. The death of Vincenzo had drained me of expression.

"Has Stanton been here all along?"

I nodded, and Will was surprised.

"They been turning people away all night. Bonino was here for a while. He couldn't find you. So was a lot of union people." He noted my blankness, my stupid stare, and said, "You look awful, Sam."

"I'm okay, but I better get home," I said.

Will Denks looked so young beside me, like twelve or ten years old. Dirt was smeared across his cheek and he had a busted lip. I reached an arm around his shoulder, and we stepped out into the night. Along the river road, the black trees made almost no outline against the blacker sky.

I stopped by Lucy's on the way up to the patch and she said the police had come by and told them the news. So Mama knew. She hadn't gone off her head, as you'd expect, but took a long draft of laudanum and crawled into her own bed at home.

Lucy had been through the first rush of pain already; her eyes were bloody, her cheeks tearstained. But she was under control, with Bonino beside her, calm and quiet. He asked me if I wanted to sleep there, but I said no, I would sleep at the river.

I gave her a hug and even hugged Bonino, who said he didn't see me at the hospital and guessed I'd gone home already.

He said nobody would tell him a damn thing. I said I was sorry to miss him. It relieved me that Mama had taken the news without getting hysterical, and that I hadn't been the one to tell her.

Instead of going home, I went back to the river, where Will Denks had got a fire going. He gave me tea with booze in it, and we hardly said another word to each other. I needed sleep as a way out of a day that would stand alone like few other days in my life. A strange, slow anger was building in me, not just toward Bing Stanton but against the miners, too: the miners, helpless and herded like sheep, who could not stop them from killing my brother. I hated their lack of fight, their fear of men they imagined to have some mysterious power over them. I didn't see how Vincenzo could get killed for people who would hardly even recognize his courage. I slept badly that night, like a coal lit up in the grate by gusty winds.

Midmorning: As I made my way home through the patch, the few people who noticed me pretended not to see me—I could have been invisible. People smell grief on someone and stay away from it.

Such a bright morning with a high blue sky and cool steady wind! The leaves clicked, bringing the first sounds of fall. The air had that clean smell of September, and though you knew that the hot, stuffy days were not done with, you also knew what was coming. Fall, with its bleeding colors, and school. The red piles of leaves and chilly mornings. The dull and darkening days.

From a distance I could see Mama in the garden. There were two acres behind the house, and half of one was dug up. The crops had been neatly laid out in sections. Cabbages, lettuce, kale. Beans. Corn. Carrots and potatoes. A big patch of tomatoes. The garden fence was strung with grapevines. In the fall, the whole fence turned blue.

Mama loved the garden for its order, its customary rhythms. The mess in her head was made up for by this order. Garden work steadied her. Inside the house, she tended to fly off the handle. Outside, she was easygoing and collected. As I came up on her now, she worked with a pitchfork uprooting carrots.

"Give a hand," she said.

I bent beside her to pull slender carrots up by their lacy green shoots. "They're awful small," I said.

"They're good that way."

She always let a number stay in the ground until winter. They did fine underground, even through frost. You could pull them up as late as March, when they would be sugary and crisp.

"How many you want?"

"Work," she said. There was a big pail, half full, beside her. "We need a lot because of the company."

Mama had needed the company when Papa died. Company helped her get through the grief. She could make herself busy, thinking about the comfort of others.

"They said you was the last to talk to him," Mama said, rocking with one foot on the fork. The carrots came up in a dirty tangle.

"He was awake when they took him down, Mama. I talked, and it seemed like he could hear me. I told him what a good job he did for the miners. I said he was a hero."

"Hero," said Mama, as she dug into the carrot tops. *Hero* wasn't a word she liked. It implied *dead*. "It was his life. I did what I could for that boy."

"You ought to be proud of him, Mama."

She grunted her rejection of this notion. Her idea was that there would always be rich and poor in the world: *Ci sarà sempre chi è ricco e chi è povero.* All she could understand now was that her son, who was living last night, was dead this morning.

She stopped digging to wipe the tears from her lashes. She wiped her hand across them, leaving a streak of mud.

"You okay, Mama?" I put my arms around her shoulders and kissed her.

"Just you don't get no ideas about that union," she said.

"You go into business." She pulled a fat carrot from the ground, tugging hard to release it from the clod. I lifted the pail for her to toss it in. "Shake out the dirt," she said. "You can't eat dirt."

"How's Grandpa Jesse?"

"He's in bed. He hasn't said nothing to nobody."

I shook my head.

"Maybe you go talk to him this morning. He likes to talk to you."

I said I would.

"He is going to blame this on himself," she said. "This is stupid. Vincenzo, he did what he wanted. He didn't never listen to nobody."

The fact that she was being reasonable somehow made me cry.

Mama put down her pitchfork and held me. "Sammy, Sammy," she said. "You're my boy and don't you worry about nothing. You hear?"

After a minute I said, "Mama, do you think people can really live—I mean in heaven or somewhere—once they're dead?" It was too awful to imagine that my brother had vanished for good, just disappeared. This was the same backyard where only a few weeks ago he had thrown baseballs harder than any man in northeast Pennsylvania.

She stepped back and squinted. "Don't be so curious," she said. "If God wanted us to know that, He'd say it. We don't know nothing, and that's how life is." She paused. "Get another pail from the shed," she said. "This one is full."

"You're not going to pick them all?"

She waved her hand. "I planted new ones this morning," she said, pointing to a freshly tilled row at the other end of the garden. "You can always get more carrots," she said, bending over; she spoke more to herself than to me now. "A garden keeps coming. You can't stop anything if you plant it right. It just keeps coming."

The way she turned to her work, I knew she wanted to be left alone. I got her the pail and went to the house.

The kitchen was empty, like after Papa had died and I sat there alone with Mama downstairs in the cellar. She went down there to cry, and her voice rang in the plumbing, rising through the house like steam. It sounded awful, like when a cat gets a squirrel by the throat at midnight. They seem to take forever just to die.

I poured a glass of milk from the icebox and cut a slice of bread. For a long time I sat there, eating, listening to a silence that filled the kitchen and expanded through the house like a balloon. You could tell the house had lost someone by that stillness, which seemed to collect on the furniture like fine dust. There was not even a fly in the kitchen, and the counters were clear of ants and spiders. The absence of living things scared me, and I bit into the bread, which was a comfort, a hunk of stored-up, unused life. I drank the milk in one long swallow, letting the coolness rinse my throat and stomach.

I rocked my chair just to make some noise and remind myself I could still move things, shake loose deadness from the air. I was humming, probably too loud to respect the dead, as I walked upstairs. I paused at Jesse's door. Poor Jesse would be ruined. His best friend was Vincenzo. I never really understood Jesse, though he'd been with us a long time. He was too odd, too involved with a view of the world taken on somewhere in the past, in another language. He couldn't bring the sense of it across the line to this country.

Jesse heard me in the hall and coughed, but my eyes kept moving toward Vincenzo's door, now slightly ajar. Before I talked to Jesse, I wanted to go into my brother's room, something I never did when he was alive, unless he was in there.

The door swung easier than I liked, and the room sparkled in too-bright sun, glittering like a chandelier. The room faced south and caught the best morning light, which doubled itself in the big mirror on the north wall. The brass bedposts glinted, and the curtains breathed in a slight wind, the windows wide open. The white bedspread looked crisp as snow. Vincenzo's floor was waxed and slippery, the oak yellowy and slick.

His clothes were hung neatly in the closet: a row of shirts

pressed for duty, work clothes on hangers, one black suit, a linen jacket for Sunday cookouts, cotton trousers. It hadn't occurred to me that Vincenzo's smell would cling, so sharply, to his clothes. Everybody has their own smell, their private odor; but I'd never noticed Vincenzo's. He was clean, almost catlike, in his habits. I never thought he *had* an odor until now. But the waves rushed over me—Vincenzo's deep, mannish smell. I swung sideways to see if somehow he could be there beside me, like another Lazarus. He wasn't, but I felt him there and knew for certain that Vincenzo, who was shot dead last night, had simply changed form and could see me plain. He could hear my thoughts, see what I saw inside my head.

I walked into his closet and buried my face in the linen jacket he wore only the night before last. I hugged it with both arms, and spoke a quiet prayer into the fabric. I prayed that I could be only half as dedicated to my own principles—whatever they would prove to be—as Vincenzo was to his. I wanted him to understand this, too, and not expect me to be exactly as he was. I never felt so different from Vincenzo as I did now, but I never felt so close, either.

I lay down on his bed on my back, the room's strange white light filling my bones. As I lay there, it seemed like I was shining.

18

Bonino helped us make the funeral arrangements. He was nice about it and bought me lunch at the Kako Diner: a salami sandwich with fried onions and peppers—the cook's special item, which tended to remind you of its specialness the rest of the day. We both drank three cups of black coffee, which made us zing.

"Sammy, kid," Bonino said. He smoked a self-rolled cigarette, and his fingers shook a little. You could tell he was a mechanic by the rough calluses. Grease had lodged itself for good under his nails, even though he had them clipped back pretty neatly. "Listen, Sam, like I'm sorry about this mess that went on here, like Vince getting killed. That stinks, don't it?"

It sure did. I ordered more coffee, figuring I might as well go nuts on the stuff.

"I been thinking about this, Sam, and it strikes me how you guys ain't going to have much, like, cash. You know what I mean?"

I just nodded.

"Right. It's a problem. Have you put much thinking to it? I figure like you're in charge now, so you'll have to get some kind of work."

"I'm still in school," I said. "I've got to finish."

Bonino looked embarrassed. "What I wanted to say, like, was that now that I got my own garage in town, you might come work for me. I could teach you to be a mechanic. I mentioned this to Lucy last night and she said it sounded terrific. Your mama would be glad to hear it."

I felt sick inside. Me—a mechanic? But what the hell was going to happen now, without Vincenzo's income? Jesse wasn't good for anything. How would we live?

"How's that sound, kid?"

"Thanks," I said. "It's nice of you to offer that." I tried to answer and be polite without saying anything too specific. You can't make that kind of decision on the spot. "I'm really glad you're willing to help," I added, kind of stupidly.

We seemed to float from the diner to the morgue, a block away, where we met the undertaker, Mr. Patruski. He had drained off Vincenzo for us and put in formaldehyde so we could show him at home. They didn't drain them in the old country, so you could hardly stand to visit a corpse who wasn't already buried in flowers. Mr. Patruski charged ten bucks, and Bonino cursed him to his face. The small-boned little Pole picked his teeth but didn't argue back. He had the money in his pocket, so he could afford to put up with some crap. Anyway, Bonino didn't look like the type who could do much damage with a punch.

We laid the body in the back of Bonino's car for its final journey to the patch, where we planned to set up in style in the front room. We borrowed a trestle table and spread it with a white sheet. The flowers had been arriving all day.

It was three by the time we got home, and there was Louis's car, a Chrysler Royal Sedan loaned him by Maccerio, parked by the house. He made it like he promised. Tonight would be

198

a family night, with all of us together. Tomorrow the public would come to pay respects. But meanwhile I felt weird about Louis. How could I face him? The stupid mess in New York City opened like a fan before my eyes, peacock-bright. I grew weak.

"Sammy!" Louis yelled, charging around the house.

"You made it," I said, faintly.

He rushed all over me, hugging and squeezing so close the air fizzed from my lips. He obviously didn't give a damn about what happened between me and Franca in New York City. After all, what's a little sex between relatives? A brother is a brother, and you don't let a dumb woman get between you. Sex brings out the worst in you, anyway, and you've got to accept that. A man isn't made of brick, so you can't blame him if he goes nuts when a girl prances bare-ass in front of him. It's just nature.

"I see you got a Chrysler," I said.

"They're good cars. Smooth as manure."

Bonino grunted, half in disagreement about Chryslers and half to say that he was standing there like the third handle on a pisspot. I introduced Louis to Bonino and they shook hands.

"We better get Vincenzo out of the backseat," Bonino said. "It's kind of hot, and he'll be stinking."

"We paid ten bucks to keep him from stinking," I told Louis. "Do you know Mr. Patruski?"

"Hell, he probably pumped Vince full of water and charged us for the good stuff," said Louis.

The sun beat down hard on our necks. Louis sweated buckets in a black suit, his face slick. We were drenched anyway, but it got worse as we slid Vincenzo carefully out of the backseat into the hot air. I held the corpse by the shoulders and Louis had the feet. Bonino grabbed him by the waist as we marched him up the front steps and through the screen door. Gino, milk-white and gaping, held the door for us.

We laid Vincenzo out nicely, folding the arms across his chest. His hands were cool and waxy like the dead frogs in green bottles at school. The rouge on his cheeks rubbed off on my cuff, and I could see where Patruski had sewn the lips shut so his tongue wouldn't loll out during the funeral. The eyelids were neatly pasted down; you couldn't see stitches.

"He looks good," said Louis. "Patruski does a nice job on the looks."

"He's been around a long time," said Bonino. "They lay them out nice in Poland. It's their tradition."

"I don't think he's the right color," I said. "Vince was darker, wasn't he?" The powdery skin upset me.

"Blood loss," said Bonino, acting like he knew something. "It whitens them."

Louis took a comb from his jacket and lifted Vincenzo's hair back from the forehead, which made him look much more like usual. He smoothed the eyebrows, too. "There," he said. "Mama will like you now." It gave me the creeps to see somebody talk to a corpse.

Mama was upstairs, thank goodness. I didn't want her to see Vincenzo before he was ready. It was bad enough he was dead without being messy.

"Anybody else want a drink?" I asked.

They said no, so I went to get one for myself, swinging into the kitchen.

"Hi, Sammy," said Franca, who was standing by the sink in one of Mama's aprons.

My jaw unhinged itself. Franca!

"Louis didn't tell you I was here?"

I shook my head.

"He should have," she said. "I'm so sorry about what happened to your brother. It's a shame." She came up and kissed my cheek. I couldn't budge. "Listen," she said, softly. "It don't matter about what happened in New York. Lou, he thought it was . . . funny."

Some joke, I thought.

"He was a little mad, but at *me*. I told him what I did, and he wasn't mad at you—not at all. He said I was sending your soul to hell and slapped me around, but then it was over. He said he was more worried about you." She stepped back. "He loves you."

This was too weird to comment on, so I didn't. Sometimes you do best to clam up altogether.

"Look," she said, holding up her left hand. She showed off a knockout sparkler, the biggest diamond I ever saw. "We're engaged!"

My first thought was how right Father Francis had been when he quoted scripture to me once about your sins finding you out. You do one really bad thing and you can be sure it will catch up. The thought of confronting Franca for the rest of my days left me exhausted.

"So ain't you glad for me?" she asked.

"Mama said Louis ought to get married," I said. "A man his age needs it."

"But . . . aren't you glad he's going to marry *me?*"

"Sure . . . why not?" I said. Sometimes the truth doesn't pay a fair wage, so you've got to lie.

Franca accepted this and sat down. I got her a glass of wine and poured one for myself, too. Now that the first shock was wearing off, I felt better about her. She was, after all, both easy on the eyes and nice to me. You could tell she felt at home here. I heard about their trip in from New York City, about how Louis had been promoted with Maccerio, about the September wedding they had planned. Our talk got so cheerful and interesting you'd never guess Vincenzo was laid out dead in the next room.

When Mama finally came down from her nap, having finally knocked herself out with some laudanum, she stepped foot by foot, gingerly, like an old woman. Everyone cleared out of the living room so she could have a little time alone with her son, whom she had never before seen dead. Sitting quietly beside him, she cried some, then talked to him like he was alive. I listened at the door as she scolded him up and down for the union work. Hadn't she told him it would lead to this? She gave him hell about making speeches in public places where you could get yourself shot. He had no business, she said, to concern himself with those things. Why didn't he just get himself a girl and have children, like other boys? Her voice grew louder as she talked and scolded.

Mama never would have talked her mind so openly to Vincenzo when he was alive. He had a wild temper as a boy. It scared everybody. Once, the worst time, he slapped Mama all over the kitchen because he thought she had taken something from his dresser, something stupid. I was a little kid then and stood, shaking, in the doorway as Vincenzo went nuts. He was maybe ten or eleven at the time. When Papa got home from the mines, he burned at both ears and carried Vince, who kicked and screamed and bit, to the garden shed for a beating. Vince managed to tear a patch loose from Papa's cheek, which left a scar on Papa for good, but he himself came back bloody in the mouth and nose, his clothes ripped like a horse had dragged him through the dirt. I can't say who got the worst of that battle, but nobody spoke to Vincenzo for weeks afterward. I don't know if he ever apologized to Mama. As I thought back now, Louis was the gentle, easygoing one. But Louis went wrong somewhere; his gate was always swung wide, and anyone could get in there, anything. He couldn't say no to anybody, not even to himself. So here he was, a crook in New York City.

I think that incident with Mama changed Vincenzo: he started to control his temper overnight. It was weird to see it happening in front of you, the way he changed colors, blotching red to purple, but restraining himself. The lines deepened in his forehead, making him look ten years older than he was at fifteen. You felt he could blow at any moment, like a dam in April when the snows melt into streams and the hard rain doesn't let up for weeks. Vincenzo created a new man of himself, a kindly one, concerned about everybody. But he also grew more distant: the price he paid for that control. Jesus, I said to myself, how strangely the end brings everything into focus.

This death, like Papa's, would knock a little more life out of Mama. You could tell that already. It had knocked even more life out of Jesse, too. It was sad if he blamed himself for my brother's death, since Vincenzo had such a mind of his own; he'd have gone ahead no matter what Jesse said. He was a man of the people. In fact, he felt about people in general the way I felt about Ellie Maynard.

Father Francis was with us, as usual, butting in where he could. His face sweat like a ham as he sat on the back porch, guzzling wine. When he ran out, he asked me to get him more from the cellar.

Following me downstairs, he said, "It's a loss to us all, Sammy, a great loss. Your brother was an unusual boy. What a priest we could have made of him!"

I grunted, trying in vain to picture Vincenzo in a priest's collar. He never even wore a tie.

"Sammy," he said. "Have you given more thought to your own vocation?"

"I have, Father."

"Good!" His round face burned in the dim light while I looked for the worst wine. There were several barrels behind the bar, which Vincenzo had built for Mama last summer out of planks left over from an old chicken coop.

"I'm not ready to make a decision like that, Father," I said. "But I'm still thinking."

Father Francis sighed. "I can understand your hesitation. If God wants you, Sammy, He will make this plain to you in time." He examined the blood-bright wine as I tapped the barrel.

I didn't know what to do now, except wait and see, to stay as open as possible. You have to feel your way through life, looking for openings, paying attention to other people and their needs. Somehow, I knew my job was to keep up something of Vincenzo's work. This didn't mean joining the union or becoming a miner, though that wasn't impossible either. I had to do what I could to see that people like those who lived in the patch, miners and plain working people, weren't battered around by the whims of a man like Bing Stanton. Some of the spirit that passed from Vincenzo's body seemed to have come to me, I could feel it—a tingling, a freshness, something like courage but undirected, waiting.

I woke early the next day—like you do when something is up. The hootch we drank too much of the night before only fueled my early rising. My head had been pounding since 5:00 A.M. and got no better, so I sat up to do some thinking, to remember the years with Vincenzo in this very house. I would hear his snoring in the night and would pound on the wall, furious, but he never seemed to notice. One time in high school he got the scarlet fever and they thought he might die. I went into his bedroom and rubbed his back down with alcohol, feeling his muscles like hard little knobs under my fingers, and he grunted as I worked. We talked about dying that night. He said that death didn't matter, but life did. He was hell-bent on life; that was clear from the start. When he was younger, he'd climb the giant chestnut tree out back like a chimpanzee. Mama said she'd beat the shit out of him if he did it, but he never listened. When he fell and broke his arm, I was the one who had to run for Mama. She was so mad she hit me first, like I was the one who'd toppled from the stupid tree. I remembered my brother as an altar boy, too: the hair that fell straight across his forehead, the dark eyes and wide, serious mouth. Women thought he was an angel; they didn't know about his temper. Vincenzo announced his lack of interest in the Catholic Church at an early age and skipped catechism. I never thought you *could* skip it, but Vincenzo did what he pleased.

It was, of course, possible that Vincenzo would go to hell. Though he may have had some secret belief in God, he kept it quiet. But I was sure God wouldn't turn His back on a man so holy that it showed through every move. Nobody tried, or was forced by his nature to try, as hard as my brother to be decent. Mass was for sinners, *real* sinners, like me; Vincenzo was already a saint, and God would recognize at the gate this one who had managed what most don't, even with help.

Taking care not to squeak the stairs, I crept down into the living room. Vincenzo's hands were crossed like we'd left them, relaxed and modest. He didn't have the sweat on his face that covers the living like a film at night and has to be washed off before breakfast. He looked clean and cool, his hair so black, glistening. The morning sun poured through the crepe curtains, filling the room, lighting his features.

I kissed him on the cheek, touched his hands, then crossed myself once for each year of his life; I knelt beside him and said several prayers. A strong feeling began in my heels and ran up through my spine and broke over my shoulders; it was God's way of telling me something. The feeling meant that God had looked kindly on my brother, I decided. He had taken Vincenzo in.

I stayed there beside him until the house started up with footsteps in the hallway, water chugging through the pipes, coughs and grunts. The bathroom door opened and slammed several times. The toilet flushed and whinnied like a mule. Then Mama was downstairs, percolating coffee. Bacon crisped the air. In spite of my brother's death, the day sparkled. This could easily have been the day of his wedding.

In the kitchen, Mama put her face to my cheek and hugged me. We didn't need words to say what we felt. She broke away only to get me coffee and a fresh roll, which she warmed in the Roper and gobbed with butter. There was a jar of Mr. Sanderini's honey out on the tablecloth—one of the dozens of gifts from our neighbors.

"Eat," she said, putting some rolls on the plate. "You'll feel better if you do. *Ecco!*"

I didn't need much persuasion. The honey gleamed on my roll as it soaked into buttery dough. The coffee was rich espresso, flavored with hot milk.

"Sammy, you ain't *never* going into no mining work. You keep that in your head," she said. "I want you to marry a nice girl and be happy."

"I'll be happy," I said. Whatever job I did, whether or not I married, the world could not take me away from myself.

"Look at that boy," she said. "My Vincenzo." She sighed into her coffee. During the night she had cried herself out, leaving her calm and dry-eyed for the funeral today. We expected more than a hundred visitors later in the morning.

I got into Mama's lap like I was four years old, letting my coffee go cold. We were alone in the kitchen, and I knew she would like this. I wanted to sit there, too. I needed her. For twenty minutes she held me and hummed like when I was a baby, an old Italian song. We broke off when Bonino's big feet came pounding up the back-porch stairs.

The coffin was brought in by the carpenter, Joe Petra, shortly after breakfast. It was custom-made, walnut-stained pine board and with a velvet lining. We had asked for it yesterday, but he needed time for the extra touches, such as the initials of the dead, which he dug into the clasp. We wanted Vincenzo to ride out in style, so we paid more and waited the extra day.

Just before the people came, we lined up at the coffin with Mama at Vincenzo's head, the last in line. She looked respectful in her black lacy dress, her hair piled high. Gino stood next to her, dressed in his suit. He was quiet, for once, and polite. He would soon be older and more like somebody you could talk to. Next came Lucy and Bonino, then me, then Louis. Franca didn't want to stand with the family, since she wasn't married yet, so she sat on a folding chair where she could make eyes at Louis. It tickled me to see Louis with a sexy woman to parade in front of all these visitors. They would come to think of di Cantini men as having sexy women, which might help my own chances in the future. Sexy women like to be around men said to attract sexy women.

The viewing started at ten sharp with Father Francis at the

door. Soon people lined up on the porch and began moving forward through the living room, all the sad, drawn, bored, respectful faces. The morning moved like a silent picture, flashing in a strange light. The faces were familiar enough, but in a way I knew nobody. None of the talk seemed real. What people said seemed written on the screen like subtitles: "I'm sorry about your brother, Sammy. This is a shame," or "Your brother was a fine young man." But what could people say? You watched them composing their big sentence as they approached you, a blank watery stare in their eyes. The old Italian ladies were the worst, and droves of them came. They loved funerals, and they hunched together like buzzards along one wall of the parlor. "*Magari fosse ancora in vista,*" they crowed. But it was their private triumph just to be alive when such a young man as Vincenzo was dead. They figured they had done something right in God's eyes to warrant so many extra years. Their custom was to dress in black all the time, ready at a moment's notice to attend a funeral.

A few people did seem real to me. One was Will Denks, who wore a black tie that belonged to Hark Wood, who stood mute beside him and just shook my hand when his turn came. You could count the pores in his big purple nose and smell the hootch on his breath.

"Thanks for coming," I said to Will. He had brushed his hair down hard and it gave off a clean, rivery smell.

"Is your mama okay?"

"Look at her," I said. She was chattering to Lucy, excited by the company. People palpitated her like coffee. She loved the attention, which helped ease her grief for Vincenzo. "She's tough," I said.

Will understood. "Hey, come for a swim this afternoon. After the burial. Okay?"

"Okay," I said. It seemed sacrilegious to talk about swimming after a funeral, but it helped to realize that the old life would continue when Vincenzo was buried. The world would not suddenly evaporate. But I would hate the moment when they lowered his coffin in the ground. It had been the worst part of Papa's going.

Miss Turner passed me, her voice full of Texas. The sight of her brought back thoughts of fall, which was near enough now. It was always hard to start school again after the summer, and with Vincenzo gone it would be somehow harder. Lucy was gone, too: married. And Jesse was hardly Jesse. Not a word broke from his lips all morning.

The patch boys filed by, trussed up in clothes too fancy and hot for August; Hitch Lima and Lobo Stansky, dumb as two pegs in a fence; Billy Shawgo, mean as dirt; the suave and clever Mike Torrentino. I felt awkward before them and just shook their hands and said nothing.

"You're doing a good job," said Father Francis in my ear. He bobbed around us, acting like a member of the family. He always enjoyed a good funeral; death brought out the best in him. "There's lemonade punch on the kitchen table, if you care for it," he said. "I'll see that your mama gets some. She's holding up nicely."

The room teemed with flowers—marigolds and carnations, dahlias. Bing Stanton had sent calla lillies, which he probably had to order special. They glowed whitely as sun poured through the sheer curtains and lit the honey-waxed floors, the legs of the wing chair, the faded wallpaper. It was at least 90 degrees and the room was stuffy as more folding chairs were brought out and set up around the room. The ladies sat down with their ankles crossed to gossip in whispers, while most of the men stood together by one wall, silent, out of place in fancy clothes, their hands folded in front like when you walk back from the communion rail. People I didn't even recognize were sobbing loudly. Vincenzo's friends chatted in one corner, trying to sit hard on laughter when a joke—almost by accident—got told. This didn't mean they weren't sad. A laugh can be the purest note of grief. My head grew large and juicy with tears, and I almost couldn't tell who was talking to me.

It was Mr. Maynard, speaking gently through his blond

moustache. Beside him, Ellie stood with her hands together at waist level, her hair tied in back like an old lady. The way the light caught her face, she had the same moustache, too. I looked at her and startled.

She stared at me without blinking, waiting for her father to finish his little speech about how sorry he was. It was an elegant speech like he made at school assemblies.

"I'm sorry about your brother," she said.

She said that plainly, and she meant it. Her eyes fastened to my own, powerfully, the tiny lines in her forehead like cracks in a china teacup. Her handshake was strangely frail.

"Thanks for coming, Ellie," I said.

"I'm your friend, Sammy. Of course I would come."

Yes, we were friends. This was a proper beginning for any good thing that might pass between two people, and I was glad for it. But when you've been expecting so much more from a girl, the word *friend* can ring a little hollow. "Maybe we can still go to Argentina together?" I asked. "In a few weeks."

"Maybe," she said. "I can speak Spanish . . . a little."

She glanced over my shoulder at Vincenzo, which shook me. You just don't flirt with a girl in front of your dead brother, who would never again have the chance to flirt with anybody. Ellie had called my attention to this sad stinking fact.

"I'll talk to you later," she said, feeling the pressure to move along the line.

I nodded, and tears wet both my cheeks. People probably figured they were tears for my brother, and in a sense they were. They were tears for all the sad, lost things in my life, including the ones to come.

I needed to get away from there, away from so many people, so I excused myself and went to the kitchen. A few people were milling about the punch, talking in soft tones. A mist of quiet sadness hung over the room. "How many boys got to die before they do something?" asked Mrs. Montoro. "*Quanti ragazzi?*" She handed punch to Sam Muncy, Maud's father.

They looked uneasy when they saw me. Close relatives of the dead are marked.

I settled by the icebox in a folding chair, and nobody bothered me. A while later, Bing Stanton walked into the kitchen with the Nipper at his side. I heard that they would be coming because Bing Stanton attended the funerals of anyone who ever worked for him. It was part of being the boss.

Father Francis followed them into the kitchen, knowing I was there. I guess he figured I might need help.

"Good morning, Father," said Bing Stanton.

Father Francis bowed slightly.

Bing Stanton must have got very little sleep lately. His eyes sagged at the corners. His hair was greasy and ruffled. He had taken a big nick out of his top lip while shaving. As he pulled a cigarette from his jacket pocket, his hands quivered.

Nobody moved. But since I was the host—or something like that—I went toward the table. It hurt me even to look at them, but I had to pretend, to act like in my own house I was in control. I drew myself right up to Bing Stanton's face. "Punch?" I asked him, holding up a glass. "Lemonade punch?"

"Oh, yes . . . thanks."

Mrs. Montoro stared at me hard, as if I had any choice about serving them.

"Nip?" I asked. "Want some?"

"Okay," he said. He was not known for manners. His lips made a faint red line across his face. Puberty was grinding him through its gears, and I noticed that acne had begun to leak through his pale skin. His chin was rosy with a pimple so big it looked like sunburn. His ears stuck out from the sides of his head like barn doors flung wide. It struck me how often angelic boys turn into ugly men. Time was strangling the beauty out of Nipper's body, and his eyes twitched in resentment.

Bing stubbed out his barely lit cigarette in a glass on the table, and the closeness of our bodies was uncomfortable. I wanted to say something, anything, but no words came. I might have said, *Mr. Stanton, because you are a real first-class bastard, my brother is dead in the parlor.*

He said, "Sam—I wanted to talk to you." He stopped, gathering words from a deep, serious place. "I . . . never should really have been, well, at . . ." He lifted his head and turned toward the screen door to withdraw, caught on the barb of some confession. The most important sentence he might have said to me was lost in a mumble.

He looked at me again in distress, like he was going to try once more to say something. But he was stuck in being Bing Stanton, unable to jerk himself loose into the open air of decent, ordinary people. His sense of himself, something he grew up with and could never get around, was a prison. He wasn't big enough, as a man, to unlock the door and walk free.

"We better be going," he said to the Nipper.

"Yes," I said, taking their glasses.

They scuttled out through the kitchen door, afraid to leave the front way, where everyone would see them. I watched them slope out, their shoulders bent forward, their eyes fixed on the floorboards as if any ripple in the wood might trip them. The blond-gray hair at the back of Bing Stanton's head was like the brown edges of a leaf in fall, a sign that the tree, however tall and green from a distance, was being eaten away at the edges, dying from the outside in.

Father Francis went onto the back porch and motioned for me to join him. He had a difficult look in his eyes.

"Let's go see your mama's garden," he said.

I agreed. It would be a relief to stand among cabbages, beans, and carrots.

"Sammy, that was *terrific*. You really handled him," he said. His voice was much too bright.

"Who?"

"Bing Stanton! You stared him down. He left here a mess, an absolute mess."

I wanted to explain that Father Francis was all wrong, but I saw that he, too, was trapped in himself.

He said, "Sammy, you're more like your brother than I realized."

I shook my head. "I'm not like Vincenzo," I said. I was like Sammy di Cantini, for better or worse. Plain me.

Father seemed not to listen. He had a distant glimmer in his eyes. "I guess without Vincenzo you're going to be in charge around here."

It was true enough. My hopes of going anywhere to college had been blown away by a stupid bullet.

"You certainly won't be able to enter the priesthood," Father went on. "I can see that now. I wasn't thinking yesterday."

This came as an odd relief, somehow. I didn't have to wiggle out of *that* anymore.

"You know, Sammy, you are going to do fine. I know it. The money will come. It will."

"We'll be okay," I said.

He half chuckled and put his arm around my shoulder like a chum and walked me back to the house without a further word, and whether or not he understood anything I'd said didn't matter. Whatever the world threw at me now, I would throw back in spades.

19

I'd been living at the river for a week now, going up to Bonino's garage every morning to pretend I really did like to twist wrenches. I would rather had gone swimming or fishing with Will Denks, who would have made a better mechanic than me anyway. Life wasn't fair. But Louis had talked to me and Mama about money before he left for New York. He had some big money coming, and he left us a check for $100. I had already told Bonino I was going back to school, but I also agreed to work for him after school and on weekends. Maybe I would, someday, wind up twisting wrenches for a living. But meanwhile, while the summer had any blood left in its veins, I wanted some of the old times back. I wanted me and Will together by the river: swimming, cooking, and talking baseball with birds cackling in the treetops. I wanted the sky a long way off, brilliant, blue. But there went the Canada geese already, arrow after arrow, heading south: black honking birds.

The trees would soon lose their leaves in the sharp wind. The river's easy gold would turn to rust, then change to blue. By October, the water would run clear; rocks would become visible below the surface; the brush would grow thin. The air itself would clarify toward winter, and then, in winter itself, the sky would drop, come so close you could touch it.

But I wanted to hold on to what was left of summer and the old life. I wanted the same scenes, the familiar repetitions: the sweet piny air drifting down from the hemlocks when you woke, the ferns by the river, the high wet grass, your bare feet paddling over moss. I wanted fried bullhead and black coffee. I wanted to talk to Will Denks like before: talk about the World Series or Hornsby's batting average.

It was still light at suppertime, though two months earlier you'd have thought it was afternoon at this hour; it was certainly dusk now—an orange-colored dusk, with a further half-hour of good light left. Clouds layered the western sky, blood-red, big horizontal stripes, as I sat on a crate that had contained Will's secondhand set of Sir Walter Scott's novels. He had the notion that he might want to go to college someday, too, which meant reading literature as well as engineering. The novels were bought at a yard sale in Pittston, over twenty volumes. I had left *Ivanhoe* somewhere in the middle, a month ago, and now the idea of reading through that crate seemed worse than mining for a lifetime.

"You really going to read those books?" I asked.

"Yep. One by one."

"That'll take you years. It only takes four years to go all the way through college."

"One by one," he repeated. "If it takes twenty years, so what? I got time."

Will Denks would turn sixteen in September, but he didn't look it. No whiskers sprouted from his chin, nor pimples either. He had the clear blue-green eyes of a child, and his voice still, though deeper, had the light firmness of a boy's. It would be just like Will to slip out of puberty's net.

"More fish?" Will asked.

"Sure."

He flipped another bullhead, butter-brown, on my plate as the fire warmed our shins. The woods were deep and dark. The night was no different from any other night of that summer by the river except that Vincenzo was dead, but somehow that made every detail shine in a new light—as if the balance of the world had shifted.

"You seen Ellie Maynard lately?" Will asked me, out of the blue.

"Yesterday. I stopped by and saw her after work. We had ice-cream sodas in Pittston."

You could tell he didn't expect that reply. I could feel myself gloating but tried to restrain it.

"You still like her a lot?" he asked.

"Still?"

"She sure screwed you around," he said.

"No she didn't," I said. I was trying hard not to swing easily with the negative drift our conversation was taking. "She never had any obligation to me. I was always the one to press for something, and she went along to a certain point." I looked at Will to see his reaction. "You can only take a friendship so far on your own." I sipped my coffee. "It looks pretty good right now." With Nip Stanton going off to New England to a prep school, the field was deep and clear for me and Ellie. There was no telling what might happen—everything, or nothing.

Will Denks reflected on my answer, digging into the nearly burnt-out sticks to separate them. Fires start quickly in the woods during August, so you can't be too careful. He poured a bucket of water on the fire, which sizzled and left a fine charcoal odor in the air.

"How about you?" I asked. "You still seeing that girl?" I pretended my remark was perfectly ordinary.

"*Who?*" He jumped sideways like a startled bird.

"Am I right or not? Just say yes or no, and you don't ever

215

have to explain. But didn't I see you here with a girl one day? You were swimming with her."

"You saw us?"

"Yep."

His lips curled up at the sides, like the petals of a carnation. "Goddamn Peeping Tom," he said, not mad at all.

"I came looking for you, but I sure ran off when I saw you had female company."

"She ain't nothing special," he said. "I met her back in Harding at the fair. She wanted to see my camp." Harding— a small town to the north—had a county fair every summer, but I'd missed it this year for the first time. It surprised me that Will Denks would have gone to the fair without telling me. He never would have done that in the old days. "It's funny," Will continued. "There ain't so many girls you can talk to. They don't talk easy."

I agreed. Ellie was one of the first girls I'd met who had much to offer in the way of good conversation.

"Maybe they don't talk nice unless they're in love," said Will. "That loosens their tongues like crazy."

"You think?"

"That's what I hear."

By this time it was getting darker, the sun shrunk to a red ball in one corner of the sky and hardly visible behind the bushy pines. I stared at a bottle of grasshoppers that Will kept for fishing, the insects jammed close and scratching against the glass in a pitiful way.

"You want a swim?" Will asked. "Ain't so many days left we can swim."

"Sure do," I said.

He grabbed a couple towels from the lean-to and tossed one over my head, running ahead of me through the trees to the river. "Come on!" he yelled, his voice glancing off tree trunks, distant already, a spirit released from Aladdin's lamp.

I unscrewed the tin lid of the grasshopper jar and turned it on its side, to watch the spindly creatures scramble, awkward and leggy, into the free air. I would hear them in the woods all night, a bleeping chorus of *thank you, thank you, thank you.*

"Hey, di Cantini!" Will's voice glanced through the trees. My name seemed to hang in the cooling air.

"I'm coming!"

When I got to the river, there he stood—one hip higher than the other, his ass small and bare, his legs as slender as a crane's. His body was copper-colored, like taffy, a color that comes to the skin only at the very end of summer. His hair, which hadn't been cut since June, bushed out white from bleaching. I became loose-kneed, wobbly with affection.

"How is the water?" I asked.

"Warm as cow piss."

"How do you know so much about cow piss?"

"I drink it for breakfast when you ain't here."

I stepped out of my clothes, too, and kicked them into a ball.

"Ain't you coming?" he said. "Or what?"

"In a minute. I'm airing out first."

"Get in the water. Your smell is killing the trees."

I said, "Answer me first: Who had the most strikeouts in one ball game—National League?"

He ran his fingers through his hair. "Christy Mathewson."

"Nope."

"Noodles Hahn," he said, firmly, "1901 or 1902."

"Nope."

"I give up."

"Charlie Sweeney," I said. "Nineteen strikeouts in one game—1884."

"*Charlie Sweeney!*"

"Yep."

"Never heard of him. You made him up."

"I didn't."

"You did."

"I didn't."

Will Denks yelled across the river. "Wake up, Charlie

217

Sweeney! Defend yourself!" And he dove into the red, slow water.

I looked up to see the moon breaking through a purple stretch of sky. Venus was there, too, winking. The Milky Way began to speckle through, a sprawl of diamonds, as the tiny swallows darted in the air more like bugs than birds. In Coxton Yard, boxcars coupled and uncoupled, echoing across the river. You could hear the distant thunder of a train.

Will disappeared, swimming to the bend in the river without taking another breath, while I sat on a rock ledge, misty-eyed, and could easily believe that Papa was alive up in that bright sky. He was up there, maybe on a cloud. It didn't matter where. And Vincenzo would be seated next to him, like in the old days at supper. They would see me below—a speck in the distance—and each have a version of the life that reached before me, and they'd each be wrong. Nobody can guess that, just like nobody can know a man's heart except himself. I stood up and waved to them. I shouted, "It's all right, fellas, it's all right!" And I dove, making a slight arc across the water. There was still enough heat left in the world for weeks of swimming, and the river would stay warm till late September.